WORNSTAFF ... LIBRARY
W9-BMA-205

"I'm not looking for someone to work a ridiculous number of hours," Wyatt said in the video chat.

"You'd have plenty of time to do your freelance commissions. I can provide space to use as a studio, as well as bedrooms for you and your nephew."

It was better than Katrina had hoped. Yet she hesitated, recalling his popularity during high school. "I know you can't make guarantees, but I'd rather not move back and immediately have to find another job and spot for us to live because you get married again."

He shook his head. "Nobody can take Amy's place. But I could make the same comment about you. It would be hard on Christie to get comfortable with someone, then have them leave right away, either to get married or go back to the city."

"I'm avoiding romance right now," Katrina said firmly. And believed more strongly that it was true.

Dear Reader,

My series Big Sky Navy Heroes pivots around a gruff grandfather who drove his grandsons away from Montana. Saul Hawkins bitterly regrets the way he raised his grandchildren and hopes to bring these navy heroes home again by offering each of them a challenge: prove yourself as a rancher and receive one-third of the family's Soaring Hawk Ranch in a trust.

Wyatt is a widower and devoted father to his young daughter. When he learns he's going to be deployed, he resigns his commission and accepts his grandfather's challenge. Wyatt isn't worried about proving himself to Saul, but he has to contend with his long-absent father's return to the Soaring Hawk...and the beautiful, forthright childhood friend he hires as his daughter's nanny. With Katrina Tapson around, anything might happen! Even a brand-new chance at love for the pair of them.

Please visit my website at sites.google.com/view/juliannamorris--author/home, where I share information on my books and other news. I enjoy hearing from readers and can be contacted on Twitter @julianna_author or on my Facebook page at julianna.morris.author. If you prefer writing a letter, please use c/o Harlequin Books, 22 Adelaide Street West, 41st Floor, Toronto, Ontario M5H 4E3, Canada.

Best wishes,

Julianna

HEARTWARMING

The Navy Dad's Return

Julianna Morris

WORNSTAFF MEMORIAL LIBRARY

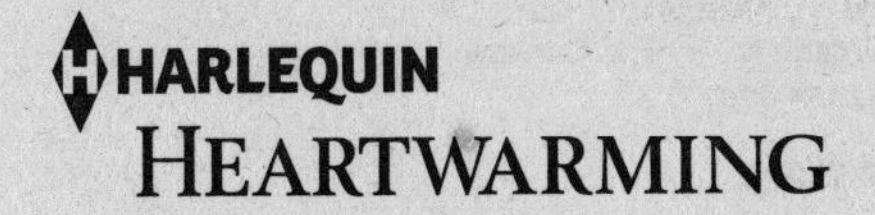

If you purchased this book without a cover you should be aware that this book is stolen property. It was reported as "unsold and destroyed" to the publisher, and neither the author nor the publisher has received any payment for this "stripped book."

ISBN-13: 978-1-335-58488-5

PLEASE RECYCLE • THIS PRODUCT IS RECYCLABLE

Recycling programs for this product may not exist in your area.

The Navy Dad's Return

Copyright © 2023 by Julianna Morris

All rights reserved. No part of this book may be used or reproduced in any manner whatsoever without written permission except in the case of brief quotations embodied in critical articles and reviews.

This is a work of fiction. Names, characters, places and incidents are either the product of the author's imagination or are used fictitiously. Any resemblance to actual persons, living or dead, businesses, companies, events or locales is entirely coincidental.

For questions and comments about the quality of this book, please contact us at CustomerService@Harlequin.com.

Harlequin Enterprises ULC
22 Adelaide St. West, 41st Floor
Toronto, Ontario M5H 4E3, Canada
www.Harlequin.com

Printed in U.S.A.

Julianna Morris barely remembers a time when she didn't want to be a writer, having scribbled out her first novel in sixth grade (a maudlin tale she says will never ever see the light of day). She also loves to read, and her library includes everything from history and biographies to most fiction genres. Julianna has been a park ranger, program analyst and systems analyst in information technology. She loves animals, travel, gardening, baking, hiking, taking photographs, making patchwork quilts and doing a few dozen other things. Her biggest complaint is not having enough hours in the day.

Books by Julianna Morris

Harlequin Heartwarming

Big Sky Navy Heroes

The SEAL's Christmas Dilemma
The Cowboy SEAL's Challenge

Hearts of Big Sky

The Man from Montana
Christmas on the Ranch
Twins for the Rodeo Star

Visit the Author Profile page at Harlequin.com for more titles.

To moms and dads everywhere

PROLOGUE

WYATT MAXWELL STARED at the orders he'd received earlier in the day, saying he was being transferred to Rota, Spain, to begin training for deployment on a navy destroyer.

Deployed.

He'd served twice on an aircraft carrier during his marriage, but now Amy was gone and he was raising their daughter alone. His brothers and their wives would undoubtedly offer to look after Christie, but how could he leave his child like that? A deployment usually lasted six or seven months and could easily go longer.

Christie was only three. She'd never understand.

His commanding officer didn't have children and his unconcerned remark that "kids are resilient" had infuriated Wyatt. Kids might be resilient, but his daughter had already lost her mother and gone through two moves in her short life, which meant new people, new day-care centers and a new home.

"Daddy, *Daddy*," Christie cried from her bedroom, almost as if in response to his thoughts.

Wyatt hurried to her. "I'm here."

"The monster is mad." She pointed to the closet.

"Sweetheart, there aren't any monsters. It's just a dream."

Christie put up her hands and pushed her palms together. "He squishes so big people can't see him."

"I'll check." Wyatt made a big show of turning on the light inside the closet, then shaking out her small clothes and shoes. "Nope, it's all okay. No monster."

His daughter sniffed and didn't look convinced. "He took Fluffy Bob."

"Nobody took Fluffy Bob. He fell on the floor."

Wyatt gave her the large teddy bear and she clutched it close as he sat on the bed and stroked her hair. It was another hour before she fell asleep again. He spent the time evaluating what he needed to do. The navy had been good to him, but he didn't see any options.

He would have to resign his commission.

Sighing, Wyatt went to his office for the conference call he'd scheduled with Jordan and Dakota. He opened the program and saw his two brothers drop into the electronic meeting. Wyatt pressed a button and their faces soon appeared on the screen.

"What's up?" Jordan asked immediately. "Is Christie all right?"

"She's okay, except she's still having nightmares. But now they want to deploy me out of the naval station in Rota, Spain." Wyatt drew a deep breath. "I've decided to resign. I can't leave Christie for months at a time."

Both Jordan and Dakota nodded, and he was glad they didn't argue that he'd lose his twenty-year retirement. What was a pension compared to Christie? She needed him at home, not on a ship.

Dakota leaned toward the camera on his computer. Despite the fading scars on one side of his face from an explosion while serving as a Navy SEAL, he was his old self, the laughter and devilry never far from his eyes.

"Do what I did," he said. "Come back to Montana and accept Grandpa Saul's challenge to work on the Soaring Hawk for a year in exchange for a share of the ranch. He's mellowed. You won't have any trouble with him. And Dad is here."

Wyatt stiffened. "I don't want to talk about him."

"Wyatt—"

"*No.* You aren't in my shoes. It hurt more than I could have imagined when I lost Amy, but I would never dive into a whiskey bottle and neglect my daughter. Yet that's exactly what Evan did after Mom died."

"Wouldn't you rather call him Dad?"

"No."

"We shouldn't argue about this," Jordan said firmly. "Wyatt, whatever you decide to do, Paige and I will help with Christie."

"So will we," called a voice in the background.

Dakota laughed. "That's Noelle. She was passing by in the hallway. Count on us, too."

Wyatt's seven-year-old niece suddenly appeared on the screen in front of Jordan, her expression excited and happy. "Hi, Uncle Wyatt," she exclaimed.

"Hey, kiddo. I can't believe how much you've grown."

Mishka giggled. "Grandpa Scott says I grow like prairie grass in the spring."

"He's right."

Grandpa Scott was Scott Bannerman from the Blue Banner Ranch, father of both of Wyatt's sisters-in-law. His brothers had each formed a good relationship with the lanky rancher and his wife.

"Say good-night," Jordan told his daughter. "You can talk to Uncle Wyatt another time."

She scrunched her nose. "You want to have a grown-up talk."

"Yup."

"Oookay." Mishka blew a kiss at the screen. She was a true child of the twenty-first century, completely at ease with communicating online. "Good night, Uncle Wyatt."

"Good night. Sweet dreams."

"So what about accepting Saul's challenge?" Jordan asked when Mishka was gone. "We all expected to go back into ranching after leaving the navy. It would be great to have the three Maxwell brothers together again.

"I've been considering it for a while. Dakota, is the original ranch house available yet?" Wyatt asked. While ranching required long periods of work, at least he'd be able to see his daughter every day.

"It will be soon. Noelle and I should be moving into our new place before Thanksgiving. The navy will take longer than that to process your resignation. I'd be surprised if you were here before January."

"About the old house. I never asked—if you love it so much, why aren't you staying?"

"We decided our living space needed to be on a single level, rather than two floors. Better for my leg."

"Oh. How *is* your leg?" Wyatt asked, uncertain how Dakota would react to the question.

"Much stronger than before. I can work all day without any trouble, but my knee still doesn't appreciate staircases. Climbing slopes is no problem, it's just steps." He'd been so angry about the injuries that ended his career as a SEAL, it was amazing he could discuss them this calmly.

"That's great," Wyatt said. "All right, I'll put everything in motion. I have to act before the permanent change of station goes through or they might not let me go."

His brothers looked pleased. It would be great to spend real time with them. They'd always been stationed in different parts of the world while in the navy. Besides, this way Christie would get to know her family and have a safety net she didn't have now. And maybe if she felt more secure, her nightmares would go away.

Or that's what Wyatt hoped.

CHAPTER ONE

KATRINA TAPSON SAT at the desk in her living room, answering emails from her family and catching up with personal business. When the phone rang, she looked at the caller ID and made a face. It was her *ex*-fiancé, an editor at the publishing house where she worked.

"Hello."

"Hi, it's me."

"Yeah, I know. I have caller ID like most people. Why am I talking to you on a Friday night? Why am I talking to you at all?"

"I wanted you to know you're getting promoted to senior artist."

Katrina made an exasperated sound. "That doesn't explain why you're calling me outside of the office. Monday would have been fine."

"I was thinking about us. We can't talk at work."

"There isn't any 'us.' I've moved on, so should you."

She knew Gordon might still have feelings for her, but she'd ended their engagement when she found out he didn't want a family. Actually, it was more because he'd pretended all along that he wanted one, only to finally admit he had just hoped she'd change her mind once they were married. The long deceit still bothered Katrina.

Shouldn't she have seen it?

A sound from the back of the apartment caught her attention and she looked up to see her nephew.

She winked and pointed at the phone, making a face. He grinned.

"Sorry, I need to get off. 'Bye." Katrina disconnected before Gordon could protest and put the receiver down. "Can't you sleep, Tim?"

Her nephew plopped onto the couch. "It's kinda noisy out tonight."

She knew what he meant. The city traffic seemed louder than usual on the street outside the apartment building. "I'm sorry."

He shrugged. "It isn't your fault."

Timothy was a good kid. Her sister and brother-in-law had taken teaching positions in Hong Kong, but Tim had been quietly miserable there. After several family consultations, they'd decided he could stay with Katrina. Except that wasn't the answer, either—he missed his friends and life in Montana. Her nephew had thought Seattle was awesome when he was visiting and going to professional sports games and the Seattle Center, but actually living here was different. Not that he'd admit it outright.

"It's late," she said. "You should try to sleep. We have a reservation at the riding stable in the morning."

He shrugged. "Okay. I just wish they didn't put blinders on the horses. They think we don't know what we're doing."

Despite the disgust in his voice, he headed for his bedroom. He didn't pass up an opportunity to ride, no matter what.

Katrina got it—she missed Montana, too. While she hadn't grown up spending weekends and summers on a family ranch like her nephew, horses and small-town life had been part of her childhood. She'd always felt out of place in the city. And now all the buildings and cars were making her feel stifled, which wasn't good for an artist.

She waited until she was sure Timothy's door had closed before going online to check the real estate and rental listings in her hometown. It had become her Friday-night ritual over the last couple of months, but she didn't want to raise his hopes unless she could make something happen.

The online housing listings were sparse. As usual, no suitable homes were for sale. A small hobby ranch had been available for ages, but even if Rafferty & Son Press offered a work-from-home option, Katrina wouldn't be able to afford it. On top of that, she didn't know that much about the real work of ranching, so maintaining it would require a steep learning curve on her part. Few rental properties were listed, either, and none that would work for the two of them. Shelton had a chronic housing shortage.

She also decided to pull up the limited job listings, something she usually didn't bother doing because if she couldn't find a place for them to live, a job wouldn't help. Then an entry caught her notice.

Live-in nanny/housekeeper needed on Soaring Hawk Ranch. Salary w/room & board. Contact W. Maxwell.

Hmmm.

W. Maxwell had to be Wyatt Maxwell.

It was hard to believe he was back at the Soaring Hawk. He and his brothers had been raised by their grandfather, better known as

Sourpuss Hawkins. Mr. Hawkins's reputation for being difficult was legendary. Even her parents, experienced educators, had been wary of him.

Katrina felt a tingle of excitement. Being a nanny would be a new experience and it included living on a ranch, which she and Timothy would both enjoy. Unfortunately the listing was over two weeks old.

She read the Help Wanted entry again and typed a note to the email address in the advertisement. Wyatt probably wouldn't want a housekeeper who came with a kid, but there was no harm in learning the details and if the position was still open. She'd never been on the Soaring Hawk, but some of those old ranch houses were huge and they might be willing to provide a room for her nephew.

A message arrived a few minutes later, asking if she was available right away for a video call. She glanced down at her oversized sweatshirt. Not exactly interview clothing, but it was a Friday night. A reasonable person wouldn't expect to see her formally dressed and she might as well find out if Wyatt was reasonable.

She smoothed her hair, then typed a reply back and clicked on the link he sent. A minute later he appeared. The picture quality wasn't great since he was on a cell phone, but she could tell he was better-looking than ever.

"Hey, Katrina. It's been a long time."

"I wasn't sure you'd remember me."

"How could I forget the girl who broke Nick's heart?"

Katrina tried not to roll her eyes. She'd primarily known Wyatt through the Shelton Youth Ranching Association. Outside of school and church youth groups, it had been the main social outlet for kids in the area. He'd been the most gorgeous boy in the county, never taking the same girl out for long. They hadn't dated themselves, but his best friend, Nick McGill, had been a charming pest, impervious to rejection.

Maybe she *should* have gone out with Nick. After all, he'd been the only boy in school bold enough to ask. Her parents were great, but her social life in high school had stunk because most of the boys had been wary of her father, the football coach, while the others wanted to avoid her mother, the principal.

"He just saw me as a challenge," she told Wyatt.

"Nah, he really liked you. We stay in touch.

He's still single and a church pastor in Helena."

"Pastor? That's hard to believe."

Wyatt grinned. "He claims to be reformed. Are you really interested in becoming a nanny and housekeeper? You were into drawing and painting when we were younger."

"Actually, I'm working as a commercial artist in Seattle. But you remember my sister, Mary, right?

"Sure, she was in my class at school."

"She and my brother-in-law are teaching out of the country for a couple of years and their son is staying with me while they're gone. He's twelve and a great kid—we're just both really homesick. Anyhow, I can be an artist anywhere. I already take a lot of freelance commissions and can continue when I have time. Art is a portable career."

Wyatt nodded. "I heard that Mary and Shawn were in Hong Kong. Sounds like a great opportunity for them."

"They love it there. Tim not so much. Tell me more about the job," she said briskly.

Wyatt looked amused. "Christie is three and a half and very articulate for a child her age. I think it's from contact with so many different day-care providers and now a large family. We returned to the Soaring Hawk in early January. Basically, I need light housekeeping and childcare."

"I thought you'd always stay in the navy."

"I was a career officer, but resigned when they wanted to deploy me again." His face tightened. "My wife died when Christie was a baby. She had some rare complications from an autoimmune disease. Being deployed meant months away from my daughter—maybe even a year or more. She's too young to understand that kind of absence."

Katrina understood. It spoke well of Wyatt that he'd resigned for his daughter's sake. Mary and her brother-in-law had debated leaving Hong Kong, but they'd realized Timothy was old enough to guess the reason and feel guilty if they left. And he *was* happier in Washington than he'd been there, he'd just be even happier in Montana with his longtime friends and more of the family close by.

"Are your parents still in Shelton?" Wyatt asked.

"They took early retirement and moved to Bozeman a few years ago. That's where my brother lives. Dad would have preferred Arizona or New Mexico, but with Cody in Bozeman and other relatives in Shelton and

Billings, they didn't want to go too far away. Luckily, they found a condo where the association hires someone to shovel snow. That was on the top of their must-have list."

Wyatt chuckled. "I remember your dad's expression when we had football practice and there was snow on the ground. He didn't complain, but his face spoke volumes."

"I'd forgotten you were on the football team."

"Mostly I rode the bench." Wyatt covered a yawn. "Sorry, it's been a long day. Give my sister-in-law a call tomorrow and she'll provide the details. I'll text her number. Paige is the Soaring Hawk's business manager and also does accounting for other ranchers. My daughter and I live in the original homestead house. The place is big and comfortable. Dakota and his wife did updates before they decided to build a new place."

"Paige is Dakota's wife?" Katrina asked, trying to sort out who was who.

"No. Dakota married Noelle Bannerman two years ago. She's a doctor at the clinic in town. Paige is Jordan's wife. Also Noelle's sister."

"I remember the Bannerman family."

"I'm getting to know them again." As Wyatt

shifted the phone, she saw a jumble of moving boxes behind him. “Katrina, I’m not looking for someone to work a ridiculous number of hours. You’d have regular days off and plenty of time to do your freelance commissions. I can provide space to use as a studio, along with bedrooms for you and your nephew.”

It was better than Katrina had hoped. Yet she hesitated, recalling his popularity during high school. “This may be sensitive, and I know you can’t make guarantees, but I’d rather not move back and immediately have to find another job and place for us to live because you decided to get married again. At the very least I’d like some solid warning.”

He shook his head. “I’m not getting married again—nobody can take Amy’s place, she was one of a kind. I can’t imagine loving anyone else. But I could make the same comment about you,” he added. “It would be hard on Christie to start getting comfortable with someone, then have them leave right away, either to get married or go back to the city.”

“I’m avoiding romance right now. And believe me, if I come home, I’m not going back to Seattle unless I don’t have any choice,” Katrina said firmly. “If we’re both agreed, I’ll contact your sister-in-law tomorrow. Once everything is decided I can give my employer their two-week notice."

"Sounds good."

They ended their call and Katrina sat back with a gleeful smile. Mary and Shawn knew she was looking for a place in Montana, so they wouldn't be surprised about her news. It just would have been easier if they hadn't leased their house in Shelton, but nothing could be done about that.

Annoyingly, the memory of Wyatt's face drifted into Katrina's thoughts.

While his older brothers were attractive, he was the one who'd made the girls' hearts stop when they were kids. Black hair. High, well-defined cheekbones. Dark brown eyes. Naturally bronzed skin and a warm, kind smile that could turn a woman into mush. From what she'd seen on the video call, he still oozed masculine charisma, so it was a good thing she'd sworn off romance while she was taking care of Timothy.

Not that there was any question of romance with Wyatt. His obvious lack of interest in her when they were younger had stung a little, but she hadn't lost any sleep thinking about it since then.

TWO AND A half weeks later Katrina knew she should be tired; instead, she was exhilarated. They were in Montana and would soon be seeing their new home. Timothy leaned forward in the passenger seat, impatiently watching the miles pass.

"It looks the same," he marveled.

She understood his excitement. Instead of a busy cityscape, there were rolling snowfields and mountains rising to the west. Patches of evergreen trees dotted hills, while leafless black cottonwoods crowded meandering low areas where water flowed in the spring and summer. The snow was deep and another storm was coming in, so ranch hands were out, laying down hay. Cattle were lined up, munching away. The scene was so familiar she could paint it with her eyes closed.

February wasn't the best time for a road trip across the Rockies, but getting out of the city had been relatively painless. She'd sold most of her furniture and a shipping company had picked up their boxes of clothes and other personal items. Wyatt had offered to pay for the shipping, which was decent of him.

Katrina turned onto the Soaring Hawk Ranch road, driving carefully on the icy gravel.

"They might already have calves," Timothy said. "No matter how careful Grandpa was about timing the breeding season, we always had some that arrived in February. Well, he didn't raise that many cows after he sold the Big Jumbo, but a few," her nephew added.

He was trying to sound wise and Katrina knew he hoped to get involved on the ranch. It wasn't impossible.

The Soaring Hawk came into view. From the photos and information Wyatt's sister-in-law had sent, Katrina knew the first building—a large three-story place built in the 1920s—was the main house. Wyatt's two-story home was on the knoll to the west. A new one-level house stood on a low hill north of the two. Each had broad porches—useless this time of year, but a pleasant prospect in warmer weather. She instantly envisioned herself out there painting.

Various other ranch buildings were mostly to the south and southwest, separated from the homes by a hundred yards or so.

A woman came down from the main house and waved, a black-and-white Border collie racing ahead of her toward the car. Katrina stopped and got out and petted the dog. "Oh, who's this? Morning, Paige."

"That's Finn. Welcome to the Soaring Hawk, Katrina. You're earlier than we thought. How was your trip?"

"Uneventful, which is the best kind. We left Seattle early so we could spend a day in Bozeman with my parents, making it a short drive today."

They'd talked several times on the phone, getting reacquainted. Katrina would have liked remaining in touch with the people she'd known in Montana, but the worlds of commercial artists and ranchers were far apart. Funny how people got swept up in their lives and left pieces of the past behind.

"I sent a text to Wyatt saying you'd arrived. He should be here shortly. Goodness, Tim, you've grown since the last time I saw you," Paige said as Timothy got out and pulled on his coat.

"Hey, Paige." He ruffled the fur on her dog's head and the Border collie wriggled with pleasure.

Just then Wyatt came striding toward them from around one of the ranch buildings. "Katrina, glad to have you here. The same with you, Tim." He put his hand out to shake and Timothy's shoulders rose at the adult greeting. "Call me Wyatt. I was hoping you might be willing to help keep our horses exercised."

Her nephew looked more excited than ever. "I sure would. And I can groom them and do all sorts of other stuff. My grandpa taught me. He used to own the Big Jumbo."

"We'll talk about it. You're welcome to go over to the horse barn." Wyatt gestured to the large barn behind them. "Your cousin, Melody James, is there. She's looking forward to seeing you. She says you're quite a rider."

"*Awesome*. I forgot she worked at the Soaring Hawk. Is it okay, Aunt Kat?"

"Of course."

Timothy raced toward the barn.

Wyatt turned to Katrina. "Move your SUV up by the house and I'll help get your things unloaded."

"Thanks, but we'll take care of it. I'd like to meet Christie. She doesn't attend preschool on Mondays, right?" Though Katrina had never been a nanny before, she knew Wyatt's daughter had to be his first concern.

"Take time to unpack," Paige urged. "Christie is fine with me. My son is a toddler and he adores her. My daughter will also be home later and they love playing together. By the way, my mother takes the kids to school and picks them up. She wants you to know she'll be happy to include Tim."

"That's nice of her. Tim is already reregistered. I had his transcripts sent from the school in Washington and spoke to the principal last week. He starts classes again on Wednesday."

"Wonderful. Go on and get settled. It'll be easier without Christie there."

Katrina shot an inquiring look at Wyatt and he gestured his agreement.

WYATT WAS SO relieved to have Katrina here, he would have agreed to practically anything. His brothers and their wives were great, but he'd already needed to leave Christie with them a couple of times in the middle of the night—once because a pair of coyotes were harassing the herd and once for a horse with colic. Recently he and Christie had even started sleeping at the main house so he wouldn't have to disturb anyone when he was called out.

He could have gotten someone working here earlier. He'd had a couple of applicants for the nanny position, but both had been former girlfriends. They were nice women, he just hadn't wanted to take the chance of them misunderstanding the situation. Particularly since one of them had acted as if she was interviewing as a potential wife.

He was *never* getting married again.

Nobody could replace Amy and he didn't want anyone to get the wrong idea and start thinking they could try. Besides, if they'd really needed employment, they would have applied for the bunkhouse cook opening he'd also advertised. Not that it mattered. Katrina was the best choice, even if she hadn't been able to start right away. She was smart, confident, swift with a comeback and had a great sense of humor.

Best of all, they'd never dated.

Wyatt briefly wondered what had put her off romance, but maybe she was simply focused on her nephew.

"At least let me show you the place," he said. "I'll bring Christie over later and introduce you. We've been staying at the main house for a few days. It will be nice to get back tonight."

"All right."

They crunched up the snowy path he'd shoveled following the last snowstorm.

The old homestead house retained a rustic feel, but it was solid and had recent amenities added. Christie also seemed comfortable here, though it was nothing like the ultramodern apartments he and Amy had favored.

"I'm afraid there's just one full bathroom on the bottom floor," Wyatt explained as he opened the door and showed the space to Katrina. "Naturally, it's yours and Tim's exclusively. My brother also installed a new half-bath down here and there's another one off the utility and mudroom. Old, but functional."

"My apartment had a single bathroom and nothing close to this size. Ooh, I love the stained glass," Katrina said as she looked inside and spotted the large window.

"That's how my sister-in-law feels, but she couldn't bring herself to move it to the house that she and Dakota built. Saul wouldn't have objected. He's quite fond of Nicole."

A thoughtful expression filled Katrina's greenish-blue eyes. They reminded him of something, he just couldn't remember what it might be. "I used to hear stories about your grandfather. He must have, um, *softened*."

"Saul is okay. We aren't that close, but he wants to bring the family back together." Wyatt gestured to three other doors in the hallway. "These rooms are for you and Timothy. Christie and I are upstairs. I thought you'd prefer having a more separate space. I had two sets of bedroom furniture delivered. They're basic, so let me know what else you need. We have a television in the living room and Wi-Fi information is in a file that Paige left in the kitchen. Luckily, it was upgraded last year. There's also a letter that says you can act on my behalf. I always had to do one for Christie's day-care providers, so I figured it was a good idea for you as well."

"Thanks."

Wyatt cleared his throat. "Uh, the house still isn't in great shape as far as unpacking is concerned. The family wanted to help with getting everything together, but they were doing so much by taking care of Christie, I wouldn't let them. I'll deal with it after calving season is over. In the meantime, please ignore the mess. Oh, I also have a new baby monitor, so you can hear Christie in her room at night when I'm out. She's been dreaming about a monster in the closet, but she has a night-light and it helps a little."

"I understand. Do you have any other preferences or instructions?"

"Not at the moment. I've never had someone living in to look after my daughter, so we'll have to take things a step at a time. Just get your own stuff unpacked and relax. It's a long drive from Seattle. I'll take something out of the freezer for dinner tonight."

"All right. In the meantime, there's no need to stay. Feel free to get back to whatever you were doing."

Wyatt restrained a smile at the way Katrina was subtly trying to take the lead, the same way she'd tried the first night they'd connected. He didn't mind. He'd been recalling even more memories of her from when they were kids. At the youth ranching association the group would often stand around, trying to decide where to start and getting nothing done, then she would step in, either giving them jobs to do or taking care of it while everyone else was talking. Of course, she'd also had a hot temper and little patience for procrastination.

Despite her temper, there was something about her that he'd always appreciated—a sparkle and zest for life that was hard to resist. In fact, if his best friend hadn't liked Katrina so much, he might have asked her out himself. She was the same, yet different now, like a picture that had come into focus. Instead of youthful roundness, her face was more defined and striking.

An odd sensation went through him with the observation. It wasn't guilt, not exactly. After all, appreciating an attractive woman didn't mean he'd stopped loving Amy.

"Are you sure I can't help unload your SUV?" he asked as a distraction to his wayward thoughts. It wasn't like him. His officer fitness reports had consistently referenced his ability to remain focused in chaotic circumstances.

"Positive. Tim and I loaded everything and we can certainly unload it ourselves. Besides, I shipped most of our stuff. There's just luggage and a few other items."

"Er, right. Feel free to explore. We have two cats, so please don't let them go out. They're indoor only. Oh, and none of the ranch's dogs are allowed in the house. Christie is afraid of them."

"No problem."

Wyatt left, breathing a sigh of relief. Things would be easier after they got used to each other. Yet busy as he was, a part of him wished Katrina had let him lend a hand unloading her belongings.

It seemed the proper thing to do.

KATRINA LOOKED AROUND with pleased anticipation, appreciating the lovely old house. The historic atmosphere was much more appealing than the tall city buildings where she'd lived and worked for years. She checked the rooms they'd been given and saw the two on either side of the bathroom had double beds. The third, on the northwest corner, contained the boxes she'd shipped, tidily stacked against an inside wall.

That was the last tidy thing she saw.

Wyatt hadn't exaggerated when he'd said he needed help. Upstairs there were three up-to-date bathrooms and four bedrooms, including a large master suite that looked as if it had been created from two other rooms while still maintaining the traditional feel of the house.

Christie's bedroom was fine, but the other three were a disaster of half-opened boxes, piles of laundry and general mess. Wyatt was even using a sleeping bag on a mattress dropped in the middle of everything. Nonetheless, she didn't think he was inherently untidy—just temporarily overwhelmed.

Katrina made a face at the furniture beneath the clutter in the master suite—like the living room furniture, the stark contemporary lines were incongruous in the historic building. But each to their own.

Snow began drifting down as she moved the SUV closer to the house and pulled out one of the three pieces of furniture she'd kept—her drafting table, another long folding table that doubled as a desk and general work area, and a swivel chair. Timothy ran over from the horse barn and lifted one end of the drafting table.

"Sorry, Aunt Kat."

"There's nothing to be sorry about. Did you enjoy seeing Melody?"

Tim nodded. "She's, like, the second in command here after the foreman and the owners. Isn't that cool? And she says Sourpuss Hawkins is really nice now."

"We shouldn't call him that," Katrina warned as they maneuvered the table through the front door. Saul Hawkins's reputation might be decades in the making, but it wasn't right to call him names on his own ranch.

"I know."

They carried the drafting table into the spare room and went out for the rest, including the boxes containing Katrina's lamps, computer and other supplies. She hadn't been willing to trust her equipment to being shipped;

they were a big investment and too important to her.

Tim had his own computer. Online classes weren't common at the school he'd attended in Washington, but according to Paige Maxwell, they'd become a popular alternative in Shelton during winter storms. "No more snow days," she'd said with a laugh.

The bedrooms were of equal size. Both had bookshelves, but one included a student desk. She appreciated seeing Wyatt's thoughtfulness toward Timothy's needs.

"You take this one," she told her nephew. "It's okay if you want to go out to the barn again. Just come back before the storm gets too bad."

"Thanks." He dashed out of the house.

The corner room where their boxes were stored had a lovely view in two directions. Great for a studio, other than not having natural light from the south. That was fine, her lamps simulated daylight and she'd likely need to do most of her work on freelance commissions at night, regardless. She moved the bookshelves from her room to the studio to use for storage until she found something better.

It didn't take long to sort out which boxes

went where. She was feeling content until she opened the refrigerator to get an idea of what to prepare for the evening meal—no matter what Wyatt had said about taking care of dinner, she wanted to have hot food ready at a reasonable time.

She found little of value aside from cheese, but the *freezer* held a variety of homemade casseroles and other dishes. All had notes with women's names and some were adorned with hearts and *x*'s and *o*'s. Or else they were signed "Love," "Miss you," and "Can't wait to see you more often." She went to look at the chest freezer in the utility room and found a basket filled with similarly marked items.

Katrina made a face.

Wyatt had assured her that he wasn't likely to get married again, but she suspected a few women in the Shelton area were still hopeful. She didn't want to be a cynic, but someone who was foreman of the Soaring Hawk Ranch and a grandson of the owner was probably viewed as a more desirable husband than a cowhand living in a bunkhouse.

Casseroles didn't make a meal, but she'd brought produce and other groceries from Bozeman, including the almond butter, jam and bread that her nephew consumed in great quantities. He'd reached an age when he had a bottomless pit for a stomach and she hadn't wanted to take a chance that Wyatt wasn't well-stocked for a preteen's appetite.

A cat meowed and Katrina looked down at the sleek black feline winding its way around her ankles. "Hello."

It blinked up at her.

"I've seen your food and water bowls. What about your litter box? I can certainly *smell* the thing."

The cat blinked again.

Following her nose, Katrina found two covered boxes in the large utility room. Beyond it was a similarly spacious mud porch. The door between the kitchen and utility room had a cat flap below its window so they could get into the enclosed area, but it wasn't enough to fully contain the stink from the very dirty cat boxes. She dumped the contents into a garbage bag and refilled them. Another black cat, this one with white toes and a fringe of white whiskers over its left eye, promptly jumped in and began scratching as if digging to the center of the earth.

Katrina grinned and metaphorically pushed up her sleeves.

Time to start work. And the sooner she put the house to rights, the sooner she could focus on her commissions again.

CHAPTER TWO

IT WAS AFTER dark when Wyatt went up to the main house to get his daughter. He found his brother sitting on the living room floor, playing a board game with Mishka and Christie.

"Wow. Candy Land." The corners of Wyatt's mouth twitched. Jordan was a former Navy SEAL, the toughest of the tough, and he was playing a child's game with names like Gumdrop Mountain and the Candy Cane Forest. And seemed to be loving it.

Jordan twirled the spinner and moved his marker forward. "Don't you play with Christie?"

"Not recently. Most of her games are still packed in a box somewhere."

"I got the rainbow!" Mishka exclaimed after taking her turn.

"Yes, you did." Jordan kissed his daughter's forehead. "And Christie got to the rainbow first the last time."

Christie ran over and flung her arms around

Wyatt. "Hi, Daddy. We found King Kandy *twice*."

"That's great. Why don't you go get your coat?"

"Okay." She trotted out of the room.

His brother got up and stretched. "Did you have a difficult calving?"

"One. It's still quite early in the season, but I don't need to tell you that storms seem to prompt labor."

Jordan hiked an eyebrow. "Yeah. I also know you don't have to help with every single calving. It's all right to trust your people and delegate. Running a ranch has many of the same principles as being an officer."

Wyatt shrugged. "As an officer I had to get to know the people under my command. And trust goes both ways. Before coming back, I hadn't worked with a cow since high school. I have to refresh my skills. The crew isn't going to respect someone who doesn't have a clue about what he's doing or isn't willing to pull his own weight."

"Nobody doubts you know the job. As for pulling your own weight? You're already working eighteen hours a day. What are you going to do when calving season really gets going, never go to bed?"

"The only reason I'm the foreman is because of the deal with Saul. It isn't as if I worked my way through the ranks."

Jordan drew him out to the foyer. "Dakota and I went through the same thing. You don't have to prove yourself in the first six weeks. Ranching is a marathon, not a sprint."

"We agreed you'd let me do this my way," Wyatt reminded him. "And you're a fine one to talk. You half killed yourself in the first few months of getting the Soaring Hawk back in shape."

Jordan chuckled. "I was hoping you'd forget that, but I suppose my wife has been telling stories."

"One or two."

A familiar pain twisted in Wyatt's chest. He was glad his brothers were happy, he just wished he could have returned to Montana with Christie *and* his wife. It was odd. Sometimes he felt as if Amy had been gone forever, and other times her loss was still new and hard to wrap his head around.

"Daddy, I'm ready," Christie called as she ran into the foyer. She was learning to run thanks to her cousin, who seemed to run everywhere.

He picked her up and hurried over to the

mud porch on the homestead cabin—a name that still stuck, even though it was no longer a cabin, but a large home.

The wind whipped loudly, creaking the tall cottonwood trees that shaded the house in summertime. Yet over it, he heard strains of music coming from the kitchen. As they shook a few snowflakes from their clothes, he saw Katrina through the window in the door. He blinked. She seemed to be dancing as she moved from the stove to the refrigerator.

Dancing.

She wore a bright batik top that showed off her slim waist and gentle curves—a cheerful flame of color after the dim twilight. And she didn't have any shoes, just a pair of red socks.

Wyatt opened the door and she turned around.

He put his hand on his daughter's shoulder. "Sweetie, I want you to meet your—"

"Salem, Blinx, I *missed* you," Christie cried, paying no attention. She plopped onto the floor as the felines ran to her, their purrs revving loudly.

Katrina didn't seem perturbed. She switched off the music and went over to sit cross-legged next to Christie. "Which one is which?" she asked.

"This is Salem," Christie said, stroking the cat who had appropriated her small lap. "And this is Blinx." She scratched under the other feline's chin, whose purr rose even louder. "Cuz he looks like he's blinking all the time."

"They're beautiful. I love cats."

"Me, too." Christie focused on Katrina. "I'm Christie."

"I'm Katrina, but my nephew calls me Aunt Kat. It's Kat with a *K*." She drew a K in the air with her finger. "Not a *C* like your cats." This time she drew a *C*.

A smile filled Christie's face. "Can I call you Aunt Kat? I have an Aunt Paige and Aunt Noelle."

"That's up to your daddy."

"It's fine," Wyatt said. He'd anticipated the usual tension of Christie meeting a new child-care provider, but Katrina had smoothed the moment with impressive ease.

"Okay. I'm Aunt Kat. My nephew is out in the horse barn right now, but he should be back soon. He's twelve and his name is Tim. How old are you?"

Christie held up three fingers on one hand and curled two of her fingers on the other.

"Three and a half is a great age," Katrina said, correctly interpreting the gesture.

"I used to know your daddy when we were growing up."

"Daddy had to get growed up too?" Christie sounded astonished.

"That's right. He needed to grow up, just like you're growing. Did you get your cats as kittens? They grew up."

"I don't 'member." Christie stuck her chin out, looking thoughtful. "That was before I got born. Daddy says the cows are having babies, but they're called calfs. I don't like cows. They're awful big."

"They need to be big. And baby calves are adorable. They kick up their heels and run around, having lots of fun."

Christie didn't look entirely convinced. She wasn't just nervous of the Soaring Hawk's cows and dogs, she was also fearful of the horses.

Wyatt leaned against the kitchen counter, watching Katrina charm his shy daughter. He was glad it was going well, yet it gave him another pang to see them together. Amy should be here, helping their child learn and develop.

People often said how much Christie took after him, but she was such an individual, he only saw his little girl. More than anything else, she had a lively imagination, which was great except for the way it invaded her nightmares. After he put her to bed, he'd sometimes hear her telling stories to Fluffy Bob and the cats about riding on clouds and floating over the land. He just didn't know how she went from that peaceful image to waking up with a bad dream, convinced a monster was in the closet.

"Are you hungry?" Katrina asked Christie after a while.

"Uh-huh."

"Good. There's food in the oven that a friend brought you and your daddy."

Christie scrunched her nose, a gesture she had learned from Paige and Noelle. Or maybe she was picking it up from Paige's daughter. Mishka was such a healthy, enthusiastic little girl, it was hard to imagine the struggle she'd faced as a desperately ill orphan. It gave him hope to see her, because it showed Christie could also recover from the upsets in her life.

"I don't like the food from Daddy's friends."

"Why is that?" Katrina asked.

"They put icky stuff in it. Archick hearts and little sour things."

"I'm not sure what the sour things are. Artichoke hearts are good when you learn to like them, but that's okay. It leaves more for me to eat."

Christie appeared dumbfounded that her new "aunt" was an artichoke lover. Wyatt tried to be flexible about what she ate as long as it was a balanced diet, so he never insisted she eat things like artichoke hearts.

"Just in case, I also made macaroni and cheese," Katrina added. "And I found peas and carrots in the freezer, which are my absolute *favorite* vegetables with mac and cheese."

To Wyatt's astonishment, his daughter gave Katrina a kiss. "Thank you, Aunt Kat."

"You're very welcome. Now go wash your hands before we eat."

Christie giggled. "Like Salem and Blinx?"

Sure enough, the two cats were studiously licking their paws and swiping them over their ears and faces.

"Cats have one way to wash themselves, people have another," Katrina said. "You wouldn't want to lick all over your body to get clean, would you?"

His daughter stuck out her tongue. "That would be icky."

"Yeah, we're lucky to have showers and bathtubs. I don't think cats like being that wet because they have so much fur to get dry."

Christy touched the thick length of Katrina's dark blond hair. "You have bunches."

Katrina laughed. "That's right, I do. But people aren't the same as cats, so I still prefer showers and baths. Go ahead while I finish with dinner."

Wyatt stayed behind a moment. "It was thoughtful of you to prepare a kid-friendly dish, but I was sincere about making dinner myself. Nobody expected you to hit the ground running."

Katrina's smile widened. "I don't know how to do anything else. Besides, as I said, the main dish is a chicken casserole from the freezer."

"Uh, yeah. Old friends have been bringing things to help out, but they forget children don't care for certain types of food."

"Here's the note that was attached to the dish."

She handed him the card signed by Gretchen Corbett, a girl he'd dated briefly in high school. One of the reasons he'd stopped asking Gretchen out was because she kept passing him cute messages like this in class, even after being warned by the teachers.

He dropped it in a trash can. "The ranch gets a weekly delivery from a grocery supplier. I have a standard list, but you should coordinate with Paige on changes or anything in particular you want. She inputs the order on Wednesday evening for both the Soaring Hawk and her parents' spread, the Blue Banner."

"Okay. How is Christie about fruits and veggies?"

"Not bad. She likes bananas, pineapple, apples, oranges—that kind of thing. Also corn, peas and the more usual vegetables. So-so on broccoli. Salad is okay if it doesn't have spring greens. Basically, she doesn't like anything bitter, too exotic or different."

"Obviously artichoke hearts are too exotic."

"Yeah." Wyatt glanced down at his clothes. After working in the barn and paddock all day, he didn't look or smell great. "Is there time for me to shower before eating?"

Katrina bobbed her head.

He took the rear staircase two steps at a time and strode the length of the hall to his room. Then stopped at the doorway in surprise. The bed was a bed—assembled and covered with a comforter, presumably with sheets and blankets underneath. The two chests of drawers and the entertainment center were against the walls and the half-empty boxes and piles of dirty clothes were gone. He actually had a bedroom now instead of a junk heap.

He was amazed by it, yet he was also reminded of why he'd decided Katrina was such a good choice to hire. She got things done faster than anyone he'd ever known and putting his furniture together wasn't even her responsibility.

He threw his clothes in the now *empty* hamper in the bathroom and scrubbed off in the shower. One of the things he'd quickly gotten accustomed to again was how grimy he got working on a ranch. After a while he barely noticed, which was quite a switch from being an officer in the navy where good grooming and a clean uniform were important.

When he ran back downstairs he heard Timothy's voice, excitedly telling his aunt about the horses on the Soaring Hawk.

"They have geldings, but also stallions and mares with some real spirit," Timothy enthused. "The ranch sells weanlings and yearlings. Maybe I can buy one someday and be a ranch hand like Melody. She says most of them have their own horses in a special barn, just for the employees."

"Don't dismiss geldings," Wyatt advised as

he went into the kitchen. "They're easier to handle when working cattle."

"Yes, sir. I mean, Wyatt. They bought really quiet geldings at the Big Jumbo after it turned into a dude ranch, so beginners could ride easier. But they kept some stallions and younger mares for the staff and better riders."

"Do they breed any of the mares?"

"Nah. It isn't a *real* ranch any longer, not like the Soaring Hawk. They raise a few cows, just for appearances, or that's what Grandpa Jim-Bo says. He was able to keep living there until a few months ago. That was part of his deal with the company who bought it." Timothy looked at his aunt. "I'll go change."

Once they were alone, Wyatt knew he had to say something about his bedroom. "I appreciate what you did upstairs, but you could have injured yourself moving the furniture around. It definitely isn't the light housekeeping we talked about."

"Most of your pieces are modular, so it wasn't too hard. You must really like the modern steel-and-black-leather style. It's in the living room, too. Don't the cats claw the leather?"

"Not so far. I guess you don't care for it yourself."

"Let's just say I'm glad you didn't get the same for our bedrooms." She took two baking dishes from the oven and put them on the old farm table, along with serving bowls of side dishes.

Wyatt fetched Christie and they all sat down to eat. But at Katrina's first taste of the chicken casserole from Gretchen, a strained expression crossed her face.

"What?" Wyatt asked.

"I know what Christie's little sour things are. Pickled capers."

He ate a bite himself and nearly gagged, remembering Gretchen's beef stew had also been loaded with capers, along with a couple of other dishes. Why anyone would put capers in stew or a chicken casserole was beyond him, though he recalled her saying something about adding gourmet touches for his "sophisticated palate."

He didn't know how she'd gotten the idea he was sophisticated in any way, unless one of his brothers had made a joke about it.

Timothy was pushing the capers to one side and gulping down the rest of his supper. At his age, he was probably more interested in quantity than quality.

Wyatt served himself a big scoop of the

macaroni and cheese, while Katrina gamely kept eating the casserole.

"See?" Christie said, happily forking up her macaroni and cheese. "Daddy's friends make yucky food."

"They mean well," Katrina murmured, though she looked as if she might choke on each mouthful.

KATRINA WAS GRATEFUL she'd only taken a small serving. She liked capers in chicken piccata, but they didn't go with this particular combination. Her stomach finally rebelled at eating the last bite on her plate, so she ate another serving of the fruit compote she'd made.

"I'm tossing the chicken leftovers," Wyatt said at the end of the meal.

Katrina didn't like to waste food, but he was right. The casserole wouldn't reheat well and the flavor from the capers might get even stronger.

"Tim, go on and fix your room the way you want," she said. "I put your boxes in there."

"Okay." Timothy got up. "Uh, Wyatt, thanks for letting me live here with Aunt Kat."

"You're very welcome."

Her nephew disappeared to the back of the house where Katrina was pretty sure he'd just lie on his bed talking with his friends on social media, rather than unpacking any boxes.

"May I get down, Daddy?" Christie asked.

"Sure. Thank Katrina for dinner."

Christie did better. She ran over to give her new nanny another kiss. "Thank you, Aunt Kat."

She skipped off and Katrina got up.

"Where did the salad makings and fruit come from?" Wyatt asked as they loaded the dishwasher, an update to the kitchen she'd been grateful to see. "Since we've been staying over at the main house this last week or so, I didn't think there was much in the refrigerator."

"I got everything in Bozeman on the way here. I love fresh produce. I used to shop at Pike Place Market on my lunches. It was near the publishing house where I worked." She was going to miss the Seattle landmark and the Puget Sound, but Washington had never become home to her.

"I'll reimburse you. And be sure to add any of your favorite foods to the grocery order. Tim's favorites, too. The delivery service offers a good variety."

"Oh. Okay."

Katrina didn't care if he paid for the groceries she'd brought, but it was nice that he was encouraging her to get food her nephew particularly enjoyed. Not that Tim was a picky eater aside from having an allergy to seafood. Like any child, he had moments of rebellion, but he was a good kid. He hadn't complained in Hong Kong, though he'd been miserable there, and had tried to be upbeat and helpful in Seattle.

Wyatt rubbed the back of his neck. "I should explain the situation here since you're going to hear about it sooner or later. I have a deal with my grandfather to spend a year showing I can manage cattle in exchange for a third of the ranch in a trust. So it's even more important than usual to do a good job, because it means security for Christie's future."

Katrina's jaw dropped. "Haven't you already shown you can be a rancher? You grew up on ranches and competed at the Shelton rodeo. Quite successfully, as I remember."

"I also have a degree in animal sciences. It's fine, though. Saul isn't being unreasonable. When he found out I wanted to hire someone to help with Christie, he said the ranch would cover salary and expenses. That's why the Soaring Hawk is officially your employer instead of me."

The sound of small footsteps returned to the door of the kitchen and they both looked over.

"Daddy, will you play a game with me?"

"Sure, we can—"

A knock on the front door interrupted him and Christie's expression fell. Apparently, she already learned a visitor at night could mean her daddy would have to leave.

Wyatt went to answer and there was a murmur of discussion before he returned.

"Sorry, sweetheart."

"I know, you hafta work," Christie said, sticking her lip out in a small pout.

"It's important. There's a mama cow who needs help."

"Can I go with you?"

A mix of emotions crossed Wyatt's face, no doubt evaluating whether he wanted his young daughter to see something as down-to-earth as a cow giving birth.

"Maybe another time. It's getting close to bedtime and you have preschool tomorrow." He turned to Katrina. "I don't think Paige mentioned it, but Mrs. Bannerman picks up the kids from the main house at seven thirty in the morning. Earlier when there's rain or the roads might be icy. But it's starting to look as if classes will be online tomorrow, which includes Christie's preschool. We get an automated call from the school district when that happens. The laptop she uses for class is in the living room."

"Got it."

Katrina held her hand out to Christie. "We should have enough time for a story after you take a bath. Do you have a favorite book?"

It seemed an effective distraction because the three-year-old lit up. "The Wild Things."

"Ooh, *Where the Wild Things Are.* That's a great story. But we need to hurry so we have time to read it together."

"Okay. Bye, Daddy."

Wyatt seemed chagrined at how easily his daughter had been tempted away from wanting to watch him help with the calving. But that was her job as a nanny, right? To take the pressure off him as a single dad.

Christie splashed happily in her bath, singing a song she'd made up about mermaids and sea otters playing hide-and-seek. After a while Katrina lifted her out and wrapped her in the plush towel she'd put by the heat register to get warm.

Soon the three-year-old was wearing pink flannel pajamas covered with playful white

Persian kittens. Pink seemed to be the prevailing color in her wardrobe. Katrina had also seen gallon cans of brilliant raspberry paint, presumably earmarked for Christie's bedroom. But when she gently teased Christie about it being her favorite, the little girl scrunched her nose.

"Pink was my mama's favorite. She's in heaven now. I like blue best."

Katrina wondered if Wyatt was subconsciously pushing the color in remembrance of his wife. She'd have to speak with him before he started painting. It was one thing to be devoted to his wife's memory, another to overwhelm his daughter with reminders of a woman she'd never known. Besides, as an artist, Katrina had studied the impact of color. The intense raspberry shade was pretty, but it could be overstimulating and might contribute to tantrums.

They sat on the bed to read together, but before they started, Christie looked up. "My daddy has to work a bunch, just like he had to in the navy. What does he *do* all day?"

"I don't know what he did in the navy, but ranchers take care of animals." Katrina felt inadequate getting into the details, and wasn't sure how much her father would want her to know. "This is the time of year that cows start having babies. Sometimes they need help. Other work is needed, like putting out food before storms and cutting grass for hay. And they have to ride around and check the herds and fences to make sure everything is all right."

"The cows and horses don't hurt my daddy, do they?" Christie asked in a fearful tone. She clutched a large stuffed teddy bear close in her arms.

Katrina was at a loss for a moment. Ranchers and cowhands sometimes *did* get hurt dealing with livestock, but she didn't think the little girl needed to hear that.

"Your daddy knows how to take care of them," she said. She opened the book and began reading, but after only a few pages, Christie fell asleep.

Katrina tucked the comforter around her and checked the position of the baby monitor. She'd tested the system earlier and was going to keep one of the receivers with her whenever Wyatt was out and Christie was in bed. Right now she had laundry to run through the washer and dryer and other things to do, but it didn't have to be finished all at once. She'd accomplished a little in Wyatt's bedroom, but the other two rooms remained filled with boxes and general mess. Part of what she'd done was to simply shift the mess and boxes from *his* room to the unused spaces.

Downstairs she loaded the washing machine again and went to check on Timothy. She tapped on his door.

"Come in."

As expected, her nephew was sprawled on his mattress, phone in hand. He grinned. "My friends are really excited I'm back. I did a grand announcement."

Katrina sat on the end of the bed. "You didn't tell them before?"

Timothy shrugged. "I wanted to wait. Cuz, like, what if something happened?"

"Cuz? Like?" She smiled. "Don't let your Grandma Edith hear that. She used to be an English teacher before she went into school administration."

"Did you and Mom have to talk all proper when you were growing up?"

"Kinda sorta."

Timothy snickered.

"Did I tell you that Paige's mother is going to drive you to school and back?" Katrina asked. "She also takes Christie and Paige's daughter, Mishka, and said you were welcome to go with them. Please be prompt before and after school and don't make Mrs. Bannerman wait."

"I don't mind taking the bus."

"It's fine. Mrs. Bannerman volunteered."

"That's cool. Since I don't start until Wednesday, Melody says I can ride fences with her tomorrow if it's okay with you and the weather isn't bad."

Letting Timothy ride during the winter made Katrina uncomfortable, but she'd talked to Mary and her brother-in-law about how much freedom to give Timothy on the Soaring Hawk. Checking on the herd was an important task at any time of the year and he would love feeling as if he was already part of the ranch.

"Sure. Just do whatever she tells you. But the storm might not be over by morning, so riding may be out."

"I know." He yawned.

"Don't stay up too late," she warned.

She was folding clothes on the kitchen table when the utility room door opened and a swirl of cold air entered along with Wyatt.

With Christie in bed and no meal to serve, it was just the two of them and suddenly everything felt more uncomfortable than before.

“Hi. How did it go?” she asked.

“Healthy calf, if underweight from coming early. Mother and baby doing well. We’ll keep them in the barn for a while, then close by for observation.”

The pleasure in his dark eyes gave her a pang of wistful envy. She’d always wanted to learn how to pull a calf. The Shelton Youth Ranching Association had been great, but “town kids” had been included mostly for the social benefits, rather than to learn about the fundamental aspects of cattle ranching. She supposed that was natural—kids on ranches were living it every day, they didn’t need the association to help them understand.

That was okay; she was determined to experience it now. Learning new things was a great way to stay fresh as an artist.

Wyatt frowned as she folded a pair of jeans and put it in the basket.

“Honestly, I said light housekeeping and I meant it. I’m aware the house looks like I’m a slob, but that’s just from the pressure of the move and transitioning into being a foreman in the middle of winter. Normally I keep everything in order.”

She waved one of his socks at him. “Laundry *is* light housekeeping.”

He looked skeptical. "Maybe stuff for Christie, but those are mostly my clothes and I know they were pretty rank from riding and dealing with animals. I expect to clean up after myself. You don't have a thing about excessive tidiness, right? This is a ranch. That won't work."

Katrina laughed as she folded the last shirt. "Hardly compulsive. I'm just going to help you get caught up. I promise, after that, dealing with your stinky clothes is up to you."

"Then we'll give you a bonus in the meantime."

She sighed. While the Maxwell brothers had different personalities, one thing they'd shared was a stiff-necked pride. Life couldn't have been very warm and cozy at home with their stern grandfather, but they'd pretended everything was fine, putting their chins out if anyone asked how they were doing.

"Why don't we consider the furniture in Tim's room as the bonus?" she suggested. "If I'd realized you needed to buy him a bedroom set, I would have ordered one myself. It isn't a problem. Mary and Shawn send money for whatever he needs."

"I'm glad to have Tim here and it was great to see him excited about riding our horses.

You're welcome to use them, too, if you're interested," Wyatt said. "But I'll want to go with you a few times to evaluate which horses would be best suited to your skill level and weight."

Katrina suppressed an illogical stab of irritation. It had been a long time since he'd seen her ride—if he even remembered her from those group outings—and he would naturally want to be sure she was still an adequate equestrian. After all, the horses belonged to the ranch and he had a responsibility to ensure their safety along with hers.

"I'll look forward to it," she murmured, though she wasn't certain how much she'd actually enjoy spending leisure time with Wyatt.

He'd changed more than she would have expected. There were shadows in his eyes and a lingering sadness. It might be her imagination, but she also had a feeling he was putting the world at a distance. Perhaps it was the combination of grief and the years of being a naval officer where a certain restraint was required.

Their initial conversation had been so comfortable, she was disappointed things seemed awkward now. But maybe that was normal. No one anticipated becoming a widower and single father at his age and now he'd resigned from the navy and returned home to show he could run the ranch.

It would be challenging for anyone.

CHAPTER THREE

Billie Bertram drove through the Soaring Hawk ranch center and parked near the employee bunkhouse.

When she'd come to interview for the dining hall cook job a few days earlier, it had been gray, windy and colder than a polar bear's nose. But this morning the sun was shining and a warm, dry Chinook wind had started. The temperature had risen by more than sixty degrees in a few hours.

The ranch was on the slope of a broad, shallow valley with a sweeping view up toward the Rockies. At this elevation there was a blend of evergreens and deciduous trees. It was beautiful, still frosted with melting snow, and she could imagine how the place would look once the grass had grown in and was blowing long in the breeze.

Mmm.

She'd traveled all over North America going to rodeos with her parents and as a contestant herself, but she didn't think there was any prettier place than a Montana cattle ranch during the spring and summer.

"I suppose you think you're a better cook than me," a voice announced behind Billie. She turned to see a seventy-something woman with short, graying black hair and an air of energetic authority.

"Not better," Billie said, unperturbed. "Just different. I'm Billie Bertram and you must be Mrs. Hawkins."

"Yes, and *I* will continue cooking for the hands. We'll find something else for you to do."

Billie closed the door of her ancient truck, giving it an extra hard shove to make the cranky latch catch. She needed to find a junkyard and get another one to replace it. Fix it herself or make do was her motto.

"That's up to Wyatt Maxwell. He's the foreman. He mentioned wanting to give you more time to spend with your great-grandchildren. Besides, I'm only supposed to cook Friday through Tuesday, and then help with other work as needed. You still have Wednesdays and Thursdays. I don't intend to cook for anyone seven days a week, not even for myself."

Her comment about Wyatt Maxwell was deliberate. Billie's new boss had said that Anna Beth—who'd married Saul Hawkins a few years earlier—was devoted to her husband and new family. So she probably wouldn't fight something her step-grandson had decided, particularly if it was intended for her benefit.

Billie felt a brief melancholy pang. It would be nice to have a close family, but she'd made her choices and tried not to regret them. She'd thought about having children, she just hadn't wanted to raise them on the road the way her parents had done with her. It had been a fun, exciting life, but some kids and spouses were miserable not having a real home. Billie hadn't minded it herself, yet after fifty-four years of being on the go to rodeos all over the continent, she was ready for less travel and more peace and quiet.

At least she hoped she was ready.

Anna Beth crossed her arms over her chest. "In that case, you're on probation. I have the cowhands behaving properly. They clean up after themselves and eat healthy meals—good, solid chow and they know not to complain."

Billie tried to keep from grinning. She'd long since learned not to back down from a challenge. "I've got strong lungs," she said. "Which means, I know how to stick up for myself. I can argue the ears off an ornery bronco, so a few cowhands won't bother me."

"You sound almost as tough as Anna Beth," said a man's voice as he walked up to them. "Hello, Billie. Welcome to the Soaring Hawk. I'm Saul Hawkins and I've lived on this patch of ground for over eighty years. Forgive my wife for being difficult. She used to be in the marines and prefers being in charge."

Anna Beth's face softened as she looked at him. "You knew I was a retired master sergeant when we got married."

He gave her an affectionate peck on the lips. "Sure did. I always meant to write to the marines and thank 'em for letting you go."

"Huh. You also know they made me retire."

"Apples, oranges." Saul waved his hand. "Billie, hiring a cook was Wyatt's idea, but I endorsed it. I wanted—"

"*You* endorsed it?" Anna Beth's annoyed question broke in.

"Sure did. I want more time with my wife. Anything wrong with that? I've wasted too many years being alone."

A smile was creeping into Anna Beth's

face. "That wouldn't have happened if you weren't so hardheaded."

He chuckled. While Anna Beth was obviously a force to be reckoned with, her husband didn't seem shy about sticking up for himself, either. It was nice. Some folks assumed older couples got married for companionship, but Saul and Anna Beth really seemed to be in love.

Wyatt Maxwell emerged from around the end of the building. "Sorry, Billie, I didn't realize you'd arrived. I showed you around the other day, so go ahead and stow your belongings in the bunkhouse. Glad to have you here."

"I baked corn bread already and have beef stew in slow cookers for the crew's lunch," Anna Beth interjected.

"Great. It will give me time to explore the supplies and kitchen," Billie said cheerily.

Anna Beth's eyes narrowed. "And there's food prepared ahead in the big chest freezer."

"That'll be convenient for the days you're still cooking," Billie shot back to head off either the suggestion she use the frozen goods, or be warned not to touch them.

Billie understood the other woman was protective of the role she'd carved out for herself on the ranch, but she wouldn't let it keep her from doing her job. She'd heard an earful about the Soaring Hawk's history the times she visited Josh McKeon's rodeo school, a few miles north. He'd even offered her work when he learned she was giving up life on the road, but that was just Josh being Josh—the school didn't need a barrel racing instructor and they already had someone cooking for them.

"I'll order a second freezer," Wyatt said, visibly amused. "One for each of you."

"Absolutely not," Anna Beth returned, her expression harassed. "I suppose there's enough room in the old one for both of us."

"Then I'll get started." Billie went to the door of her camper, reached inside and pulled out a duffel bag of clothing.

She'd sold her horse trailer, but didn't intend to get rid of the camper on the pickup. She liked the security of knowing she had a home on wheels available. If the Soaring Hawk job didn't work out, she could move to somewhere new without wondering whether she had a place to sleep at night. That camper was like an old, trusted friend.

"Christie wants to know if you're having a party," said a young woman, walking up with a small child on her hip.

Billie smiled at the kid, who promptly hid her face. She was awfully cute.

"Not a party, Katrina." It was Anna Beth, her expression changing from disapproving to cordial.

"We have a new employee," Saul added. "This is Billie Bertram."

"Hi, Billie. I'm also new," Katrina explained. The little girl was still hiding her face. "This is Christie and I'm her nanny. I started a week ago." She stroked Christie's hair.

"Hi, all. Nice meeting everyone, but I better get to work now. Lots to do."

WYATT FELT A wry acceptance that Anna Beth had confronted the new cook without consulting anyone. She did things her own way. Luckily Billie didn't seem to be intimidated because she jauntily carried her duffel into the bunkhouse and closed the door. Her blithe confidence when she interviewed for the position had impressed him. He'd warned her that Anna Beth might have her nose out of joint about him bringing in a cook, but he hadn't thought his "new" grandmother would challenge Billie the minute she arrived.

"Daddy, please give me a hug," Christie

said, obviously more comfortable now that the stranger was no longer there.

Wyatt lifted his daughter from her nanny's arms and held her close.

He and Katrina had barely said more than "good morning" and "good night" since the day she'd arrived, yet each time he returned to the house for a shower or to sleep, he found everything in better shape. But true to her word about just helping him get caught up, after she'd unpacked, organized and scrubbed an area, she hadn't gone back to do more than light cleaning.

He'd been curiously reassured to find the clothes hamper with dirty laundry and his hastily made bed left as it was, however askew the comforter might be. Katrina didn't seem concerned about proving anything, which he appreciated—she was just taking care of business.

"Wyatt, Saul and I want to take Christie up to the house for the day," Anna Beth said. "I don't think Katrina has had a minute to herself since she got here, not with the kids having online classes because of the weather and the broken water pipe at the school. Hopefully they'll get everything dried out this weekend."

"That's fine. Thank you."

He was annoyed to realize that while he'd assured Katrina she would have regular days off as a nanny, he had done nothing to make it happen. It wasn't as if she'd worked months without a break, but she might be wondering if she had gotten into an impossible situation with unreasonable expectations.

Anna Beth reached for Christie, who heaved an exaggerated sigh. "I know, Daddy has to work." She kissed his cheek and accepted being shifted into her great-grandmother's embrace. "I see you later, Aunt Kat."

"See you later," Katrina echoed and watched them leave. "That wasn't necessary," she said when they were alone, "I knew you're busy with calving and other stuff. I partly came over to find out if you minded me taking Christie into Shelton when I visit family or shop or go to the post office to ship finished artwork to my clients. Obviously not the digital projects, those get sent online, but the pieces that are painted or drawn. Oh, and before long I'll need to get my Montana driver's license again."

"It's fine if you take Christie, but please use my SUV. I bought a Volvo before Christie was born because I like the safety features. Anyway, the child car seat is there and I'd rather not have it moved back and forth between vehicles. The keys are on a hook in the kitchen."

"It'll be a few days before I go, but I wanted to check. Um, if you're planning to ride fences today, is there any chance I can go with you?" Katrina asked. "There's an idea I want to discuss."

Wyatt glanced across the landscape and the blue sky, punctuated by sculpted clouds. While Chinook winds could cause hazards, even tornadoes, they weren't predicted to get that bad. It was a fine day and he wanted to make things up to her for failing to give her a break.

"Sounds good. I'm going to check on our herds to the north this morning. Do you have riding boots?"

"Yup. I often went to a riding stable in Washington, even before Tim started living with me. I'll get them."

"Then I'll see you by the paddock."

KATRINA HURRIED BACK to the house to put on her boots and grab a precautionary jacket before Wyatt could change his mind.

Because of the weather, Timothy hadn't been able to ride the previous Tuesday as planned, but he and Melody had gone Saturday and he'd helped clean the horse stalls afterward. Then his great-grandparents had come by on Sunday morning to take him to church. Basically, aside from having to attend online classes his first few days back instead of seeing his friends in person, he was ecstatic to be in Montana.

At the barn she found Wyatt had chosen a small chestnut mare for her. Angel was older and didn't seem to have much zip, but she was attractive and affectionate.

Three of the ranch's dogs raced up before Katrina mounted, excited and happy. She crouched to give them a good pet and glanced up at Wyatt. "When I lived in Shelton, Border collies were the popular dogs. But these beauties look similar to Australian shepherds, except for their floofy tails and being less stocky."

"My brothers call them Aussie collies, which is a mix of Border collie and Australian shepherd," Wyatt explained. "I'm told it's a highly desirable crossbreed. My grandfather bought several blue merle Australian shepherds for Jordan when he first returned. Then when Jordan married Paige, she brought her Border collie. He's responsible for the mix."

"They're beautiful."

"The dogs are remarkably helpful. I've been trying to get Christie interested in adopting one of the puppies that were born a few weeks ago, but she's even scared of them."

"Maybe she'll want to once she's gotten more accustomed to Soaring Hawk. It's all new to her."

"I hope so."

Katrina mounted Angel, determined to show she was competent on horseback, though she wasn't sure why it was something she wanted to demonstrate to Wyatt other than getting his approval to ride when she had time available. They rode forward, the dogs running along with them, and she sniffed the air with pleasure. She didn't know why, but everything always seemed sweeter and fresher when she was on a horse.

A man stepped out of the calving barn and gave them a tentative wave. Katrina waved back, only to spot a tight expression on Wyatt's face.

"What's wrong?" she asked.

"Nothing."

"Hardly nothing. You look as if you've eaten a sour lemon. Or maybe Gretchen's chicken and pickled caper casserole."

Wyatt's eyes were chilly. "Fine. That was my father."

Katrina blinked. She doubted there was anyone from Shelton County who didn't know Evan Maxwell's early history—he'd become an alcoholic after his wife's death, ultimately losing custody of his sons. He'd also been a wild, prank-playing teenager, though that was before she was born.

"I didn't know he was back in the area."

"You've been away yourself. Saul, of all people, found my father and offered him a job a couple of years ago." Wyatt seemed to hesitate. "Evan is also an artist. He does wood carvings."

That was interesting. "I'd love to see some of his work."

"You're welcome to ask, but I don't want him anywhere near Christie. She doesn't know who he is and I want it to stay that way as long as possible."

"You don't want her to get acquainted with her grandfather?" Katrina asked, shocked.

"No. At least not until I'm convinced he's really stopped drinking and won't upset her. Anyway, there's no guarantee he'll stay. The last thing Christie needs is someone disappearing from her life without a word. Which is exactly what Evan did to me and my brothers."

"Yeah, but sooner or later she'll figure it out. Daniel is too young to say something revealing, but Mishka must talk about her grandfather."

Katrina had met Paige's kids when she'd come over between weather fronts to visit, along with Anna Beth and Saul and other members of the family. She'd tried to be friendly with her neighbors in Seattle, but it hadn't been easy. Here she had already met most of the people on the Soaring Hawk, arranged for playdates between the children, and discovered a mutual interest in the British tradition of afternoon tea. They were going to take turns hosting a tea every month or so.

"Look, I understand that Mishka will eventually say something about Evan. If she hasn't already," Wyatt acknowledged. "And I'd never ask my niece not to be herself. But at her age, I doubt she's long on details. At the very least, I'm hoping to put off any explanations about my father until Christie is old enough to understand. Maybe by then I'll feel more assured he won't disappoint her."

Katrina opened her mouth, then shut it quickly. She had a tendency to speak before she thought things through. After all, she'd never been in Wyatt's shoes and couldn't know what kind of father Evan Maxwell had been when he was intoxicated.

Or sober.

Wyatt could have good reasons to keep his daughter away from him, though as she recalled the story, Evan couldn't have talked to his sons about leaving because there'd been a restraining order preventing him from having contact with them. That was life in a small town: everybody knew your business, almost as soon as you did. Though she'd partly known because her bedroom had been above her parents' home office and the old-style air vent had broadcast all of their conversations.

She focused ahead and saw cows drowsing blissfully in the warm wind blowing down from the mountains. A small number had nursing calves close by, while most must still be waiting to give birth. That was something else she wanted to know—how to tell a cow was pregnant. To her they all looked the same, with the possible exception of being rounder in the middle. Yet the nursing mothers also looked round. The differences must be more subtle than she knew how to spot.

She tipped her head back, reveling in the

sunshine on her face and neck. The temperature change had already dramatically reduced the snow pack on the ground—it might even be gone by the time the weather shifted again and dumped a new load of white. Yet they could also have an early spring.

"What did you want to talk to me about?" Wyatt asked after a while.

"Oh, right. I thought I could bring Christie out to the barns when you're working so she can watch and learn what ranching is all about. She keeps asking questions, including whether the 'big animals' are going to hurt you. I wouldn't let her get in the way, but it would be nice if she understood why you have to be gone so much. And this way she'd get to see you more often and maybe grow less nervous of the animals here on the Soaring Hawk."

"I don't know. She's young to see some of that stuff. What if we lose a calf when she's there? And it might be upsetting when I can't focus on her, instead of on what I'm doing."

Wyatt gave the impression of being overprotective, so it was the reaction Katrina had expected. Still, she suspected he might have to eventually accept that kids living in rural areas got exposed to the facts of life much younger than some children.

And that included grandfathers who were less than perfect.

"Then I have another suggestion," she said carefully. "When I'm not taking care of Christie, why don't I come out and watch you or the other ranch hands work? Better yet, let me get involved so I can learn by doing. I've already asked Saul to teach me how to throw a rope and I'd really like to help with some calvings and other tasks. That way I can explain and do illustrations to help her get a better idea of what you're doing. To be honest, I'm not overly familiar with ranching myself."

"How is that possible? You grew up in Shelton County and were involved in the youth ranching association."

"I was a town kid. I heard the broad strokes, not the nitty-gritty details. As for our association, it was hardly an education in farming or ranching. If you think about it, we had a bunch of parties, worked on community projects, went riding and had picnics and decorated floats for parades. But we never watched a calving or got involved in basic ranch operations. For that matter, I've only seen haying from the road while driving by. If I was more familiar with what happens, I could explain to Christie as I draw the pictures."

Wyatt shook his head. "You're already doing too much. Despite my inattention this last week, I promised you'd have plenty of time to work on your freelance commissions. I intend to keep that promise."

Katrina sighed. She didn't need him or anyone else protecting her.

"I wouldn't have asked if I thought it was going to impact my commissions. As a matter of fact, it could help. I might even write and illustrate a kids' story about ranching. The drawings for Christie could be the foundation for a picture or middle-reader book. Or both."

WYATT WAS TORN.

Spending time with Katrina held an appeal—she was an old friend as well as his daughter's nanny. At least he wanted to think they were friends. And her idea wasn't bad, as long as she didn't draw anything too graphic when it came to calving or other aspects of animal care.

But he also wanted to be fair and not ask too much. Cowhands were accustomed to long hours; it was the nature of the job. But she wasn't a cowhand. In all honesty, you had to love the life to work on a ranch. The Soaring Hawk was now paying one of the best salaries to cowhands in the state, but even with the addition of room and board, they weren't getting rich. And the ranch still needed to modernize and expand the bunkhouse to enhance living conditions.

"Come on, Wyatt," Katrina said in a coaxing tone. "You'd be doing me a favor."

"Adding work to your week doesn't sound like a favor."

"I don't see this as work. Think about it. Saying no might mean I'd never win the Caldecott. That's one of the most prestigious awards for children's books. I was fortunate to have illustrated a Maitlin blue ribbon book six years ago and I—" She broke off, a peculiar expression on her face.

"Yes?" he prompted, wondering if he'd missed something.

Katrina seemed to shake herself. "Nothing. Just imagine how bad you'd feel if you kept me from winning the Caldecott."

"Look, I know you're an artist and have that temperament thing going, but I don't see—"

A small burst of laughter interrupted him.

"You used to have a much better sense of

humor," she said, grinning. "Seriously, lighten up. Artists don't fit into one emotional category and I'm teasing, regardless. There's no way to set out to win the Caldecott aside from doing your best work possible. It would be fabulous to win someday, but I'm not holding my breath."

Wyatt was chagrined. He *was* taking things too seriously. It was a pattern he'd fallen into before Christie was born. The strain of Amy's illness had taken a toll on both of them.

"I just wanted to be sure you weren't making the offer solely for my daughter's benefit," he said, which was partly true.

"Not solely. I got the idea when I was sketching a horseshoe for her, but it quickly developed into more."

Wyatt looked surprised. "A horseshoe?"

"She didn't want to put on her shoes because Mishka had told her that cows don't wear shoes, so I explained cows didn't walk or run as much as people and horses. That led to showing her what type of shoes horses wear. I could have pulled up a picture on the internet, but it was cleaner and faster to do a sketch. She was fascinated."

"It wouldn't have looked like much if I was

the one doing the drawing. I'm probably the only kid who ever flunked finger-painting in kindergarten."

"Don't exaggerate. Anyhow, everyone has different abilities. Life would be boring if we didn't," Katrina said. "Imagine every artist painting like Picasso, or every writer writing like Hemingway. Variety is the spice of life."

Wyatt looked ahead. He'd been watching Katrina and was reassured about the way she rode, moving easily with the mare. She held the reins well, neither too loose nor too hard, and seemed able to direct Angel in the right direction with just a small movement of her fingers and pressure of the knee. Possibly a born horsewoman, though he believed that anyone could learn to ride if given enough time and practice. Still, you couldn't teach an instinctive communication with horses and that was what distinguished an adequate rider from an exceptional one.

"What do you think about my idea?" Katrina prompted.

"I'll give it some thought."

Yet Wyatt knew he would probably agree. The situation should benefit both of them, over and beyond the question of a salary and services rendered. Christie wasn't going to need a nanny forever and Katrina had to consider her future.

EVAN MAXWELL RETURNED to sanitizing the calving area in the barn, trying not to worry about his youngest son. He wouldn't blame any of his kids for hating him—it was why he'd stayed away for so long. Drinking had been an escape from his troubles when he should have been focused on raising them. He was fortunate to have made his peace with Jordan and Dakota so quickly.

Wyatt was a different story. He wouldn't talk about how he felt and was determined to keep his distance, which included keeping Christie away.

The thought of his granddaughter brought instant pride and pleasure, the same as Evan felt about his other granddaughter and grandson. And soon there would be more children on the ranch since both of his daughters-in-law were expecting. Dakota and Jordan were fortunate. Noelle and Paige were wonderful women.

Despite the tension with Wyatt, Evan was more excited about the future than he remembered being in decades. Children had an enthusiasm that adults took for granted. If he could be a small part of giving his grandkids a good life, it would be enough.

"I missed breakfast. I'm going to grab something to eat," he told Eduardo Reyes who was keeping an eye on the pregnant cows they'd moved closer to the main ranch.

"Sure thing."

Evan headed to the dining hall. He'd worked in the calving barn a good part of the night and morning. The ranch hands were on their own if they didn't make it to a meal—which was fine since Anna Beth kept the refrigerator stocked with easy-to-grab items, either to heat and eat there or take with them.

"Who are you?" asked a woman as he stepped into the kitchen. She was slim, lithe and within shouting distance of his own age. Fine-looking, too.

"Evan Maxwell." He tipped his hat.

"Billie Bertram. Are you related to the foreman? His name is Maxwell."

Evan wished she hadn't made the connection so quickly. "Uh, yeah, I'm his dad. Just looking for a bite. I didn't get breakfast. I was busy with a calving heifer."

"I'll fix something for you." She took a bowl of eggs and other items from the fridge.

"That isn't necessary. I don't want special treatment."

It was true—he liked being just a member of the crew. He did his best job and didn't think much beyond that. No lost nights of sleep, wondering if beef prices were going to crash. No stewing about the cost of feed. No payroll to get out or tax issues to juggle. All he had to do was the job he was assigned, and apply initiative or get help if he saw a problem developing.

Billie shook her head. "Hardly special treatment. I'm the new cook and general help."

He whistled. "Anna Beth isn't going to like that."

"Already know it. We talked when I arrived." Billie looked amused.

"Are you from Shelton County?" Evan asked, wondering if they'd met in his murky past.

"I haven't spent much time in Shelton, though I've traveled through here periodically," Billie said. "I'm a rodeo chaser, have been since I was born on the road. Always been one rodeo, then on to the next. My folks never made it big, but they had good times and put a little money aside. I kept going after they decided to settle down—very reluctantly,

I might add, but it was time for them. They got a place up in Great Falls."

Evan looked at Billie with even greater interest. "Did you do barrel racing?"

"Sure, along with roping and other events. When I didn't earn enough purse money from competing, I'd pick up temp jobs and get my travel money that way. Often cooking, though I've done everything from working in the chutes to shoveling horse and bull manure. Lots of manure at a rodeo. Goes with the territory. I tried traveling with another rodeo performer to share expenses, but I preferred being on my own."

"I've moved around a bit myself. What made you stop?"

"My horse was getting older and I hadn't been training a younger one, so I decided we should both retire. Lilly Jane is living the good life at a rodeo pal's ranch here in Shelton County—great care, green grass in the summer, and a warm stall in the winter. I'm going to visit her whenever I can. That mare could practically read my mind. She's the reason I looked for work in the area. That and my folks being not too far away."

"Rodeo pal? That wouldn't happen to be

Josh McKeon, would it? His wife is friends with one of my daughters-in-law."

"Yup. He owns McKeon's American Choice Ranch. I know both Josh and Kelly from my rodeo days, along with Kelly's mom and dad." While chatting, she was moving around the kitchen, cracking eggs into a pan, putting bread in a toaster and doing other tasks. She had the balanced grace of a barrel racer.

"You're going to get in trouble with Anna Beth by cooking for me outside of mealtimes," Evan protested, albeit halfheartedly since he hadn't found any appetite at dinner the night before.

Between storms and calving starting early, they were busier than usual, so his youngest boy frequently ate with the ranch hands. Evan understood it was important for Wyatt to treat his father the same as everyone else, but it got uncomfortable and sometimes he could barely choke down a few bites. Problem was, he wondered if his lack of appetite might make Wyatt suspicious he was drinking in secret.

But Evan was determined to never consume another drop of alcohol. He had a weakness and he knew it. He attended online AA meetings at night in one of the barns for privacy—

going in person when possible—and he stayed away from stores and restaurants where they sold liquor. He'd been sober for over seven years and had no intention of backsliding.

Billie plopped a loaded plate on the counter along with a bottle of hot pepper sauce. "I'm not saying you'll get this kind of service again, but Mrs. Hawkins already has a stew going for lunch, leaving me with time on my hands. Think of it as a first-day-on-the-job special. Any which way, I like staying busy."

Her no-nonsense manner was reminiscent of Anna Beth and Evan wondered how well they were going to get along. Being too similar wasn't always a good thing—they'd be like pieces of steel and flint striking sparks off one another.

Though the words "duck and cover" came to mind, it would be interesting to watch the two of them wrangling. He admired strong-willed people who didn't back down from a fight. Others might call it pure ornery cussedness, but on a Montana cattle ranch, it could be a valuable quality.

In fact, Billie might fit in just fine.

CHAPTER FOUR

"PLEASE TELL ME you aren't painting Christie's bedroom that color," Katrina said early on Friday morning.

Wyatt kept stirring the contents of the gallon can he'd pried open. "Why not? Considering the clothes you wear, I would have assumed you like bright colors."

"I do, but not necessarily on walls."

Though Wyatt shrugged, his doubts had been growing from the minute he removed the lid from the paint. "The renovations my brother and his wife did on the house are terrific, but Christie loves pink and I want her to have a room that feels special and personal."

"You just think she loves pink because..."

Katrina stopped and pursed her lips into a little bow as if she was throwing a kiss. The gesture was cute, even more appealing than the way Paige and Noelle scrunched their noses.

"That is, most of Christie's clothes are pink,

along with her sheets and pajamas," Katrina continued. "Not to mention her coats. Even if she adores it, she should have some variety."

"You think she prefers something different?"

"She's mentioned liking blue. I've studied the impact color has on people. Vivid pink won't encourage Christie to sleep. Imagine getting stirred up, right before climbing into bed."

It was a point he hadn't considered. "I'll ask what she wants."

Katrina gave him a look he was beginning to recognize. "Don't ask or try to influence her, just let her choose, preferably between pale shades. They're more versatile and easier to repaint. You can always accent with deeper tones."

Wyatt pressed a finger to his aching temple. He'd found few free moments since arriving in Montana and they would become even scarcer now that the crew was coming down with the latest seasonal virus. He hadn't heard so much coughing and sneezing since he'd been deployed at sea—close quarters tended to spread germs quickly.

It was too late to do anything for this winter, but he mentally upped the priority on building a new bunkhouse before the next cold and flu season. Private bathrooms probably weren't feasible, but he'd like to provide small individual rooms with a common area for relaxation.

"Tell you what, I'll get some paint samples on my next trip into town," Katrina suggested. "Then you can sit down with Christie and let her pick."

He looked at the open can again; the color was even more intense than he remembered. It even seemed irritating for some reason, though it was an attractive shade and one his wife had often worn. The clerk at the store had expressed doubt about his selection, saying it might be too much for a child's bedroom, but he'd insisted.

"Okay," Wyatt agreed, tapping the lid back down with a rubber mallet to be sure the seal was tight. "But let's go now. All of us. I don't know when I'll have another time to paint. Just give me a few minutes to notify the crew that I'll be away from the ranch."

Katrina looked surprised. She must have anticipated a longer debate. "I'll get Christie into her coat."

By the time Wyatt had returned, his daughter was buckled into her car seat and the engine was running, heat pouring from the vents. The warm Chinook wind had ended as quickly as it began and freezing temperatures were the norm again. But they hadn't gotten more snow, which was helpful since the cattle could easily reach any forage still available.

"Sorry it took longer than I expected. I'm glad you got the heat going in here," he said as he slid behind the steering wheel.

"It was mostly for Christie. I've noticed she gets cold easily. For me, one of the nice things about being in Montana is the lower humidity. Seattle has a fair amount of humidity year round, except when an arctic weather front moves over the area, so I'm not as affected by temperature extremes here. At least right now. Not that I don't feel the chill, but I'm not miserable, either."

"I know what you mean. But Christie takes after her mother. Amy felt cold in nearly every season, wherever we lived."

"My sister is the same. Unless it's at least eighty degrees, Mary wears leggings and camisoles under all her clothes. I would collapse from heat exhaustion. I put on extra layers when I'm riding or hiking in the winter, but that's it."

As Wyatt drove toward Shelton, he tried

to mentally calculate how much protein cake and hay remained available on the ranch and if more would be needed. Yet another part of his mind was astonished that he'd mentioned his wife without the fierce pain that usually came with Amy's memory. Was that good or bad?

"You're a million miles away."

He glanced at Katrina. "Just evaluating our winter feed situation." It was partly true.

"How much feed do cows need in cold weather?"

"Up to thirty-six pounds of forage or hay daily, depending on a variety of factors. A nursing mother is at the top of the range. We also put out protein cake."

She stared. "That's a lot of food."

"Food is energy. But my brothers started sowing cover crops a couple of years ago after haying was finished, so our herds do pretty well unless the snow is too deep or there's a bad storm. It's still tricky, though, and feed is needed for at least the equivalent of a month or two. Winter started early and there's no telling how much longer forage from the cover crops will last."

Soon they were passing the Shelton city limits and Wyatt mused that the small community hadn't changed much since he was a kid. The feed and seed place was bigger, but the schools, churches and stores were the same, including the Bibs 'n' Bobs shop that sold something of everything.

"Some towns seem to get run-down over time, but Shelton is doing well," he said as he parked in front of the hardware store. "Must be due to the rodeo. I've heard it's bigger than it used to be."

"That's right," Katrina agreed. "I used to spend half of my vacation time each year coming to the rodeo. They have big names competing now, including a few national champions from both the United States and Canada. It's a real boost to the economy, with thousands of visitors. Everyone tries extra hard to keep the town attractive to encourage people to come back."

Wyatt unsnapped Christie from her child's seat and lifted her into his arms. "National champions? It must be discouraging when someone outside of the area walks away with most of the prizes."

"They still have the silver memorial buckles, which are exclusively for competitors from Shelton County. Mishka is certain she'll win one someday."

"Jordan and Paige are going to let Mishka

compete?" Wyatt couldn't keep the shocked note from his voice.

"She's already competed. The Shelton Rodeo Daze committee has added a third category with age divisions from two years to thirteen."

"*Two years old*?" Wyatt cast a look at his daughter; she was listening intently. Little seemed to escape her inquisitive young mind. He lowered her to the ground and took her hand.

Katrina nodded. "Yup. Don't worry, two-year-olds aren't riding broncs or bulls, they do roping and other activities. Your nephew will be eligible this summer to barrel race with his stick horse. It's one of the most popular events at the rodeo, along with mutton busting, when kids ride or race sheep."

Barrel racing with a stick horse was a whole lot more reassuring than some of the other possibilities, but Wyatt wasn't so sure about mutton busting. In high school he'd cracked a rib riding a bronco. He'd pretended he wasn't injured in order to compete in the finals—not something he'd recommend to anyone. And the fall from a sheep for a young child could produce the same injury.

"Don't tell me Tim wants to compete."

"Starting at nine, kids are allowed to ride steers. They aren't as volatile as bulls, but they still buck. I told Tim to ask his parents for permission, not me."

The corner of Wyatt's mouth twitched at the conflicted emotions in Katrina's face. However confident, she was glad to leave this particular decision to her sister and brother-in-law.

Inside the hardware store, she made a beeline for the racks of paint samples, selecting color chips in light shades and circling the lightest colors with a pen before handing them to him.

"Christie, I'm going to paint your bedroom and it should be the color you like best," he explained, spreading them out to show his daughter.

She bit her lip. "My mama liked pink."

"I know, sweetie, but it's fine if you prefer a different color."

Christie shifted from one foot to the other, looking anxious. "But pink makes you happy."

Wyatt winced. His child shouldn't be worried about making him happy. "I promise, I want whatever you want."

Katrina knelt to look into Christie's eyes. "Tell you what. If you'd rather have a different color from pink, I'll paint a picture with pink in it to put on your wall. Maybe wildflowers on a hill or a sunrise. You'd like that, wouldn't you?"

Christie vigorously bobbed her head and started to go through the samples. Finally, she selected a pale blue. "Cuz it's the color of the sky," she explained. "My mama is in heaven and that's like being in the sky."

The clerk had finished with her other customer and mixed the new cans of paint without comment, though Wyatt suspected she was secretly laughing. Dark or intense colors on walls might be popular in modern decorating, but he doubted they were common in Shelton County. People tended to be traditional here.

"Never mind," Katrina leaned over and whispered. "Maybe you can add blue to the raspberry and make purple."

"What would I do with three gallons of purple paint?"

"I'm sure the calving barn can use some sprucing up. Do cows like purple?"

He gave her a sharp look and realized she was joking. His sense of humor was going to get a workout around Katrina, but he didn't mind. Today was the most he'd enjoyed himself in longer than he could remember.

"I think cows are partial to green. I'll have to speak with their interior decorator."

Her grin made him feel good.

As they were putting the cans of paint in the back of the SUV, a car horn tooted and an older couple pulled into a nearby parking space. Wyatt remembered them from when he was a kid, although Angus Bell's hair had been ginger back then, not mostly gray. He was just as tall, however, towering above his petite wife.

"I didn't know you were back," Katrina exclaimed as they got out and hugged her. "Wyatt, Christie, this is my aunt Bettina and Uncle Angus. They've been on a long vacation in Hawaii."

"I remember the Bells." Wyatt shook hands with them. "You must be retired by now."

"Aye, right, our daughter and her husband have taken over the shop. They're both pharmacists," Angus said in his distinctive Scottish brogue. He looked down at Christie. "Eh, you're bonnie, lass."

"What does 'bonnie' mean?" she asked, curious enough to peek out from where she'd hidden her face against Katrina's waist.

"Bonnie is how we say pretty in Scotland. That's where I was born a verra long time ago. My Scottish clan say that I sound as if I'm from Montana now."

Katrina and her aunt laughed. It seemed to be a family joke. Even Wyatt had to smile, because even if Angus had picked up a few idioms from his adopted home, he still sounded distinctly Scottish.

KATRINA WAS DELIGHTED at the unexpected encounter with her aunt and uncle. It was a reminder of why she'd wanted to move back to Montana. Video calls were okay when you didn't have anything else, but family had been a daily part of her childhood and you couldn't hug someone online.

Yet she knew Wyatt had to be restless. He'd shown amazing patience while his daughter was choosing which color she wanted, but he must be anxious to return to work, either to begin painting Christie's bedroom or to his job as foreman.

"It was wonderful seeing you, but we should get going," she told her aunt and uncle. "Wyatt needed something at the hardware store and we rode in with him."

"That's quite all right," Aunt Bettina said

as they both hugged her again. "It's lovely to have you and Tim back home. Seattle was just too far away."

Christie gave them a polite goodbye wave and eagerly got into the SUV.

The phone rang while they were on the way back and Wyatt pressed the answer button on the steering wheel.

"Hi, boss," Melody said in a raspy voice. "You wanted me to let you know if anything changed. There's a heifer having trouble with calving. Nothing to worry about, we've got it handled."

"I'm sure you do, but we're on the way back. I'll be there in half an hour or less."

Melody went into a fit of coughing and couldn't talk for a minute. "S-sorry," she finally choked out. "Eduardo, Carmen and your brothers are out checking on the herds, but Rod is here with me. Your fath...uh, *Evan*, is in the horse barn along with Stedman. I can always ask them to come over, so there's no need to—" She began coughing again and Wyatt told her to get off and catch her breath.

"Melody sounds awful. She should be in bed," Katrina murmured after the call disconnected.

"That probably isn't going to happen with a

cold. You wanted to learn how ranches operate," he said wryly. "The reality is that ranchers and cowhands generally have to keep working, even when they're sick. Animals don't stop needing care."

She lifted her chin. "Sorry, but if Tim gets a cold, he's staying in the house and getting plenty of rest and fluids. You don't want to answer to Mary if he comes down with something serious. *Or to me.*"

Wyatt laughed. "I don't expect a kid to do chores when he's sick, though I admit my grandfather was pretty strict in that department. We did our work, no matter what. But… well, since I rarely catch anything, it wasn't much of an issue. In the navy they loved that I rarely went on sick call."

Katrina wondered if there was something Wyatt was holding back. She liked Saul, but there had been whispers around town from his employees when she was a kid, suggesting he was cold and demanding with his grandsons. Even so, it seemed Wyatt had genuinely forgiven his grandfather.

She cleared her throat. "You don't seem to resent Saul."

"He was hardest on Jordan. Probably because he looks like our father. But after he enlisted, Dakota and I were allowed to do stuff outside of school and the Soaring Hawk. And Saul is making a real effort to make up for the past."

Katrina glanced into the back seat at Christie and saw her head was bobbing sleepily. "You seem to have a decent relationship with him now."

"Yeah. He's a funny old guy, but Anna Beth and Paige keep him in line. Just don't be surprised if he starts hinting we should get together. He isn't above attempting a little matchmaking."

She blinked. "Why should he do that? He must know you don't want to get married again."

"Saul wants to see his grandsons happy and has decided a wife is the answer. I'm told he wasn't subtle about trying to push Dakota and Noelle together three Christmases ago."

Katrina shook her head. "He hasn't said a word to me and probably won't. Paige grew up on a ranch and Noelle is a doctor. Either would have sounded more promising as a prospective granddaughter-in-law to a rancher than an artist."

"Don't put yourself down. Saul may still get around to suggesting it to both of us."

"I'm not putting myself down, I'm being realistic. Ranchers' daughters and doctors have more to contribute on a ranch."

"You're probably right. Noelle was working for an international relief organization when she met Dakota, but my grandfather must have figured she might be willing to practice medicine in Shelton if she and Dakota fell in love. And that's exactly what happened."

Even though Katrina didn't see Wyatt as a potential romantic partner, the relieved look on his face was almost an insult.

Stop, she ordered.

She found Wyatt attractive, but that was as far as it could ever go. And she couldn't help remembering what he'd said about her batik tops. She also had a few eye-popping tie-dyed ones. After years of working for a publishing house with a conservative dress code, her leisure wardrobe had become even more vibrant than it might have been otherwise. Gordon hadn't appreciated her choices, preferring her clothes to be more conventional when they spent time together. His attitude alone should have told her they weren't compatible.

Even if Wyatt was looking for a wife, there was a good chance he'd feel the same way.

That wasn't how she wanted to live her life,

always feeling as if she wasn't measuring up to someone else's ideas. The shock was that she'd dated and been engaged to Gordon for so long. He wasn't a horrible guy, but when everything was added up, he was totally the *wrong* guy.

"You have an odd expression," Wyatt said as he turned onto the Soaring Hawk Ranch road toward the main ranch.

"Something you said reminded me of my ex-fiancé."

"That doesn't sound like a compliment."

"Just consider it extra insurance I won't start whispering sweet nothings into your ear or subscribing to bridal magazines."

"Great. That is—" He released a heavy breath. "I'm sorry. But we're friends, right?"

Katrina lifted her chin and gave him a cheerful smile. "Right. Friends."

WYATT WAS RELIEVED Katrina didn't seem too upset about her ex, or that he'd reminded her of the guy for some reason. The things you accepted in a friend were different than a loved one.

"It looks as if I won't be painting Christie's bedroom right away. Maybe later, after the calf is born, if something else doesn't come up," he said. "We really aren't in calving season yet, but a few are being born premature. I'm also told a bull got loose and found its way to a group of cows earlier than planned last year, which means more full-term calves are coming earlier than usual."

"I can do the painting."

"*No.*" Wyatt sighed, immediately regretting his sharp tone. "It isn't that I don't appreciate the offer, but this is something I want to handle myself. If necessary, I can put Christie to bed in my room and paint then. She'll have to sleep somewhere else for a few days while the fumes dissipate, regardless, and I can bunk on the couch."

"Don't you believe in sleep?"

"You're a fine one to talk. There's a light in your studio window nearly every time I have to go out at night."

"I'm excited about my projects. That's all."

Wyatt parked near the homestead cabin and as they were getting out, Paige came over from the main house. "Hey, everyone. Christie, would you like to come play with Daniel?"

Christie yawned and agreed.

"Daniel can spend the day with me," Katrina offered.

"Can I take you up on that on Monday instead?" Paige asked. "Anna Beth and my mother have plans to shop in Bozeman and I've got four of my ranch accounting clients scheduled for appointments. They don't object to my son being around, but it's more efficient to focus on business without him."

"Monday is fine. I ordered a stack of children's art supplies, so be sure he's wearing something that washes well."

"Everything he owns washes well. And maybe this way, you'll get a chance to watch Wyatt and the cowhands working today."

Her grin suggested she knew all about Katrina's request to observe him on the ranch. Wyatt still wasn't sure if it was a good idea, but he could give it a try for a few hours.

"For a while," he said.

As they headed for the calving barn, Eduardo came out. "We just delivered that calf, boss. Melody is putting the mama and baby in a pen. Rod radioed in to say they found repairs needed in the far south pasture and won't be able to check the herds to the west." He sneezed, suggesting he might be coming down with the seasonal bug running through the crew.

"That means no one has been there since

the weather turned cold again. What about Jordan and Dakota?"

"They went north toward the Circle M."

Wyatt gave Katrina an inquiring look. "Interested in going for another ride?"

"I'd love to. Just give me a few minutes to get ready."

True to her word, she was at the horse barn before he'd finished saddling the horses.

"This is Stormy," he explained, patting the mare he'd picked for her to use. Katrina had handled Angel so well their first time out, he'd decided to let her ride a younger, more spirited animal.

"She's gorgeous. I've never seen a horse that color before. Outside of a picture, at least."

"Stormy is a blue roan."

As she'd done with Angel, Katrina approached Stormy from an angle, coming in from the front left to be sure the mare saw her.

"You're a beauty," she murmured. "Do you want to be friends? Cuz I'd love that."

Stormy swung her head and nudged Katrina's shoulder.

"What a friendly girl."

Katrina put a gentle hand on the mare's halter and continued talking to her. After another minute of quiet communication, she climbed into the saddle.

"Are you glad to be back in Montana after so many years in the navy?" she asked Wyatt as they headed west, four of the ranch dogs racing ahead of them. Their energy was astounding.

"I'm pleased not to be working in an office so much," he said. "But I didn't mind being deployed, other than having to be apart from my wife. There's a sense of peace on the ocean, even with a few thousand fellow sailors onboard. More time for reflection and reading. When I was off duty and flight operations weren't taking place, I'd find a quiet spot and read or write letters. Sometimes I'd just watch the waves or study. There's always more to learn about ships and their equipment."

"Sounds nice. The Seattle area has a number of ferries. They aren't the same as being on the open ocean, but I loved going on them. *Especially* when a school of dolphins would swim along with us."

"We have hawks here instead." Wyatt pointed to a bird diving toward the ground, probably going after a mouse or vole. He'd already seen several of them in hunting mode and it made him wonder if another storm could be brewing. As he recalled, birds seemed to get quieter right before the weather began to turn, but they were also more intent on feeding.

"We should pick up our pace," he said, urging Flash into a faster trot. "I expect to move a few of the pregnant cows closer to the main ranch and it will take some time."

Wyatt wasn't concerned about having to move a dozen or so cows alone—he couldn't count on Katrina, she didn't have any experience—but he had the Aussie collies. In the weeks since he'd returned, he had discovered they were a valuable part of the team.

Trying not to be obvious, he began checking his satellite phone for weather updates. The predictions remained the same, but as the sky became less blue and more diffused with white, his gut told him a storm was coming into the area. Weather was unpredictable, especially this time of year.

"Hey, what's up?" Katrina asked after spotting Wyatt looking at his phone for the fourth time in an hour.

"It feels as if a weather front is developing, but the predictions still say clear skies for tonight. Don't let it bother you. I'm probably making a mountain out of a molehill."

"Is that why you're moving some of the cows?"

"Not because of the weather. It's just a good idea to move the ones that aren't thriving or are closer to delivery to where they can be watched more easily."

Katrina patted Stormy's neck, admiring her black mane against her seemingly blue coat. She knew it wasn't actually blue, just an optical illusion of black and white hairs.

She straightened. "How do you *know* when they're getting close to calving? I look at them and don't see anything different. Even the few nursing mothers I've seen are roundish in the middle."

Wyatt shrugged. "Various signs. For example, their udders may swell or they look narrower because the calf is shifting into the birth canal. Another indication is bulging on one side of their abdomen. I suppose some of it is just a feeling."

A yip from one of the dogs caught his attention and he turned his horse to check on a cow complaining by a pond. With an economy of motion, he dismounted, pulled on water waders, took a hatchet from a saddlebag and chopped a wide space free of ice for the animals to drink.

"Do you have to do that very often?" Katrina asked when he'd finished and ridden back. Even with the water waders, it must have been a frigid, hard task.

"Often enough. That's one of the reasons we come out regularly, so the water supply can be evaluated. Cows eat snow, but we don't always have snow on the ground through the winter. And ponds in shade don't necessarily melt, even during a Chinook."

Katrina ducked her head, not wanting him to see the admiration in her eyes. She'd never considered it before, but there was something quite sexy about a guy who worked that hard. No fuss, just getting the job done and focusing on the next task.

Careful, she warned herself.

This was the first time since high school that she'd been around a man who handled rugged outdoor tasks. It would be easy to start thinking she felt something that wasn't real. And, since Wyatt was a confirmed bachelor, it was also unwise.

But as the air grew steadily colder, Katrina still found herself watching Wyatt as much as the cattle. He might fumble sometimes with his daughter, but he was utterly comfortable in the saddle, seemingly aware of everything around him at once. No one would ever guess that he'd spent so many years away from cattle country wearing a navy uniform.

She wanted to paint him. He was the epitome of a Western cowboy. His easy charm as a teenager was less ready now; instead, a quiet self-confidence had taken its place, making his appeal climb higher. When she thought about it honestly, there were moments she hadn't completely liked him as a kid, particularly when he hadn't paid her much attention. At the time she'd just thought she was a touch envious of the other girls.

At the edge of the Soaring Hawk property, Wyatt sent the dogs after certain cows, rounding them up. They bellowed a protest, but the Aussie collies determinedly chided them forward.

Katrina wasn't sure how to help, but she rode to the opposite side and tried to keep any individuals from breaking away from the small herd, yelling and waving her hands, similar to what she saw Wyatt doing. The cows obviously wanted to stay put.

A flake of snow hit her cheek. She glanced upward...and shivered. The sky was no longer blue, and behind them it looked as if a wall of white was descending from the Rockies. It was the first time in her life that she'd been vulnerable and exposed to an approaching storm so far from a safe shelter. Stories about cars trapped on mountain passes and hikers lost in storms flitted through her mind.

"We're fine," Wyatt called as if reading her thoughts.

"Uh, okay."

Katrina had to take his word for it. Anyhow, he inspired trust. She pulled an extra scarf from her pocket and wrapped it around her throat and across her mouth. Her gloves weren't the best for handling reins, but they were heavy, lined and rated to subzero temperatures. She was particularly glad she'd put a heavy sweatshirt on underneath her coat and taken the time to don leggings beneath her jeans—ironic considering her earlier conversation with Wyatt about being less susceptible to Montana chill.

Who would have guessed a few hours later they'd be in an impromptu cattle drive in the midst of a gathering snowstorm?

Wyatt rode back and forth to check on the cows huddled against windbreaks, giving hand signals and verbal commands to the dogs. They gathered more animals as they moved eastward toward the main ranch. The return pace was slow.

One of the dogs stayed close to Katrina, helping to keep the cattle moving. She thought her name was Kiki.

"Kiki?" she called.

The Aussie collie looked up and yipped, a happy expression on her face, despite the icy wind. Apparently, this was just a grand adventure from her perspective.

Katrina had heard working dogs were happiest when they were out with their people. Kiki and the others seemed to be living proof of that. Perhaps play and work were one and the same to them.

"How are you doing?" Wyatt called as he rode up.

"I'm fine. I'm not sure how to illustrate this for Christie, but I'll figure it out."

"I apologize. A storm wasn't predicted, or I wouldn't have brought you with me. Maybe I shouldn't have let you come along, regardless."

Katrina was immediately worried. Wyatt still hadn't agreed to let her observe ranch operations and she didn't want him finding an excuse to say no.

"Nonsense," she said stoutly. "If I stop trying new things because something might happen, I'd miss out on everything. I love doing new stuff."

"Even herding cattle in a blizzard?"

Katrina blew a snowflake from her lip. "Hardly a blizzard yet. And I can't claim to be doing much herding. Kiki is working the hardest. Mostly I'm yelling at cows to get back with the others and gesturing wildly to convince them I mean business."

Wyatt smiled faintly. "Close enough. Just don't try anything creative. Two cowhands are riding out to help and the others are distributing hay and protein cake to the more crowded pastures near the main ranch. Forage is less available there. Predictions have changed. We could get several inches of snow this afternoon and tonight. Not a true blizzard, but enough to cause problems."

He rode away again and Katrina focused on the noisy group of cattle. She was warm enough, though the cold would creep in after enough time had passed. Yet it was exhilarating to be part of the actual work of the ranch.

Kiki yipped and Katrina smiled at the Aussie collie. She was going to play a big role in any story Katrina painted and wrote about ranching.

And so was Wyatt.

CHAPTER FIVE

EVAN RODE WEST along with Carmen Melendez, one of the other ranch hands. He couldn't help being concerned that his son was out in the storm alone with an inexperienced tenderfoot to watch after, along with a herd of pregnant cows.

It was illogical.

Wyatt knew what he was doing. He had GPS on his satellite phone and his location could be tracked from the main ranch or on one of the other cowhands' phones. Not only that, the dogs with him could find their way back to the Soaring Hawk, solely on instinct. Besides, it was just a small herd being moved.

Evan didn't know much about the young woman who was with Wyatt, except that she was taking care of his granddaughter and had never lived or worked on a ranch. He remembered her waving when riding away with Wyatt the other day—a friendly, uncomplicated wave at a moment when he'd particularly needed it.

The swirling snow lightened, improving visibility, and they finally spotted a group of cattle moving their direction, along with two people on horseback.

"Helloooo," Evan called.

He directed his gelding around the southern edge of the herd, knowing from the rider's size it wasn't Wyatt, who might be displeased to see his father was one of the hands who'd ridden out to help.

The young woman smiled at him. "Hi. You're Evan, right? I'm Katrina."

"Evan Maxwell. My daughter-in-law sent this for you," he said, extending a thermos and insulated travel cup.

"That's nice of her, but Wyatt needs it more. He chopped out a frozen waterhole earlier and has been moving back and forth constantly in this wind."

Evan realized his concerns had been unjustified, at least about Katrina. She might be inexperienced, but she had a sound head on her shoulders.

"No problem," he said. "Carmen has a thermos for him."

"OKAY."

Katrina was doing all right, but the wind *was* starting to crawl under her clothes. She'd have to get one of those long coats she often saw on ranch hands; they probably kept out the chill better.

She poured a cup of the coffee and took a sip. It was strong, sweet and creamy, intended to provide both a warm jolt of caffeine and calories to a chilled rider.

When she'd swallowed a fair amount she looked at Evan. "Mishka showed me a wood chest you made with animals carved into it. She keeps her special treasures in there. I don't do carvings, but I paint and sketch and do graphics on the computer."

"Carving keeps my hands busy."

Evan was watching the herd, as well as peering across the sea of animals to where his son was riding. It was hard to be certain under these conditions, but Katrina thought she detected a wistful longing in his face. He was a handsome man, but he appeared older than his years.

"You're very talented," she said. "I hear you have a workshop in one of the barns. Is it all right if I take a peek sometime when you're there?"

Evan focused on her again. “You’re welcome to take a look, whether I’m there or not. Most of us have something to keep us occupied when the ranch work is slower.”

“I was under the impression ranching never slowed down.”

Evan chuckled, sounding so much like Wyatt that Katrina was startled.

“Sometimes there’s a quieter period after the fall market. The size of the herds is nearly half of the summer peak and that helps. But animals always need tending and maintenance is needed. You can’t do much when there’s bad weather, particularly at night, so having a distraction is helpful.”

“Is wood your favorite medium?”

“My *only* medium. I never got into carving stone. I like wood. It’s organic and something I can take anywhere. The workshop is only needed for larger projects.”

“I tried both carving and sculpting in art school. Also pottery. They suggested I stay focused on computer graphics and painting.”

Evan laughed again. “I started out with a stick of wood and a hunting knife. I have a range of tools now, chisels and the like. No computer unless you count my cell phone.”

Katrina nodded. She didn’t want to bring up

Wyatt or Christie, which could get awkward, but it would be great to connect with a fellow artist. "Truth be told, I prefer a paintbrush over my computer. Maybe we'll find a chance to get together soon and compare notes."

"I'd like that."

Evan headed off to chide a cow forward and Kiki darted over to help. The herd continued growing and Katrina marveled that Wyatt and the other ranch hands could see which cows should be moved, and which could stay.

She drank more coffee and gathered as many impressions of the day as possible, though not all of them could be shared with Christie. The little girl might become more fearful than she was already.

The question Katrina had was whether Wyatt's protectiveness contributed to some of his daughter's anxiety. Christie was afraid of all the animals on the Soaring Hawk, she was nervous of new people—which was why she didn't go to church with her cousins and the rest of the family—and seemed to worry about her father's safety an inordinate amount. Nearly every day she asked if her daddy was all right and if the big animals on the ranch would hurt him.

Maybe it was normal after all the upsets in Christie's life, but Katrina had to wonder.

THE STORM HAD blown over by morning and Wyatt spent the time checking on the herds, along with his brothers and part of the crew.

Wyatt would prefer bringing all the animals into shelter during bad weather, but that wasn't possible with such a large herd, so they kept a close watch for any that were struggling. New calves were the most vulnerable. This morning two chilled newborns had been found that needed warming at the main ranch, but both were treated quickly and returned to their mothers.

By three o'clock Wyatt was assured the herds were doing well and he headed home to give his daughter a hug, only to find no one there. The Volvo was parked outside, along with Katrina's SUV, so they couldn't have gone far.

Blinx had been asleep on the couch and slanted him a disapproving look for interrupting his nap. The feline yawned and settled down again as Wyatt belatedly recalled Jordan mentioning a tea party being planned at the main house.

Play tea parties with her cats had become

one of Christie's favorite activities before they'd moved.

The cats had been less enchanted with the activity.

Wyatt headed to the main house, smiling at the memory of his daughter trying to convince Blinx and Salem to sit at a small child's table in order to consume imaginary treats. Luckily, on the Soaring Hawk Christie had resident playmates with her two cousins. And while Daniel was too young to appreciate pretend tea parties, Mishka probably loved them.

He resisted knocking on the front door—his sister-in-law had declared he was family and should come right in. But she was accustomed to a multigenerational home with lots of coming and going, while Wyatt's years in the navy and life in cities had made him uncomfortable with that much informality.

"We're in here," called Paige from the living room.

His eyes widened as he went in and saw everyone dressed in what his mother would have called their Sunday best. Low tables offered real food on pink glassware, including biscuits and a tiered server holding small sandwiches. This was no imaginary tea party with reluctant feline companions.

Christie waved. "Hi, Daddy."

"Yippee, it's Uncle Wyatt!" Mishka cried.

The two girls ran over, each grabbing one of his hands with both of theirs and dragging him to a chair.

"Uh, what's all this?" he asked.

"Afternoon tea," Noelle said. "We decided to start having them as a break in the routine. Paige and Anna Beth wanted to host the first and they've done an amazing job. They even got out the old Depression glass that belonged to your great-grandmother."

"That's nice. Don't let me interrupt. I just came by for a minute."

"You hafta eat, Daddy."

A chorus of agreement from everyone else followed.

Wyatt shifted uncomfortably. He wasn't as grimy as usual, but he was hardly presentable for a party. Besides, it was too reminiscent of formal social events in the navy when he'd needed to wear full dress whites.

"Sorry, Christie, I really need to go back to the barn." She looked so disappointed that he sighed. "But I suppose I could stay for a while."

His daughter smiled and wiggled with pleasure. The others were smiling with her and didn't seem the least troubled by the appearance of a casual guest in the middle of their gathering. He glanced at Katrina. She was wearing a greenish-blue sheath dress that matched the shade of her eyes. It was quite a switch from her usual bohemian batik tops and jeans.

Both styles were attractive, but the change made him uncomfortable—maybe because of his years in the navy where a certain discipline and routine were expected. Katrina was all over the board, like a burst of fireworks. He didn't know how to deal with someone so unpredictable. Perhaps he wasn't as flexible as he'd thought.

"Wyatt?" Anna Beth's voice broke into his thoughts and he saw she was offering him a plate loaded with small, crustless sandwiches beside squares of cake and biscuits.

His new grandmother was another mystery and the last thing he'd expected was to see her wearing a dress and hosting an English tea party.

"Uh, this is fancy," he said, uncomfortably trying to balance the plate on his knee, along with a teacup and saucer from Paige.

Katrina moved a small round table next to him and he gratefully set the delicate glassware on its surface. He focused on her again and saw her eyes were dancing with merriment.

Okay. He was out of place in his cowboy boots and coat in such a formal setting. But if he took off the coat, it meant he'd need to stay longer and he had work to get done.

Wyatt blew out a breath, recalling what Katrina had said about him not believing in sleep. Truthfully, he couldn't remember the last complete night of undisturbed rest he'd gotten. None since returning to the Soaring Hawk, that was certain. As a matter of fact, it had been days since he'd even *sat* longer than a few minutes. He didn't care except for wanting to spend more time with his daughter. Nonetheless, it was better than being deployed on a ship when he wouldn't be able to see her at all.

"These biscuits are great," he said after munching one down.

"They're huckleberry scones," Katrina leaned over to whisper. "Anna Beth used frozen huckleberries instead of currants."

"Oh, right."

The niceties of an afternoon English tea were lost on him. But surely a scone was simply a biscuit by another name. Then he recalled that cookies were usually called biscuits in England.

A dog's bark and smaller yips suddenly came from the back of the house, making his daughter jump.

"That must be Dixie and her puppies," Wyatt said casually. "Do you want to visit them, Christie?"

Christie stuck out her lip. "Uh-uh."

He wanted to ask if she'd changed her mind about adopting one of the puppies, but it seemed clear from her face that she was still opposed. Whenever Christie was visiting one of his brothers, they thoughtfully kept their dogs in a separate part of the house to keep her from being scared. If only she could get past her fear of them, it would be easier.

Wyatt ate the last of the small sandwiches and realized it was mostly cucumber inside. Well, there was a first time for everything.

The others had finished eating and they insisted on piling his plate again as if he was in the last stages of starvation. Christie helpfully dumped several teaspoons of sugar into his second cup of tea, which he managed to gag down anyway. She tried to fill his cup again, but Katrina diverted her with an impish expression on her face.

Wyatt had wondered if his daughter's new nanny would find life tedious on the ranch after so many years of living in the city. But she was obviously finding outlets for her seemingly boundless energy.

Now he mostly wondered how far he was going to get dragged into her various pursuits.

KATRINA HAD TO give Wyatt points for being a good sport. He rushed over as often as possible during the day to see Christie and give her a kiss or hug, depending on the state of his clothes. But he couldn't have expected a dressy afternoon tea.

As the party wound down, Anna Beth and Paige wanted to send the surplus they'd made home with her, Paige's mother and Noelle, but Katrina shook her head.

"Thanks, but not for us. Some of the sandwiches are salmon. Tim developed an allergy to seafood when he was in Hong Kong. I don't want to take a chance of having any trace of it around, especially after the drama at school a few days ago. Anyhow, there's still stuff in the freezer from Wyatt's, um, *friends*."

"What happened at school?" Noelle asked.

"They promised me that the cafeteria didn't serve any seafood, but Tim got hives at lunch on Tuesday. So after everything settled down, I made a pest of myself at the cafeteria kitchen. Turns out they'd used a commercial pasta sauce seasoned with a little anchovy paste. That's all it took."

Paige's eyes widened. "I had no idea his allergy was so serious."

"I'm not crazy about seafood, anyhow," Anna Beth confided. "But I found some online tea menus that included salmon sandwiches, so I went ahead and made them. Chicken or ham would have been fine."

Noelle leaned forward, still in her concerned physician mode. "Did you bring him to the clinic?"

"Yes. He saw Cheyenne Wycoff, not her father."

"I hope Tim carries an EpiPen. He seems mature enough to understand how and when to use it."

"He has one, but he forgets to bring it with him more often than not," Katrina explained. "His parents also keep ordering medical alert bracelets, which go missing almost as soon as they arrive. I didn't think it would be as much of a problem here in Montana—Seattle is known for its seafood, not Shelton. Guess I was wrong."

"I'll talk to him if you'd like," Wyatt broke in. He'd been gulping his food, no doubt hoping to get out the door as fast as possible. "Maybe I can convince him to carry what he needs to stay safe."

"Sure. That would be great."

She would never have asked Wyatt to help with Timothy, but her nephew already idolized the ranch foreman and if he was going to offer, she'd accept. Wyatt might be the only person who could convince him that wearing a medical alert and carrying an EpiPen was simply a question of good sense. So far, she and his parents had been unsuccessful.

Paige and Anna Beth refused her help in cleaning up, so she suggested she take all the kids back to the other house for a Saturday-night sleepover.

"Yippee!" Mishka exclaimed.

"I don't think Daniel is ready for sleepovers, but Mishka can go," Paige said. "We keep a backpack ready for outings. Slumber parties are popular at school, just like when we were kids."

Soon Katrina was shepherding both girls into their coats and taking them across the yard to the homestead cabin. The minute they'd run upstairs to play, Wyatt opened the front door, rubbing dirt from his boots on the mat.

"I should have objected to the sleepover," he said in a low tone.

She blinked. "Why?"

"Because now you've got two kids to watch and you also agreed to take care of Daniel on Monday."

Katrina laughed. "Daniel and Mishka are terrific and no trouble at all. As a matter of fact, they keep Christie entertained. Especially Mishka. They have playdates and visit often on the computer during storms. Isn't that part of why you wanted to come back to Montana, so she'd have family close by?"

"Yes. I just don't want you to feel taken advantage of. Not that I think Paige would intentionally do that."

Sheesh. Sometimes Wyatt acted so proper and correct, he could still be wearing his navy uniform and expecting the Secretary of the Navy to drop by for an inspection.

"It's nice you're concerned, but I'm the one who offered," Katrina reminded him. "And just so you know, I found a baby cam in a box I unpacked. Do you want me to set it up?"

Wyatt rubbed his forehead. "That isn't necessary. Are you tech savvy, too? Seems unusual for an artist."

"More stereotypical ideas about artists?" Katrina hung up her coat and took off the overshoes she'd worn to cross the yard. "I love painting and sketching, but I also use a high-tech computer for my digital art. Because of that, I took IT courses so I could repair and upgrade my own equipment."

"Then you're doing better than me. Is Tim around? I could talk to him now about the allergy issue."

"He's spending the night with my grandparents. He said to tell you that he'd done his chores this morning and will be back tomorrow afternoon to help clean the stables."

"Tim is doing a great job. The challenge is keeping him from taking on too much." Wyatt cleared his throat. "By the way, about me showing you some of the ranch operations—I'm on board if you're sure it's something that will benefit us both. And if you haven't changed your mind after riding for hours in a storm yesterday."

Katrina almost threw her arms around Wyatt's neck in her excitement, but she didn't want him thinking she was hitting on him or anything. She'd resisted pushing for an answer and was delighted he'd agreed.

"I'm positive. Yesterday was an adventure. Christie is already asking questions about it. She enjoys watching me draw and always wants me to explain what's going on in the picture. I can develop a story narrative depending on what she responds to the best. I should be paying you for the research opportunity."

Wyatt looked rueful. "I'm still coming out ahead in this arrangement. You were quite helpful with moving the cattle. Tuesday morning then, after Christie leaves for preschool? I don't know what I'll be doing—you never know what's going to happen between the weather and calving. As you've already seen."

"I'll be sure to dress appropriately."

"You'll mostly be observing, though the outfit you're wearing right now wouldn't survive long, even as an observer."

Katrina brushed her fingers over her lace-and-silk sheath. "We wanted to make our first afternoon tea an event. This was my maid of honor gown when Mary and Shawn were married. I'm glad she didn't ask me to wear something hideous that couldn't be used again."

"Are ugly bridesmaid dresses a thing at weddings?"

"Not with the people I know. I've been a bridesmaid five times and after minor modifications, I ended up with five nice cocktail dresses. Considering the number of cocktail parties I expect to attend from now on, they should keep me supplied until I'm a very old lady. Did you have a big wedding?"

Pain filled Wyatt's eyes. "No. Amy wasn't close to her family and preferred a small civil ceremony. It's just as well. I'm not reminded as much when I have to attend weddings now."

"Sorry, I shouldn't have brought it up," Katrina apologized awkwardly. "But Christie is also asking about wedding pictures of you and her mother. She sees the photos Paige and Noelle have displayed and wonders."

"That's all right—I prefer people not walking on verbal eggshells around me. There are a few pictures from our wedding day, but I'm not sure which box they're in. Though the navy accepted my resignation, my commanding officer wasn't happy I was leaving, so he loaded extra assignments on me through my last day. I'd pick up Christie from day care, come home, stuff a few boxes and fall into bed."

The loosely packed boxes made even more sense now, along with so many being opened, but not emptied.

"That wasn't very nice of him."

"We saw the world differently. He didn't have a life outside of the navy and couldn't understand why anyone would want one. Most of the officers I've known are really decent people."

Katrina pushed away a lingering wistfulness at the devotion Wyatt still felt for his wife. It wasn't envy, more a wish she could experience that kind of love for herself. The more she thought about it, the more she knew she'd never really loved Gordon. But how did she get to the point she trusted herself to recognize the real thing?

The sound of children laughing filtered down from the second floor and she pointed at the ceiling. "Time to change my clothes," she said, forcing a smile. "And check how things are going up there. See you later."

WYATT STRODE TOWARD the calving barn, his head spinning.

Katrina had that effect on him.

He hadn't paid attention when they were younger, but now he wondered how she managed to be so enthusiastic about everything. He liked working with animals and had been happy to get married and see his daughter being born, but for the most part he put his head down and did what he needed to do without investing too much emotion.

Maybe it was from growing up with Saul, who had been a grim guardian, worried his grandsons would turn out the same as their father. Ironically, though Saul had been hardest on Jordan, it was Dakota who had inherited Evan's wildness and appreciation for practical jokes. Being a Navy SEAL had helped channel Dakota's energy, but it was Noelle who'd brought him real peace.

Wyatt had felt that way about Amy. When they'd met, all the mismatched pieces of his life had fallen into place, only to scatter again when he lost her. He'd been trying to pull himself back together ever since, but it wasn't easy.

One thing was certain, he never wanted to risk that kind of loss again.

He walked the length of the barn, evaluating how much space was available in case another storm arrived right away. A few cows were in pens where they could be watched.

"Everything is fine," said a voice as he returned to the calving area.

It was his father.

"I thought Eduardo was on duty out here this afternoon."

"He's congested from that chest cold. I suggested he take a hot shower and get a bite before coming back. I was just checking the calves in the pasture for issues and now I'm going to clean the calving chute."

Wyatt worked to keep his face neutral. After all, his father's initiative was a good thing. When someone was sick, taking a break could keep them going more easily. He was lucky to have a crew who supported each other, though it was through no credit to him. His brothers had brought the Soaring Hawk back from disaster after Saul's age and stern temperament had wreaked havoc on the place. They now had a solid crew of cowhands working for the ranch.

He and his brothers also owned their father's old ranch, the Circle M, obtained by paying off unpaid taxes when they were in the navy. Since their return, Jordan and Dakota had put the Circle M land back into production and expanded the size of the herd. A good thing since the two spreads were now supporting four families, six ranch hands and a cook.

Wyatt just had to keep things going. Even on a ranch this size, every single animal made a difference. His brothers continued to work hard, but they were stepping back from the foreman's role, letting him run things for the next year.

Well, they were *trying* to step back, Wyatt mused, recalling the discussion he'd had with his eldest brother the day Katrina had arrived. Letting go couldn't be easy for Jordan or Dakota, particularly with their backgrounds as Navy SEALs. And it wasn't that he didn't appreciate Jordan's concern, but they each had their own style.

"That sounds good. Say, does anyone in your artist guild make medical alert dog tags?" Wyatt asked, remembering the earlier discussion about Timothy's seafood allergy.

Evan nodded. "Joey Pascall does that type of work. He's located in Miles City."

"Do you think he'd be open to a rush job?"

"Things are slow in the winter, so he should have the time. I'll send you a text with his number and let him know you might be contacting him." Evan took out his phone and sent a couple of messages.

Wyatt's phone bleeped and he glanced at the information. "Thanks."

"No problem. Son, I'd really like to—"

"I need to check the pregnant mares," Wyatt said quickly, recognizing the expression on Evan's face.

He wanted to talk and clear the air, but Wyatt wasn't ready to hear whatever excuses his father had to make for abandoning his parental responsibilities.

EVAN SIGHED ONCE he was alone. He'd told himself not to push, but the temptation had nearly gotten the better of him. The funny thing was, it was Jordan he'd expected to have trouble forgiving him, not Wyatt.

"I thought you had the afternoon off to work on your wood carving."

Turning, Evan smiled at Billie. She was quickly settling into life on the Soaring Hawk, despite the ongoing power struggle between her and Anna Beth.

"It didn't feel right taking the time with some of the crew being sick."

"I know what you mean. Eduardo sounds as if he's swallowed a tuba. But the fridge is stocked with ginger ale and orange juice to keep them hydrated, and I have a slow cooker filled with chicken soup for the patients. And of course there's always coffee."

He chuckled. "What does Anna Beth have to say about a slow cooker full of soup?"

"Not much. Paige mentioned Mrs. Hawkins does the same thing when folks aren't well. Paige is a real sweetheart. She adores Anna Beth, but she's fair."

Evan bobbed his head. "Noelle is a charmer, too. Never thought I'd have a daughter-in-law who's a doctor."

Billie nodded. "Even on days Noelle works at the clinic, she checks on everyone who's sick, telling them to slow down, drink more fluids and get more rest. Not that they listen when it comes to resting."

"Cowhands are ornery. We have to be."

"I figured that out real quick. You're almost worse than rodeo performers." She stopped and seemed to reflect. "I take that back. Rodeo performers are worse, but your lot comes a close second."

Evan laughed.

He and Billie had gotten into a habit of sharing a pot of decaf joe late at night in the dining hall when everyone was asleep. Neither of them were good sleepers and he also had trouble settling down after attending one of his online AA meetings. Working on a ranch made it a challenge to attend in person—there wasn't enough time to drive somewhere every day—but online groups gave him a safe place to talk and get things out of his system.

He was still working on recovery. Making amends for his behavior might be his biggest hurdle. He'd wanted to return for years, to find his boys and tell them how sorry he was, but facing them had seemed impossible. Now he was doing what little he could to help make their lives better, and those of their families.

Yet he wasn't being entirely up front with Billie about his drinking problem, which wasn't right, either. Everyone in the county knew he'd had a problem, except he hadn't told her about AA and attending meetings every day. It wasn't that he was ashamed of the meetings—they helped keep him on track—but it was difficult to reveal so much of himself to a woman he found attractive.

He shoved the thought away. "Don't forget, you're like a cowhand now. You don't just cook."

"Hey, buddy, there's no 'just' about cooking," Billie said tartly. "If an army marches on its stomach, then cowhands ride on their tummies, not to mention their stubborn back—"

"You know what I mean," he interrupted with a grin.

"Don't forget it. And don't forget I knew how to ride a horse before I could walk. I can rope and ride with the best. The things Lilly Jane and I could do in the arena would astound you."

Evan didn't doubt that was true.

BILLIE BEGAN CLEANING soiled straw from the calving chute. Evan worked alongside her and then mixed up a batch of disinfectant.

She liked the quiet camaraderie, though she half expected him to say something about his son. She'd waited for Wyatt to leave the barn before coming in herself, not wanting to accidentally overhear anything being said between them.

Family relations on the Soaring Hawk were interesting and more than a little complicated. But Billie was loving it all. She was making inroads with Anna Beth and Saul was a fun old guy—in love with his wife and embracing his golden years with his family around him.

"Thanks for grooming Stormy after the storm yesterday," Evan murmured after they'd applied the disinfectant and were waiting. "Katrina wanted to do it, but she's never groomed horses before and I told her she could learn another time."

"I can groom horses in my sleep. Stormy reminds me of Lilly Jane—her personality, that is."

"What kind of horse is Lilly Jane?"

"An American Quarter Horse. A palomino. She's a beauty. Fast and agile. Smart as a whip. I'm going to go visit her as soon as I have a couple of hours free. Want to come with me?"

The tips of Evan's ears turned red. "Isn't that like taking me to meet the family?"

Billie snickered. "Hah. We barely know each other. I just like showing her off to people."

"Either way, I'd love to go. Consider it a date."

A date?

Now it was Billie's time to feel warm. She hadn't dated that much, too focused on her rodeo career and getting from one venue to the next to think about men. Her socializing had mostly been with fellow competitors, going to a movie or bowling or barbecuing a burger together. She would have been better off money-wise continuing to have a travel buddy to share expenses, but she'd liked her freedom.

Now Evan was making her think about some of the stuff she'd missed over the years, like romance and companionship.

CHAPTER SIX

KATRINA WAS FRUSTRATED the next day when Paige brought over three additional dishes prepared by women from the church. She was trying to use everything from the freezer as fast as possible and now there was more?

"Don't they understand Wyatt has someone cooking for him and Christie?" she asked in exasperation. "And that he also knows his way around a kitchen?"

Paige gave her a sympathetic smile. "They want to be supportive, but I can't deny the ones doing the cooking are single or divorced and aware he's a widower with a young child. They assume that sooner or later he'll want to get married again."

"They're wrong. Wyatt has made it very clear he has no interest in marriage."

"How do you feel about that?"

Katrina made a face. "I haven't been here long enough to form an opinion, aside from being convinced he means every word."

"People *can* change their minds. I decided *I* wasn't ever getting married, then I met Jordan. Now he's adopted Mishka, we've had a son, and are expecting again." Paige's finger stroked the small curve of her stomach. She was just starting to show. "It isn't unreasonable for someone to think Wyatt may change his mind."

"Is that why you adopted Mishka, because you didn't expect to get married?" Katrina asked.

She was trying not to be envious of Paige and Noelle, who was also pregnant. She just wished they'd complain a little about swollen feet or morning sickness; it might make her less wistful.

"That's right," Paige said. "I'd had a couple of unhappy relationships in college and Noelle kept telling us about the orphaned children she'd seen when she was doing international relief work. I knew adopting was something I wanted to do."

Adopting as a single mother hadn't occurred to Katrina before, but it was a possibility. A plan immediately started forming in her mind. She could spend the next few years taking care of Christie and getting even better established as a freelance artist. By then, Christie might not need a nanny.

The adoption process could take a while, but it wasn't as if she didn't have time. And by working from home—a house would surely become available by then—she wouldn't need to worry about day-care costs. She could start looking into the possibility once her sister and brother-in-law returned from Hong Kong.

"Well, how do I stop all this food from coming?" Katrina asked. "The thought is appreciated, but honestly, it isn't much help. I think they're trying too hard, using too many herbs and unusual ingredients. Before I ever arrived, Christie had decided her daddy's friends made yucky food, so I always have to fix a second main dish."

Paige scrunched her nose. "I'm not sure what you can do. They all dated Wyatt at one time or another, which makes them feel a connection to him. They're nice people. I wouldn't want to give any offense."

"Neither would I," Katrina affirmed.

She'd gone to school with the women sending gifts of food and there wasn't a stinker in the lot. She liked to think it showed good taste on Wyatt's part, though why it mattered to her was a mystery.

"I'll think of something," she added confidently.

"I'm sure you will." Paige left, taking Christie, who wanted to play with Mishka.

Katrina tapped her foot as she contemplated the stack of empty bowls and baking dishes on the end of the kitchen counter. She had labeled the ones she'd emptied with the owner's name, thinking Wyatt might want to return the items personally, or at least take them to the community center where they could be picked up more easily. But he seemed oblivious to the growing pile.

Granted, he spent few waking hours at the house, though he'd painted Christie's bedroom the previous evening. The walls were now a soothing pale blue. He'd closed the hallway door and cracked the windows to let any fumes escape. Instead of giving up his bed, Katrina had suggested creating a blanket fort in the living room for Christie and Mishka, who had both loved the idea.

Making up her mind, Katrina wrote out a list, then transferred the new food into different containers, washed them and hauled everything out to her SUV. Luckily the empties from before she'd arrived were also marked with the owner's name.

"Going somewhere?" Wyatt called as he walked up from the horse barn.

"Christie is spending the afternoon with Mishka, so I'm returning these containers. Want to come? The food was cooked for you and Christie, so it would be courteous to offer a polite thank-you."

"Some of that food was barely edible."

Katrina firmly closed the rear door of her SUV. "If you're going to act that way, then you *aren't* invited."

"I didn't say I wasn't coming."

WYATT SNAPPED HIS mouth shut, realizing he'd basically agreed to go along.

How had Katrina managed that?

He regarded her warily. She was such a forthright person he didn't even think she'd done it deliberately, but the result was the same. So instead of updating the stock records in the ranch office, he would be returning empty food containers.

"Why didn't they use disposable pans?" he grumbled.

"Probably because it's more personal and homey this way. Here's the list. You can be the navigator."

They got into her SUV and she backed

around while he called Melody to tell her his plans. Going into town twice in three days for personal reasons made him feel he was being a neglectful foreman, yet he detected a note of relief in Melody's voice, however hoarse from her cold.

"Sure thing, boss. Everything is fine. It's below freezing, but the sun is shining and the cattle are foraging well. A lot of the snow has dry evaporated."

"All right, but I won't be too far away."

"Gotcha."

He got off and looked at Katrina as she drove up toward the highway. "I feel slothful."

She laughed. "Slothful? You must be channeling your grandfather. You're working eighteen hours a day, but you're being slothful to spend part of an afternoon doing something that needs to be handled?"

"It was one of Saul's favorite expressions when I was a kid," Wyatt admitted. "I could swear Melody sounded glad I won't be around for a while."

"Nobody likes having someone looking over their shoulder every minute. Melody is the second in command, but you're the third foreman she's dealt with in the last four or five years. Have you ever thought the Soaring

Hawk crew might be concerned about their jobs?"

"Why should they worry about that?"

"Because you and both your brothers are here now, along with six other employees. Didn't Jordan start by hiring five people?"

Wyatt settled deeper into the passenger seat. "Yes, but the Circle M land has been put into production and the herd is larger. You just saw a small portion of the ranch and herd the other day. We need the help."

"You might remind them of that. People like having job security. They also want to know you trust them."

Katrina was talking about morale as much as anything. He supposed she was right.

"I'll think about it." He looked down at the sheet of paper she'd given him. The list was neatly organized, with names and addresses and the dishes to be returned to each. "This shouldn't take too long. Most of these addresses are in town."

"And half the stuff goes back to Gretchen Corbett. That's why I put her first."

Katrina's wry voice made Wyatt chuckle. "She must have bought every pickled caper in Montana."

"Everyone has different tastes. Maybe she loves them."

The Corbett house was on the south end of Shelton—a huge two-story Arts and Crafts home that was a showpiece in the community.

"You know the theory about the Corbett fortune, right?" Wyatt asked as she drove down the long driveway lined by stately trees, their leafless white and gray branches standing out against the blue sky.

"Supposedly they were ruthless land speculators back in the 1800s."

"Actually, I heard a much more scandalous story about a Vivienne Belle Corbett making her fortune in Paris and touring the United States as a famous cancan dancer. Under an assumed name, of course."

"Don't repeat that," Katrina said hastily. "I happen to know Gretchen took serious grief over the rumor, which turned out to be fabricated by another girl who was jealous."

Wyatt wondered *how* Katrina knew, then realized it must have come from her parents. Being the daughter of the principal and the football coach would have had both perks and drawbacks.

Gretchen stepped onto the porch, smiling

as they got out of the SUV. Wyatt carried a large box of containers to her.

"Hi," Katrina said cheerily. "I don't know if you remember me. I'm Katrina Tapson."

"Of course I do. Your sister and I were good friends."

"Wow. Not many seniors remember a junior classmate. Anyhow, I started work as Wyatt's housekeeper and Christie's nanny a couple of weeks ago. It was thoughtful of you to help with meals before I arrived and I wanted to be sure you got your containers back."

"Oh." Gretchen seemed disconcerted and put the box on an outdoor chair. "I'd be happy to do more. Cooking or taking care of Christie. Whatever. I love children and I've heard your nephew is there as well."

"You're generous to offer, but I'm doing fine. It's easy to cook for kids. Their tastes are simple and Wyatt mostly eats at the bunkhouse dining hall. I hardly see him." Katrina leaned forward and spoke in a confidential tone. "I think he might be miffed I suggested he come along today. What a workaholic."

Wyatt tried not to laugh.

Seeing Katrina deftly parry Gretchen's attempts to get more involved in his life was worth a few hours away from the Soaring

Hawk. It was also an education, because nothing she'd said was unkind or strictly untrue.

"I don't know if Mary has heard about my divorce," Gretchen murmured. "I'd hoped we could reconnect, but I moved back after she left for Hong Kong. My ex-husband was a workaholic, too, which is why we aren't married any longer. I wanted time for us and to start a family, but he only had time for his business. He's in imports and exports."

"I'm so sorry. I've met my share of workaholics. I was even engaged to one before I came to my senses."

"Then you know what I'm talking about. Can you come in for a cup of tea?" Gretchen asked.

"Maybe we could go out to lunch one of these days instead. I don't want to hold Wyatt up any longer than necessary—he's obviously convinced the Soaring Hawk will fall apart if he isn't there every minute, keeping an eye on everything."

Gretchen made a face. "I understand. I'd love to get together. Just call and let me know when you're available. It would be great to catch up."

Wyatt stared, disconcerted by the exchange.

Suddenly he had gone from being marriage bait to practically invisible.

The remainder of their deliveries were the same. Katrina's breezy I'm-in-charge-now manner was a clear message to everyone involved that while their contributions had been appreciated, they were no longer needed.

"How long have you been planning this?" he asked as they got a cup of coffee from the Shelton market. The store had an excellent deli and despite his desire to get back as soon as possible, Katrina had talked him into stopping.

"I didn't plan anything," she said in a low tone. "But another three casseroles were sent home with Paige after church and there was that stack of pans and stuff on the kitchen counter getting in my way. When Christie wanted to go over and play with Mishka for the rest of the afternoon, I decided to deal with them."

Wyatt nodded, grateful. Katrina had the strategic abilities of an admiral.

"Hi, Mr. Reyes," Katrina said in a louder voice to the man behind the deli counter. "I didn't know you were here on Sundays."

"We're shorthanded right now. Welcome

home, Katrina. You, too, Wyatt. My son loves working at the Soaring Hawk."

"Eduardo is a fine cowhand. Good instincts."

Mr. Reyes's smile widened. "He gets them from his mother. Tell the cashier that the coffee is on me. Along with these." He handed them a pastry box he'd filled.

A couple came up wanting food from the deli case, so Wyatt and Katrina nodded their appreciation and stepped away.

"Do you want to relax for a while and enjoy our coffee?" Wyatt surprised himself by asking.

"Sure."

There were several customers in the sitting area, but they found a quiet space in one corner.

"This is new," he said, looking around. The cozy space didn't have a trendy café décor, but the setting was pleasant, with historic photos on the walls, along with old-fashioned cooking implements. Outside the windows he saw a fenced garden that probably provided an outdoor eating area in warmer weather.

"A lot of things have changed since we were kids."

Wyatt nodded, thinking Katrina was one

of those changes. She was still herself, yet different. He'd been fascinated by her lively personality as a teenager, but now? Perhaps it sounded corny, but she made him want to be a better person. It made him wary and drawn to her, all at the same time.

"Are you actually going to have lunch with Gretchen?" he asked as Katrina poured more cream into her cup.

"Of course." She looked surprised that he'd asked. "I wouldn't have suggested it otherwise. I don't know if we have much in common, but even though she was one of the popular kids, she wasn't unkind to the younger students. I can't say that about everyone in school."

Wyatt wanted to ask if he'd behaved badly at that age, but wasn't ready to find out.

"Good afternoon, Katrina," interrupted a hearty voice.

"Hi, Dr. Wycoff." She stood and gave him a hug. "I brought Tim to the clinic the other day but didn't see you."

"Cheyenne told me what happened. The school cooks are certified in food safety, but we're planning a refresher course, emphasizing allergies. There are hidden sources of allergens—even most Worcestershire sauce brands have anchovies in them. Tim is doing all right, I trust?"

"He's fine. Do you remember Wyatt Maxwell? I'm his daughter's nanny."

"Great to have you back in Shelton, Wyatt." The two men shook hands. "Your sister-in-law has been a fine addition to the clinic. I always hoped Noelle would end up practicing medicine in Shelton."

"We're fond of her, too."

Dr. Wycott chuckled. He had been Katrina's childhood doctor and remained an active physician for the community. "I'm sure you are. I'd better get going. I promised to bring home chile rellenos for dinner and don't want to forget."

Wyatt took a long drink of coffee from his cup once they were alone, wondering how many more of Katrina's friends they'd encounter. Despite her absence from Shelton, she seemed to know everyone and they all wanted to say hello.

"By the way, I've ordered a medical alert ID tag for Timothy," he explained. "Your name and number will be on it as his emergency contact. Basically, it's going to look like a dog tag. I always had to wear one in the navy and thought that might be less objectionable than a bracelet. I'll wait until it gets here to speak with him."

KATRINA WAS TOUCHED that Wyatt had come up with an option that might be more palatable to a twelve-year-old kid. He was a good person and a good father, though she still thought Christie might be better off if he didn't fuss so much about her.

What was the balance between encouraging a child to be more adventurous and protecting them from the genuine dangers of the world? And was it any of her business, even though she was watching Christie as her nanny?

"That's thoughtful of you."

"Not really. I know what it's like to be different at his age. For any reason."

Wyatt didn't add to his comment—he didn't need to. Growing up as the grandson of Sourpuss Hawkins couldn't have been easy. Yet Saul had turned out to be a nice guy beneath it all. If only he could have discovered that part of himself while Wyatt and his brothers were kids, then everybody would have been happier.

"I had a nice conversation with your father while you were moving the herd," she said, then winced. Wyatt's dad probably wasn't the best subject to raise. "I hope you don't mind. We talked about his wood carving."

Wyatt shrugged. "As I said, getting acquainted with Evan is your own business. But I haven't changed my mind about him being around Christie. He might also try to use your friendship in order to see her."

"Uh, yeah. I understand. Tim mentioned a number of the ranch's mares are carrying foals," Katrina said, deliberately seizing on another topic. "I hope that doesn't include Stormy. Moving cattle in a snowstorm wouldn't have been easy on her, pregnant or not."

"She isn't having a foal this year. All the pregnant mares are in one of the new barns. But I doubt she noticed carrying you, regardless."

"Hardly."

Wyatt cocked an eyebrow at her and she rolled her eyes. "You just think I'm smaller because you're over six feet and packed with muscles. Besides, except for Aunt Bettina, my family is tall. By growing up with them, I've had to learn creative problem solving."

He grinned. "That's obvious. You stopped Gretchen in her tracks. I doubt she's looking at me as a prospective husband any longer. For which I'm very grateful. Friendship is fine, but nothing more."

Katrina felt a little guilty. "That wasn't my intention. I just wanted her to quit sending those awful casseroles."

They finished their coffee and tossed their cups in the composting bin. The cashier waved them out, saying she knew the coffee and pastries were from Mr. Reyes.

Outside the sky was a clear, deep blue and the breeze cool, rather than chilly. Katrina drove to the ranch and parked next to the house.

"Thanks for going with me. And look at that." she pointed to the clock on the dashboard. "It took less than four hours, even with a coffee break. Now you can go do your ranch foreman thing again."

Wyatt grinned another time. "I wouldn't have missed seeing the way you handled Gretchen for the world."

"I didn't handle her," Katrina said, exasperated. "I just let her know what was going on."

"I suppose. Do you still want to observe me on Tuesday?"

"More than ever."

AS SOON AS Christie and Timothy left for school on Tuesday morning with Mrs. Bannerman, Katrina walked over to the main equipment building where she'd arranged to meet Wyatt.

She found him loading heavy sacks into the back of a truck.

"What's up for today?" she asked.

"Cattle need mineral supplementation. The tubs in the pastures have to be checked regularly and refilled. It isn't a glamorous task, but the rest of the crew is busy. Sometimes the guy in charge has to do the fill-in jobs."

"Returning baking dishes wasn't glamorous either," Katrina said with a shrug.

If he thought he was going to discourage her, he was wrong.

The truck jounced heavily as they drove out to the first location and refilled a tub with a blend of minerals and cottonseed meal. Then another and another.

"Do you know where all of the tubs are?" she asked at their fifth stop.

Wyatt finished mixing the contents of the tub and leaned against the hood of the truck with a remote expression, his gaze fixed on the cows in the pasture. "Yup. They're in the same locations as when I was growing up, though these tubs are new. You know, my grandfather has his faults, but he's a true cattleman. He has a degree in agriculture, but his biggest asset is having a gut understanding for what it takes to raise healthy herds."

"I'd say his biggest assets right now are you and your brothers and their wives. And his own wife, of course."

The ghost of a smile curved Wyatt's mouth. "Anna Beth still isn't happy I hired a cook, but it seemed the best way to give her more time with the family and Saul."

Wyatt continued to focus on the cattle and though Katrina wanted to ask more about the mineral supplement, she remained quiet, stepping on the front bumper to sit next to him on the hood. Sometimes silence spoke more clearly than words.

Katrina loved all the seasons in Montana, but winter particularly intrigued her as an artist. Maybe it was because aside from evergreens, the season stripped everything down to the bare bones, tree trunks and branches standing out in stark relief. Undergrowth was minimal and features of the landscape weren't softened by long grasses.

The land was asleep, hunkered down against wind and rain and snow, while the animals either slept with it, or had adapted to survive in a harsh environment. And now everything was poised, waiting for spring, however long it would take to arrive. That sense of anticipation was difficult to capture in art, but it didn't stop her from wanting to try.

"Saul was reluctant to spend money for a long time," Wyatt said after a while, "though he was always willing to buy good horses and get whatever the herds needed. I've learned some of the Hawkins family history since I returned, which explains why he was so tightfisted. They had serious financial struggles through much of the twentieth century. Guess it made him determined to hang on, no matter what."

"Except sometimes holding on too tight destroys what you're trying to protect."

"I suppose."

Katrina ached to hug Wyatt. Or more accurately, she wanted to hug the little boy who'd grown up in an austere household with a miserly grandfather. Saul was a nice person now, but that didn't change Wyatt's childhood. The surprise was that he'd opened up to her a little—a tiny crack in the wall he kept between himself and the rest of the world.

"It must have been hard on you as a kid," she said.

"We survived. He didn't pay us for our

work on the ranch, seeing it as a family responsibility, but Jordan found a way to get spending money to me and Dakota after he enlisted," Wyatt explained. "He also sent us one of those prepaid cell phones. We had to keep it hidden from Saul, of course. Mostly we texted when no one else was around."

"Saul has changed."

"Yeah. Dakota stuck around for a year after he graduated so I wouldn't be left alone here. It's funny how memories come back. You asked about the tub locations and suddenly I'm recalling all sorts of things I haven't thought about in years. I don't even know if I've ever really thanked Jordan and Dakota for what they did for me."

Katrina gazed up the valley to the blue mountains beyond. She could see how the ranching life could become addictive. It was hard, unending work, but the beauty of the land and the challenge must be nearly irresistible.

"You never know what's going to trigger a memory," she said softly.

"Maybe, but don't get the idea I resent my grandfather. He was lonely and unhappy for decades. That's a terrible price to pay."

She believed Wyatt *had* forgiven Saul, it

was his father's failures he was struggling to understand. She got it. When Wyatt lost his wife, he dedicated himself to his daughter's well-being, while his dad hadn't been able to cope with his grief. But Evan's failures didn't mean he hadn't loved his sons, or that Wyatt hadn't loved Amy with all his heart. They were just two different people.

The cattle around them nudged snow aside and munched on the forage beneath. A few had calves, while most were probably still waiting to deliver. She tried to spot the signs of impending birth that Wyatt had talked about, but could only see one cow that seemed to be acting any different than the others.

"That cow over there," she said, pointing. "Is she close to having her baby?"

"Yes. I've been watching her. She's been lying down, then getting up, and lying down again. It's one of the possible signs. Think I'll take a closer look."

He held out a helping hand, but Katrina slipped and he caught her as she slid down the length of his hip and leg. "Oops. Sorry." She looked up and saw his pupils had dilated, likely from annoyance.

"Uh. No problem."

Wyatt headed for the cow and she sighed.

At least she hadn't mashed his foot. He could say what he liked about her being just as she was, but he'd feel her entire weight landing on his toes, even protected by a boot.

She hurried toward the expectant cow, who was bellowing loudly now. But before Wyatt had a chance to examine her, a wet calf was delivered onto the snowy ground. The mother quickly got up and began licking her baby.

"Wow."

Katrina's impulse was to move the calf somewhere warm, or at least to a surface that wasn't frozen, but even if she didn't know that much about ranching, she knew range cattle were protective mothers. This one wasn't going to let anyone near her new baby; she was mooing and pawing the ground in warning, all while tending her newborn.

"Even an unassisted birth is messy. Are you sure you want to learn how to pull a calf?" Wyatt asked.

"More than ever. That was *amazing*."

"There should be plenty of opportunities with the size of our herds. We're going to sort them out next week, getting the rest of the pregnant cows closer to the main ranch, and separating ones that have calves into less crowded areas. The peak of calving is usually at the end of March and we have to be ready."

"Is the Soaring Hawk considered a big ranch?"

"We've become one of the largest in the area." The pride in Wyatt's voice was unmistakable. "Adding the land from the Circle M helped, but the potential has always been here for a bigger herd."

"Can I be part of moving the cattle?"

Wyatt regarded her narrowly. "It isn't the safest job in the world and you're inexperienced."

"Billie hasn't worked on a cattle ranch before and she's out checking on the herds right now with Evan."

"She isn't inexperienced. Billie has spent her life around rodeos, where they have an abundance of rambunctious steers, bulls and broncs. I can ask her to do almost anything the other hands are doing."

"I have to start somewhere. Besides, you said I was helpful the other day."

Wyatt looked exasperated. "Yes, you helped. But I don't want you to get injured. I expected to move a few cows, and instead it turned out to be over a hundred head during a snowstorm. It still bothers me I put someone without any cattle know-how in the middle of that."

"Your protectiveness is sweet with Christie. Not with me," she said.

"You're impossible." Despite his protest, he was beginning to smile. "All right, you can participate."

Katrina controlled her own grin as Wyatt headed back to the truck. He needed to relax. It was obvious that running a ranch was one of the toughest jobs in the world, but he was making things harder on himself—he didn't have to oversee all the operations on the Soaring Hawk, every single day.

Paige had confided that letting go of such tight oversight on the ranch had been one of Jordan's biggest challenges, the same with Dakota, and it appeared to be an issue for Wyatt as well…just for different reasons.

In the navy Jordan and Dakota had commanded SEAL teams and been responsible for life-or-death decisions. Wyatt must have also made life-or-death decisions while serving, but Katrina suspected he was also trying to regain the sense of control he'd lost when his wife died.

CHAPTER SEVEN

ON THURSDAY MORNING after Christie left for preschool, Katrina rushed to the barn where Saul Hawkins was going to teach her the basics of grooming a horse. He had turned out to be such a nice old guy, she hadn't hesitated to accept.

She didn't like asking Wyatt to show her everything and Saul had offered when he heard she wanted to learn. He seemed eager to pass on his knowledge.

It was cold, the wind sweeping down through the main ranch, channeling between the buildings into stronger gusts. She closed the barn door tightly behind her to keep out as much chill as possible.

Down at the end of the long building she saw Saul and Evan sitting on hay bales, deep in conversation as they rubbed oil into their saddles. You would never know they'd been bitter enemies for most of their adult lives.

"That's a fine old saddle," Evan was saying

as she came close enough to hear, gesturing to the one Saul was oiling. "I like it better than the new styles."

"This was my first as a young man. But some of the newer ones distribute the rider's weight more evenly, which is easier on a horse for a long day of work. I wouldn't want the synthetic stuff though. Leather just gets better with age and care. Gotta pay for what you want with horses and saddles."

"I don't know." Evan looked thoughtful. "I've seen people get lucky when it comes to horses. Auctions can be a good place to find a bargain. It can work out pretty well, though I'm not in favor of them. Too hard on the animals."

"Right. I prefer buying direct from the owner. But there aren't any bad horses, only ones that have been badly handled. We just don't have time to rehab 'em here on the ranch."

Katrina hated to interrupt.

What would it have been like when Evan was a wild young man, courting Saul's daughter? If only they could have seen into the future and realized that after all the tumult of their lives, someday they'd be sitting and peacefully exchanging thoughts on horses and saddles. How sad that they might have been friends all these years instead of combatants, with their families torn between them.

Evan looked up. “Hello there, Katrina.”

Saul waved her over. “Right on time. Ready for your lesson?”

“Absolutely.”

“Fine, fine.” He put his saddle aside, along with the rag he was using to work the leather. “I’m glad you don’t expect someone else to take care of yer horse.”

“I felt terrible when I had to leave Stormy for someone else to groom.”

Saul’s approving smile widened. “Stormy is a fine mare, but she isn’t a true cutting horse—that’s a horse trained to separate cows from a herd. Wyatt spoke to me and we both think you should ride Banana Split from now on. She’s spirited and the right size. You can learn how to groom with her. It’s a good way to bond with a horse and learn some of their personality quirks.”

Though Katrina had become fond of Stormy in a short time, she was pleased to have any horse to ride. During her years in Seattle, she’d spent a small fortune at riding stables in the area. Being able to ride for free was a terrific perk of working for the Soaring Hawk.

"I'm looking forward to meeting her."

"All right then. Come along." He picked up the bucket sitting next to him on the hay bale.

Katrina followed Saul to one of the stalls. She knew the horses were inside the barn today to protect them from the wind and low temperatures. A horse poked her head over the stall and nickered as they approached.

"Hello, girl." Saul patted her neck. "Banana Split is a buckskin Quarter Horse," he explained.

The mare had a sandy yellow body and brownish-black points, with a stripe down the middle of her back as if she'd been painted with dark chocolate syrup. And she had something Katrina had never seen before—stripes on the backs of her legs.

"Hey, there," Katrina said. Banana Split eagerly nosed her shoulder and she chuckled. "No need for long introductions, I see."

"She's a sweetheart, but with plenty of energy," Saul said. "Loves people. The grooming tools are in the bucket, so open the stall gate and fasten her lead rope. She cooperates, but you still don't want her moving around too much."

He demonstrated how to do the tie with a quick-release knot.

Then Katrina learned how to use a pick for Banana Split's hooves and wield a curry comb. After that there were various brushes, a different comb for her tail and mane, and soft cloths for cleaning her face and rear end. The mare pricked her ears as Katrina murmured continuously, offering reassurances and praise.

"You did good," Saul announced when Katrina was finished. "Talkin' to her, that's key. Glad I didn't need to tell you to do that. Shows you got real horse sense. My wife never rode horses before coming to Montana, but she's getting there."

Plainly, horse sense was important to him and Katrina had earned his approval.

Katrina recalled what Wyatt had said about his grandfather doing some matchmaking, but she didn't think Saul would start seeing her as a potential granddaughter-in-law, simply because she enjoyed horses.

She rubbed Banana Split's nose. "I felt as if she was talking to me, too, in a way. I suppose that sounds ridiculous."

"Nope." Saul's aging, work-hardened hands stroked the mare and Katrina immediately wanted to sketch them. Anna Beth had mentioned he had arthritis, but it didn't seem to stop him from being more active on the ranch now that his hip had been replaced. "Horses are smart and sensitive. Once upon a time I dreamed of being a famous horse breeder. Guess my grandsons will take care of that for me. They're off to a fine start."

Saul's face was peaceful, seemingly without regret at the mention of his old vision for the future. But while he didn't appear to mind that it hadn't come true, she thought of the saying about life happening when you were making other plans. It was one of the reasons she'd supported her sister and brother-in-law when they talked about spending a few years teaching overseas. They were farther away, but doing something exciting and interesting they'd always wanted to do.

"My nephew hopes to buy a weanling or yearling from the Soaring Hawk," she said. "But he'll need his parents' permission. The biggest problem is that Mary and Shawn have a house in town, so he wouldn't have a place to stable it once they come back from Hong Kong."

"Wyatt speaks well of Tim, so he should be responsible enough to own a horse," Saul said seriously. "We can reserve a future foal for when he's older and he could do some work on the ranch in exchange for its board."

"I'll let them know. It will be a while before a decision can be made, but I doubt he'll change his mind about wanting a horse since his paternal grandfather used to own the Big Jumbo. Tim practically grew up there on weekends and during the summertime. I think if he'd been older and closer to being able to take over, Jim Bonner might have kept the ranch instead of selling."

Saul grimaced. "It was a good spread. A shame Jim-Bo let it get turned into a *dude* ranch."

The disgust in his tone made the corners of Katrina's mouth twitch. There was good money in guest ranches, but a man like Saul wasn't likely to approve. He was an old-school rancher and proud they worked their cattle with horses the "traditional" way.

"I think he should have considered his niece to run the Big Jumbo," she said in a casual tone. "Melody obviously has what it takes. A fair number of women are ranchers these days."

Saul made a dismissive gesture. "He's probably too conservative for that. You have to keep up with the times."

Katrina rubbed the back of her wrist over her mouth to hide her increasing amusement. Saul was trying to show he'd embraced the twenty-first century. And maybe he had. His wife and granddaughters-in-law weren't likely to put up with any nonsense.

"That's true," she said finally. "Well, I need to get back to my studio. I have a commission to polish and send to a client."

She looked over in time to see Evan's yearning expression. Inviting him to the house was a possibility since Christie was at preschool, but Wyatt probably wouldn't approve.

She had to respect his determination to keep his father and daughter separate. Something like that was much more fundamental than the color he painted Christie's bedroom or the clothes he bought her—though Katrina *did* think Wyatt should get his daughter something other than pink to wear. Perhaps she would order a few T-shirts to give Christie some options. Paige had also offered to share some of Mishka's old clothes, saying children grew so fast, they usually didn't wear them out.

The offer had given Katrina a lovely image of ranch families living close by and working together. It was a seductive vision, but she needed to remember she wasn't a Maxwell or a Hawkins, though there'd never been an attitude of "you're an employee and not one of us." Even *Wyatt* treated her more like an annoying younger sister who was simply on the Soaring Hawk to help out…who sometimes got in the way and told him things he didn't want to hear.

Yet a part of her was starting to want Wyatt to see her as a woman, which was dangerous since his heart still seemed buried in the past. It meant she needed to guard her heart so she didn't start hoping for something from Wyatt that he wasn't able to give.

Katrina squared her shoulders and pushed her troubling emotions to one side. She'd never gotten crushes on guys or fallen in love easily.

"But if you have time, Evan, I'd love to see your workshop first. I'm sure it's nothing like my studio."

He brightened. "That would be fine. I can take a few minutes. I need to service some of the ranch equipment out there, anyhow."

FROM THE RANCH OFFICE, Wyatt watched his father and Katrina emerge from the horse barn talking animatedly. They walked together across the large open area between the buildings and were soon out of his field of vision. He didn't think Katrina would take Evan up to the house, knowing his feelings about it. At least that's what he hoped.

Dakota had been looking out the window as well. He sat back and sighed. "Dad is going a good job, Wyatt."

"I never said he wasn't."

"But he really wants to get to know Chri—"

"It isn't our decision, Dakota," Jordan interjected.

He was being still the "big brother," trying to keep peace. It wasn't necessary. Wyatt could look out for himself and he wasn't going to agree to his father spending time with his daughter until he was more comfortable with the situation. She was his top priority.

"Dixie's puppies are fully weaned and will soon be old enough for adoption," Jordan added in a less-than-subtle change of subject. "Are you sure Christie doesn't want one? We have takers for all of them, but Christie can still have her pick of the litter. Family first."

"I appreciate that, but she was scared of them before, and I don't think anything has changed."

Wyatt didn't know how his little girl could have been nervous of the sleeping puppies, even with their watchful mother standing by. Yet Christie had shrunk against him and begged to be picked up as if faced with a basket of snakes instead of five puppies with their eyes still closed. Didn't kids usually love baby animals? That's what he'd anticipated when moving back to Montana.

"Let us know in the next couple of weeks if you want to try her with them again. After that, we'll let them go to their new homes."

Wyatt nodded absently. He'd been distracted ever since that moment in the pasture when Katrina lost her perch on the hood of the truck and had gone careening along his body. An abrupt reminder that he was still fully alive, even if Amy was gone.

Katrina hadn't intended to do it, but ever since, he felt as if he was waking up. And like a limb that had gone to sleep, there were pins and needles in his heart. But he didn't *want* his heart to wake up. It was too painful to have those emotions again. Not to mention Katrina wasn't looking for anyone at the moment.

Yet it was curious to realize that he absolutely trusted her. She hadn't been trying to entice him, she'd simply skidded off the slippery hood of the truck while trying to avoid taking his hand. She wouldn't have touched him at all, but he'd worried she would hurt herself, so had caught her as she descended.

He shook his head and focused on the stock records he and his brothers had been discussing. They were debating possible avenues for the fall market, including keeping more of the heifers for breeding stock. It meant a smaller paycheck for the current year, but a chance of increased revenue for the years ahead.

Though purely guesswork at this point, it didn't keep them from coming up with strategies. Wyatt suspected his brothers were also trying to get him to take a breather, but they weren't much better when it came to working hard.

Still, it was great to be a team again. Older now. Maybe wiser and a bit more banged up than when they were boys.

But still a team.

Wyatt leaned forward in his office chair. "Jordan, is there any chance of Christie spending Friday night with you and Paige? We have a few cows close to delivering and one or two will likely need help. Katrina wants to learn how to help pull a calf and I don't want to ask her nephew to be a babysitter while we're in the calving barn."

A speculative smile grew on Dakota's face. "You've been spending a fair amount of time with Katrina lately. Is anything interesting going on that we should know about?"

Despite his earlier thoughts, Wyatt narrowed his eyes. He wasn't going to make a mountain out of a molehill or a romance out of an awkward moment by a truck.

"Katrina simply wants to learn about ranching, though her interest may wane if she has to get up at 3:00 a.m. or stay up all night. Still, with so much of the crew sick with colds, it might be good to have an extra pair of hands, even amateur hands."

He didn't want to admit that he also enjoyed her company, however exasperating she could be at moments. Besides, none of it meant he had changed his mind about getting involved with someone.

Jordan seemed to be having trouble keeping a straight face. "Katrina doesn't impress me as the kind of person who loses interest easily. But we're happy to have Christie at any time, you know that. Mishka adores having sleepovers."

"Then I'll let Katrina know."

PAIGE CAME BEFORE daylight on Friday morning to get Christie for her sleepover with Mishka, saying it was best to take her over to the other house before the incoming weather hit.

"Are you sure you want her to stay?" Katrina asked. "She woke up with the sniffles."

"It's fine. I had a talk with Wyatt a few minutes ago because Mishka is the same, along with my husband. I've got gallons of orange juice, ginger ale and other food for the patients. Daniel came down with it a couple of days ago and is already feeling better. Kids don't seem to be hit as hard as adults with this one. Anyway, Noelle will check on everyone when she gets home from the clinic."

"Okay."

It left Katrina with time on her hands. She couldn't see trying to take a nap ahead of the evening, and focusing on one of her projects was difficult when she knew the ranch was gearing up to feed the herds.

She hung around the house for less than ten minutes before hurrying out to where the crew was assembling.

They were a miserable lot.

Wyatt and his father were healthy, but everyone else, including his two brothers, were in various stages of coughing, watery eyes, congestion and generally feeling lousy. Presumably, whoever was staying at the main ranch to keep an eye on everything was in an equal state of misery.

"I want to go along," she announced, smiling at Evan and the others.

Wyatt shook his head. "Christie needs you. Besides, you're planning to be at the calving barn all night."

"Christie is spending the day with Paige at the main house," Katrina said quickly. "Come on, you can use an extra pair of hands. I can drive a truck or whatever else you need, including one of the old tractors. Melody taught me how a few days ago."

"Let her help," Carmen said after a fit of coughing. "Kat can drive one of the caking trucks while I shovel out the protein supplement. Then someone else can go with the haying teams."

"All right, but I'll team with Kat—er, Katrina," Wyatt said. "This way you can stay here with Stedman."

Carmen looked ready to protest, then started coughing again and signaled agreement with a relieved expression.

The sky was still clear, but the temperature was dropping, even as the sun began to rise. Katrina kidded around with the Maxwell brothers and other cowhands as they drank a last cup of coffee and made sure their thermoses were filled.

It was interesting to watch them load the hay on the flatbeds and hear why they created lines of feed rather than piling it in one spot. It meant more cattle could get to the food quickly. Her job would be driving behind one of the haying teams while Wyatt shoveled out protein cake. Then they'd refill the vehicles and go to another area. The Soaring Hawk had so many cattle spread out across the ranch, it would take a while getting to all of them, which was why two teams were assigned to the job.

She was relieved her responsibility would be driving beside a line of hay already laid down—less chance of doing something wrong that way. What made her nervous was the thought of Wyatt standing in the bed of the truck shoveling out feed while she drove over bumpy grazing land.

"I'm thrilled to help, but what if I hit a pothole?" she asked Wyatt. "That is, a prairie dog hole, or whatever they're called out on the range. Or a cow runs in front of the truck and I have to slam on the brakes?"

"I'll try not to fall off, promise."

Katrina narrowed her eyes at him. "I don't think that's funny."

He leaned close and she almost thought he was going to kiss her. "Hey, you usually have a good sense of humor. I know Christie woke up with a cold, but you aren't getting sick too, are you?"

"Hardly. Don't worry about Christie. Paige says Daniel is nearly well already, so it seems to be mild for kids and over quickly."

"She mentioned that. Say, what's this about Carmen calling you Kat? Tim and Christie call you Aunt Kat, but I thought that was a nephew and honorary niece thing."

"It's a family nickname and a few friends called me Kat when I was in school."

"I like it. Is it all right if I do the same?"

"Sure." Katrina rather liked the idea. Nicknames suggested a kind of closeness.

She got into the cab and slid the rear window open so she could hear Wyatt if he called to her. One team had already left; now the hay feeder moved forward and she followed behind them.

The gates were basically fencing wire attached to a pole and hooked over a post. Someone got out at the first gate and dragged it to one side, then dragged it back after they'd all driven through.

"The cows associate the truck with being fed, so they'll start coming when they see us," Wyatt said. He was crouched by the window and it felt strangely intimate. "Just give the horn a few taps every ten feet or so. That will alert the ones further away."

Katrina clenched the steering wheel as they bumped along.

It'll be all right, she told herself.

By following the tracks of the tractor and flatbed carrying the hay, she could try to avoid any deep holes. And surely Wyatt wouldn't have let her drive if he thought she would put him or any animals at risk.

The sound of Wyatt's shovel scooping up the protein cake started and she focused even harder on keeping the truck as straight and steady as possible. It might not be a glamorous job or as exciting as helping birth a calf, but it was part of the ranching cycle, one she was determined to experience.

Then a scary thought occurred—it was also a way to spend time with Wyatt.

"THE ART IS knowing when to pull, and when to let the cow do the work," Wyatt explained much later as Katrina half lay on the barn floor in the early-morning hours, bracing her feet on a post to get better traction.

As the calf slid out, the mother bellowed and Katrina's heart thumped with sympathy. Birth wasn't easy, even when everything went the way it was supposed to go.

She let go of the chain handles and turned over to check the calf along with Wyatt, clearing his mouth and nose to help him breathe. He snorted out some fluid, looking sorry for himself.

"That's a big bull calf," Wyatt said. "No wonder she was having trouble."

They carried the baby to a pen and gave him a shot to prevent disease. When reunited with her calf, the mother eagerly began licking him, this time a low moo coming from her chest.

Something about that contented sound made Katrina gulp. Motherhood was busting out all over, unlike spring which seemed to be arriving late.

"Is something wrong?" Wyatt asked.

She cleared her throat and tried to keep her eyes from tearing. "I'm fine. Kind of amazing to know you helped save a life."

"Seems like more than that is going on."

Katrina blew out a breath. Now was a fine time for Wyatt to get sensitive.

"I just...well, I thought I would be starting a family this year or next. That's all. And here I'm surrounded by expectant mothers of every species, being constantly reminded that my plans got derailed."

"From what you said to Gretchen, I thought you broke up with your fiancé because he was a workaholic."

"Gordon being a workaholic was just one of our problems."

Wyatt was obviously waiting for more and Katrina looked around as a precaution. Timothy had come in earlier and talked with Wyatt about his seafood allergy. In the end, her nephew had decided it might be cool to wear dog tags, even if they contained medical alert information.

But she thought they were alone now in the huge barn, except for a few animals. The last thing she wanted was for Timothy to figure out that he'd had anything to do with the end of her engagement. It wasn't his fault. In fact, he'd saved her from being married to the wrong guy.

"It's...well, I found out Gordon didn't want a family," she said finally. "I mean, he *really* didn't want a family. He didn't even want me to take care of my nephew for a year or two."

"What's wrong with the guy? Tim is a great kid."

"I know. I love having him with me. When Gordon and I got together and became serious, I was very clear about wanting children. He said he felt the same. But when I began talking about the possibility of Tim living with me for a while, Gordon was against the idea. I kept pushing for the reason and he finally confessed—it wasn't because he didn't want someone else's kid around, he didn't want *any* kids. Basically, he was just hoping I'd change my mind about a family after we got married."

"Seems to me you're better off without him."

Katrina took off the long disposable gloves she'd used during the calving. "I agree. But shouldn't I have guessed he was deceiving me? There should have been some indication. Maybe I just wasn't paying enough attention."

"It's possible he didn't see it as a deception."

She narrowed her eyes. "I hope you aren't going to defend him."

"Not at all. If you can't be up front about

what you want before getting married, what chance do you have to make it work after the wedding?"

"None. He isn't a bad person, just determined to have things his own way. We dated for years and had a long engagement, but I thought we were just building our careers before settling down. The funny thing is, I wasn't that upset about breaking up with him, except with myself for being fooled for so long. And now I keep wondering..."

WYATT NUDGED KATRINA'S shoulder when she didn't continue. "Keep wondering what?"

"The day when I talked about the Caldecott, I realized it was right after I won a different award that Gordon started asking me out. He's ambitious. Determined to be a force in the publishing world. Maybe he decided it would be advantageous for us to get together."

"You think that's why he became interested in you?"

"Possibly. And, well, I'm more the girl-next-door type, while Gordon's preferences lean toward tall, gorgeous and sophisticated. Similar to your tastes—women who take after Gretchen."

The comment made Wyatt uncomfortable,

though Katrina was simply being honest. This wasn't the first time she'd suggested he had something in common with her ex-fiancé and it bothered him even more now than it had before.

"No matter what the reason," he said, trying not to take offense, "that doesn't mean he wasn't genuinely in love with you."

"I know. I would just like to think something more personal appealed to Gordon initially, rather than me winning an award. A little feminine ego and self-confidence is involved here, I guess."

Wyatt was at a loss. Katrina was so filled with excitement for life, it was hard to imagine her ex-fiancé failing to appreciate her amazing qualities.

"For the record, you're very attractive," he said, hoping his sincerity was reflected in his tone. "And it's remarkable how enthusiastic you are. It's rare. Including in myself."

"Maybe that comes from your childhood with Saul."

"More likely my basic personality. Marrying Amy and having Christie have been the high points of my life. I care about my family and like ranching, but I'm not the same as you—passionate and curious about everything."

Katrina cocked her head. "I think you have passion, you've just kept your feelings under a tight rein for a long time."

"Which means I'll probably never learn to let go."

"I don't know about that. You seemed elated when you returned after a calving that first night we got here."

True enough.

Katrina would undoubtedly love to see more of the ranch's operations and he was disconcerted to realize he was looking forward to experiencing it with her. Maybe he could absorb some of her natural zest, which would be good for Christie, as well.

"I'm really sorry about what happened with your fiancé," he said.

"Thanks. All that time together and it turns out I didn't know him at all. And he didn't know me. I mean, six years with a guy who thought I'd just change my mind about wanting kids. Why didn't I see that?"

Wyatt was surprised by the outrage he felt on her behalf.

"I get how you feel about children," he said slowly. "My wife and I tried and tried to have a baby. Then when Amy was finally expecting Christie, she was diagnosed with an autoimmune disease that led to one complication after another. She only had a short time with her daughter before she was gone."

"That's so awful."

"Yeah." He almost laughed because Katrina's comment was succinct and lacked the protestations of sympathy he'd heard so often from strangers.

It was awful that Amy had died.

It was awful that she'd only had a few weeks with her child.

And it was awful that Christie would never get to know her mother.

What else needed to be said?

Katrina focused on him. "Look, you don't need to worry about me leaving right away to get married or chasing you or anything. I want a family, but I want one with the *right* person, not just anybody. Once Mary and Shawn return I may look into adoption, the way Paige adopted Mishka."

"I'm not worried," Wyatt said easily.

Curiously, he wasn't bothered to find out how much Katrina longed for children. She was much too straightforward to have ulterior motives about their living and working situation. Yet her comment was also making him think about the former girlfriends he'd been trying to duck, assuming they were looking for a husband.

Any husband.

Maybe that assumption had been unkind.

It could be they were mostly looking for the right person, too.

KATRINA PUT HER hands on the railing and gazed at the calf she'd helped bring into the world. He was drying quickly under his mother's careful attention and looking less disgruntled by the minute.

She understood. One minute he was warm, if cramped, and the next he was being dragged out by the feet and delivered onto a cold, hard floor. From his perspective it had to be completely unfair.

"How long do you think winter is going to last?" she asked Wyatt. Some years they'd had spring weather by now in Montana, but the chill and storms were lingering. Chinooks didn't count—in fact, they were sometimes called a false spring.

"No telling. Predictions say well into April."

"I guess the groundhog was right."

"Excuse me?"

Katrina grinned. "Didn't the groundhog see its shadow in February? That meant six more weeks of winter. Though around here, it's more like ten to twelve more weeks."

"The groundhog? Seriously? You probably believe there are pots of gold at the end of rainbows and that finding a fairy ring is good luck."

"A little whimsy isn't a terrible thing."

"Not much of that in my life, now or ever, except for stories Jordan used to tell me and Dakota when we were small. I'm trying to keep Christie grounded. It's how Amy and I decided to raise her before she was born, because that way she'll have fewer soul- crushing disappointments later in life."

Sheesh. Katrina pursed her lips. She'd never fully believed in the good luck of fairy rings or rainbows ending in pots of gold, any more than she'd genuinely believed in Santa Claus or the Easter Bunny. But it was a game her family played and she suspected the adults had as much fun as the kids.

"You realize her favorite book, *Where the Wild Things Are*, is basically a fantasy."

"I know. It was a gift from Jordan and Paige, so I couldn't refuse to read it to her.

But I remind Christie that the story is just make-believe."

Hmmm.

"At the very least you're going to do the tooth fairy routine with Christie, right?" Katrina asked. "I've never heard that visits from the tooth fairy lead to soul-crushing disappointments, except if you *don't* have a visit."

"I haven't decided."

"Not to put any pressure on, but Mishka gets gifts from the tooth fairy and so will Daniel when he's old enough. Christie might feel left out, which could be a big disappointment. Almost soul-crushing. I imagine Noelle's baby will also have visits from the tooth fairy. Eventually."

"Almost soul-crushing?" Wyatt gave her an exasperated look. "Is that your idea of not putting pressure on me?"

"Hey, I haven't mentioned the dragons and unicorns all over Mishka's bedroom or the mixed messages Christie might be getting between your practical approach and the fun that Mishka is having with a pretend fantasy world. That is, I haven't mentioned it until now."

He laughed. "All right, you win. I'll be the tooth fairy. But I refuse to spend money on a spangled tutu in my size. It just isn't going to happen."

Their gazes locked and a renewed flicker of awareness caught Katrina. He was sexy, handsome, and the hint of brooding around his eyes was appealing, partly because she wanted to make it go away. Transforming a tragic hero into someone happy had never been her romantic ideal, but she was starting to understand the allure. It required deep, compelling love, the kind she'd always hoped to find.

Too bad Wyatt's heart wasn't free.

Katrina turned toward the mother cow and baby again.

She enjoyed fantasy figures. They were fun and inspired the imagination. But she was trying to be realistic about romance. Especially now. She didn't love Gordon any longer, but he had taught her to be much more wary. Not to mention the blow he'd given to her self-confidence.

The calf was already trying to stand and reach up to suckle.

"That's incredible," she murmured.

"It never fails to amaze me."

She felt better watching the calf's efforts. He was wobbly after such a tough birth, but he finally made it to his mother and started to nurse. He bumped his head against her udder and soon his little tail began to swish.

After a stretch of dedicated nursing, the calf lay down with a drizzle of milk on its muzzle. His mother gave him another licking and his coat finished drying, despite the chill.

His large brown eyes blinked sleepily and Katrina rested her chin on the railing, trying not to think about anything except the wondrous sight of new life. Then the loud bawl from a cow on the other side of the barn aisle made her look around.

She followed Wyatt over to the pen.

"Looks like you're going to have another chance to learn," he said after giving the heifer a quick exam.

That was fine with Katrina.

She liked keeping busy, especially when her emotions were so unsettled.

CHAPTER EIGHT

LUCKILY, KATRINA WAS able to shower and take a nap on Saturday morning before Paige brought Christie back from her sleepover. The three-year-old's sniffles had progressed to a stuffy nose and a light cough, but she was cheerful, so she couldn't feel too bad.

"Did you have fun?" Katrina asked.

"Uh-huh. I had a...a *splendid* time." *Splendid* was one of Christie's new words from preschool. "Thank you, Aunt Paige."

Paige kissed the top of her head. "It was our pleasure." She smiled at Katrina before heading back to the main house.

"Where's Tim?" Christie asked as they ate lunch. Timothy had quickly become one of her favorite people.

"He's spending the day with an aunt and uncle." Now that they were back in Montana, Katrina didn't see her nephew nearly as much. He was too busy going out on horseback, helping on the ranch or spending time with his friends and the rest of the family.

On a private video call with Katrina, her sister had claimed that her son would rather stay at the Soaring Hawk than live with his parents once they returned from Hong Kong.

"Not at all. He misses you," Katrina had assured Mary, though she'd known the comment was mostly a joke. "He's just thrilled to be doing the things he used to do before your father-in-law sold the Big Jumbo."

"I know. I'm glad Tim's happy. You seem happier, too. Have you met someone?"

Katrina had groaned. "*No.* I love being back in Montana. But it took a while to figure out that city life isn't for me and then do something about it."

"The same with doing something about Gordon," Mary had returned in a droll tone. "I never understood what you saw in that guy."

Katrina hadn't tried to admonish her sister. It wouldn't have done any good, but it had made her think. However attractive and intelligent Gordon might have been, the family hadn't liked him. Mary had been the most outspoken after the engagement ended, but Katrina had the impression that everybody breathed a collective sigh of relief.

For the rest of the afternoon she did art projects with Christie, along with making plans for an online art course she'd volunteered to do for Mishka's class. She would have preferred teaching the class in-person, but it seemed best to keep the days when Christie was in preschool as free as possible. That way she could work on her freelance projects or continue to learn about ranching.

A corner of Katrina's mind wondered if she was making even more excuses to spend time with Wyatt.

Maybe she was. Friendship was important and she liked him. A lot.

Though she was still tired after putting Christie to bed for the evening, she went to her studio to work on a new freelance job. Designing a logo wasn't the kind of art she preferred, but the company had been referred by another client, so she'd accepted.

The front door opened and she went out to find her nephew had arrived home.

"Hi, Tim. I thought you were sleeping over with Aunt Bettina and Uncle Angus and going to church with them tomorrow."

"I was, but since so many of the cowhands are sick, I wanted to be here in the morning.

I can do extra in the horse barn and help out that way."

Katrina marveled at the mature expression in her nephew's face. It felt as if he was transforming from a boy into a young man, right in front of her eyes. His parents were going to be shocked the next time they saw him and she hoped they wouldn't regret how much they'd missed. They would see him this summer though—he was meeting them in Japan for ten days of sightseeing.

"That's thoughtful of you," she said softly.

He shrugged and looked embarrassed. "Uh, thanks. I'm going to bed so I can be up extra early."

Katrina had explained to him that it was all right to accept a compliment, but Timothy still struggled. She suspected it was connected to puberty and his parents being away. At least living on the Soaring Hawk had offered a way for him to feel good about himself.

She went back to her studio and erased the digital design she'd begun. If she was going to give the client something, she wanted to offer a logo that was fresh and interesting.

A while later a faint whimpering sound came from the baby monitor Katrina kept on her belt at night, so she hurried upstairs. Before she got to Christie's bedroom, a wailing cry of "Daddy, Daddy," came down the hallway.

The three-year-old was tangled up in her covers on the bed, sobbing. The cats had leaped to the floor and were watching warily.

Katrina sat on the edge of the mattress and stroked Christie's face. She was warm, but not feverish. "Hey, it's okay," she said softly. "Everything is okay."

Christie's eyes opened. She sat upright and threw her arms around Katrina's neck, her favorite stuffed animal falling to the floor. "Aunt Kat, the monster is mad."

"The monster?"

"Uh-huh. He sits in the closet and growls."

"Oh." Katrina thought fast. "I don't think he's mad, I think he's hungry. That's his stomach growling."

Christie drew back. "His stomach?"

"Sure. Doesn't your stomach growl when you get hungry?"

"Not so loud."

"That's because you aren't a monster, hungry for fruit. They adore fruit, but nobody ever thinks to give them any. And they're too polite to ask or take some for themselves."

"Poor monster."

Katrina stroked her hair. "I know. They sit there and hope someone will realize they don't mean any harm, they're just longing for their favorite snack. What do you think we should do to help?"

"We have apples. We could bring him some."

"That's a good idea."

Christie scrambled out of bed. "Let's go. Do they like peanut butter with apples?"

"They might. It would be very thoughtful to include a little peanut butter, just in case."

Together they went down the kitchen staircase and prepared a plate of pared apples with a spoonful of peanut butter. Back in Christie's room, Katrina got a chair and put the apples on a high shelf, pushed clear to the back—out of sight of a curious child's eyes.

"Why up there?" Christie asked.

"Because monsters feel safer eating where no one can reach them. They're scared of people."

"Oh."

"And I don't think he'll feel comfortable about eating his snack until you go to sleep. So don't be surprised if his stomach growls again. What do you think he's called?"

Christie looked thoughtful. “I think his name is JoJo.”

“Okay, say good-night to JoJo and try to sleep so he feels safe to eat his snack.”

“Okay. ’Night, JoJo.” Christie sniffed and yawned widely, then settled down with Fluffy Bob in her arms. Within a couple of minutes, her breathing had evened and she seemed sound asleep.

Katrina tucked the covers in closely, her heart aching. Being a nanny wasn’t the same as being a mother and there were times she wondered if becoming a mommy would ever happen, even if she tried to adopt.

She got up and was startled to see Wyatt in the doorway of the bedroom.

He was obviously upset.

Katrina brushed past him and headed downstairs. If they were going to have a disagreement, it shouldn’t be within hearing range of his daughter.

WYATT HADN’T BEEN able to believe what he’d heard coming up the main staircase. He’d taken a break to check on Christie, only to realize she must have had another nightmare.

“What do you think you were doing?” he asked when they reached the living room.

"Dealing with Christie's nightmare." Katrina's expression was unbelievably calm. "You said she had them."

"I've always told her the monster isn't real, now you've given him a snack? And a name? I've told her over and over, *there aren't any monsters*."

Katrina looked at him narrowly. "Yeah, you were obviously successful with *that* reasoning, which I didn't even know about. The monster is real to Christie. Dismissing her fear isn't going to make it go away."

"Neither is feeding an imaginary monster. You know how I feel about keeping her grounded in reality."

"And yet you refuse to let her experience reality, like watching a cow give birth or letting her meet a less-than-perfect grandfather," Katrina retorted, keeping her voice low. "As for monsters, there are all kinds. And I'm not talking about the ones that are green or blue or have tails and fangs and six eyes, but things she'll have to learn how to handle. Like unfair teachers or supervisors or situations."

"I'm aware of that. But she's only three."

"Well, tonight she learned something about problem solving and helped to come up with a solution. And need I point out that she went right back to sleep?"

Wyatt rubbed his face. He needed a good night of rest before discussing this any longer. Katrina seemed capable of countering any argument he could devise—maybe because she was right. He *had* been dismissing Christie's fear. A monster in the closet might seem ridiculous to him, but obviously wasn't to her.

"I suppose I should have connected what you said about not wanting her to believe in fantasy with how I handled the nightmare," Katrina added in a more conciliatory tone. "But it didn't make sense to say the monster wasn't real when she clearly believed it was. To be honest, after all the changes in her life, I'm surprised she doesn't have more bad dreams."

He groaned. "Perish the thought."

Katrina grinned. "Perish the thought? I haven't heard that one in a while."

"Yeah. I grew up with an old-fashioned grandfather. Remember?"

"Hey, guys. Is everything okay?" Timothy asked as he wandered into the living room. He was wearing pajamas and blinked at them sleepily.

"Everything is fine," Wyatt replied. "Sorry

we woke you up, Tim. I didn't realize you were home. You've been spending Saturday nights with family or friends."

Timothy yawned. "I got up for a glass of water and heard you talking. Great-Uncle Angus brought me back because I wanted to be here early to help with the horses."

He was a good kid.

"That's great, Tim, but don't overwork. School comes first. And your aunt will never forgive me if you catch a cold from not getting enough rest."

"I'll be okay. G'night."

"Good night."

As Timothy disappeared down the hallway to the back of the house, Wyatt shook his head. "I honestly don't understand that ex-fiancé of yours. How could he not want—"

Wyatt gasped as Katrina flung her arms around his neck and pulled his head down for a kiss. She was so warm and sweet, he instinctively responded.

A few seconds later, she withdrew a scant inch. "Sorry about that, but please don't say anything about Gordon when my nephew might hear," she breathed against his mouth. "I don't want him getting the wrong idea about me breaking my engagement."

Realization dawned. She hadn't truly been kissing him, she was protecting Timothy. To Wyatt's dismay, he was disappointed about the reason, though he'd probably be glad later.

"Uh, sure. I understand."

"Good." She let go of his neck and stepped back, appearing calm and collected. "About Christie's nightmares, I don't know how we're going to work this out. I can't go in now and tell her the monster isn't real, not when I don't believe it's the right approach. But you don't think my way is okay, either."

Wyatt was revising his opinion in light of how quickly Christie had calmed down. He was also chagrined at the way he'd behaved. One of the reasons he'd wanted Katrina as his daughter's nanny was her independence and decisiveness.

"I might be changing my mind."

A relieved expression filled Katrina's eyes. "That's nice to hear. You know, if she starts resolving one of her fears, it might help her resolve some of the others."

Wyatt couldn't disagree. His wife had rejected fantasy and fairy tales because she'd grown up in an unhappy home and felt it was best to see the world as it was. But Amy's death had changed everything—she wasn't here and he had to raise their daughter alone.

What had seemed right for them as a couple raising a child wouldn't necessarily work for him as a single father. A pang of guilt followed the thought, but that was something he would have to deal with later—along with the fact he liked Katrina far too much for a man who'd decided he wasn't ever taking the chance of falling in love again.

"I think you're right about the nightmares," he admitted. "And I'm sorry about overreacting."

"That's okay. You're tired and probably feel bad about working such long hours and being away from Christie," Katrina said. "I bet you felt the same way when you were in the navy. But now she doesn't have to go to a childcare facility and can see you sometimes during the day. You're doing your best."

Katrina's response was so generous, Wyatt wanted to kiss her again.

And again.

He cleared his throat. "Look, if it comes up, I'll find a way to tell Christie that I'm sorry I couldn't see her monster. She's always told me he squishes down so big people can't see him.

But what are you going to do if she wakes up again and says he's still growling?"

Katrina's smile, warm as summer sunshine, flowed over him and he was illogically annoyed that she seemed so unaffected by their kiss. But then, it hadn't been a real kiss to her, she'd just been keeping him from saying something her nephew shouldn't accidentally hear.

"I'll tell her it's his way of purring after getting his favorite snack."

Wyatt let out a small laugh. Katrina was creative and quick-thinking. Purring? That would be far more reassuring to Christie than a growl.

"If it helps," she said, "I used to be afraid there was a wild animal beneath my bed. For months I would leap onto the mattress from two or three feet away, convinced something was under there, waiting to bite my toes. Then I'd sleep with the covers over my head. In the morning I'd jump out the same distance and sprint to the bathroom so it wouldn't nip my heels. So that was *my* monster."

"What did your parents do to reassure you?"

"I never told them," Katrina admitted. "I must have liked the adrenaline rush or something. Or maybe I thought they'd say I was being silly. Which, of course, I *was*."

Wyatt frowned in thought. Katrina's story had made him see why he needed to listen to Christie's fears and not brush them away. He wanted his daughter to tell him if something was wrong or bothered her, not keep it to herself.

He yawned. Lately he was mostly getting quick snatches of sleep in the calving barn or his office. It was one thing to say that on a ranch everyone worked through illness, another to ask miserable employees to put in those kinds of hours. He couldn't do it and had taken on their tasks. "I want Christie to feel safe, but she's even afraid while sleeping. Do you know anything about the meaning of dreams?"

"Not really, but when I was getting close to graduating art school and applying for jobs, I dreamed about earthquakes a lot. I figured it meant I was uncertain about what was going to happen."

"Makes sense."

"Yeah, especially since my brother, Cody, had told me a thousand times that art school was impractical and nobody made a living at it. Not that I let him stop me from going."

Katrina made a face. “Honestly, I hope Cody meets someone who shakes him up—he needs to see the potential of the future, instead of limitations. Nobody ever truly has control of their lives, so why not do your best and enjoy the good things when they come, right?”

Wyatt was practically mesmerized by the expression in Katrina’s eyes. They saw the world in different ways and he envied her way. Maybe it was the quality that had intrigued her ex-fiancé—the sense of limitless possibilities and adventure she saw. It fascinated Wyatt as well, though he also felt a healthy dose of attraction. After all, when she smiled, her entire face lit up. He’d be a fool not to find that appealing.

He shifted his feet, knowing he had things to do. “Cody seemed pretty serious when he was a kid.”

“He’s still serious.”

“You said he should see the possibilities. But what do you do about limitations?” Wyatt asked curiously.

“Limitations are like boulders in a stream. Finding a creative way around them can mean something better happens. But whatever happens, at least you move forward. Look at me. Instead of being married to the wrong guy, I'm on a ranch, learning things I always wanted to know."

It amazed Wyatt that Katrina hadn't even let the experience with her ex-fiancé change who she was as a person, though she must have been deeply hurt by what had happened.

"We're glad to have you here," he said, unsure of the best way to respond. "About Christie, she's usually cranky the morning after one of her nightmares and it could be worse tomorrow since she doesn't feel at her best."

"That's okay. I'll get out the finger paints. She loves doing that. Maybe she'll paint a picture of JoJo."

"That might be interesting. I'll go back to work now," Wyatt said reluctantly. "Melody is there. She's better, but I don't feel right about leaving her alone too long."

"All right. Good night."

He stepped outside the house and trudged to the calving barn, his emotions in a turmoil. Katrina had seemed like a perfect choice to be Christie's nanny and he hadn't changed his mind.

He just hadn't expected to be drawn to her this much or to start questioning his decision to stay single.

"HEY, BILLIE," EVAN SAID, stepping into the dining hall kitchen on Sunday.

"Hi." Billie didn't look up right away. She was measuring corn meal into a dozen different bowls and didn't want to lose track. "I'm making my own corn bread mixes," she explained. "I'll bag them up so I can be ready to go if time is short. Coffee is on."

Evan poured himself a large cup. As usual he put his phone on the counter where he could get to it quickly. Technically, they were all on call in case they were needed in the calving barn or elsewhere.

"You're earlier than usual," Billie commented. "Don't you normally spend another hour in the sack, still trying to sleep before giving up?"

He shrugged. "Actually, I don't try to sleep first. I go to an online AA meeting on my phone. Usually up at the equipment barn if the weather isn't too bad, otherwise in my truck. Every night."

"Oh."

"It helps keep me centered," he added.

"Is alcohol still a big temptation?"

"Usually not, but I don't want to slip. So I attend my meetings and remind myself of what I have to lose if I start drinking again."

Billie tried to keep her face from revealing anything. She hadn't thought about Evan needing to attend AA every day. It made sense, though, and brought home that his sobriety was a daily choice.

The door from the utility room opened and they both looked over.

"Cooking after eleven o'clock?" Anna Beth asked. "Can't you keep up? I've noticed you're in here late nearly every night."

Billie pressed her lips together to keep from grinning. The other woman could be difficult, but she respected her. "I'm not having a problem keeping up, I just don't sleep well. All those years on the road, I suppose, traveling at late hours to get from one rodeo to the next. But I don't watch much television and prefer staying useful. Right now I'm preparing ahead so I can do even more on the ranch."

"Then I'll cook additional days."

"Thanks, but it seems important to Wyatt that you have more time with the family. Nevertheless, I was wondering something..."

"Yes?" Anna Beth crossed her arms over her stomach, her eyes narrowing.

"Well, Eduardo's birthday is on Tuesday and he's raved about your lemon barbecue meatloaf. Says it also makes great sandwiches.

Seems like a good birthday meal, so I was wondering if you'd swap a day with me, or be willing to share how you make it. Or we could trade cooking just one meal."

Anna Beth's expression softened. "It isn't difficult."

"Not for you, but I can't cook meatloaf worth eating. Mine is too dry, no matter what I do. So I usually don't."

"I suppose swapping days would be all right. Best to do a whole day so we don't joggle elbows preparing the other meals."

"That would be great." Billie began dumping the finished mixes into plastic bags and sealing them. "I also started putting more sugar into my corn bread the way you make it."

Anna Beth got an oatmeal chocolate chip cookie from the jar Billie kept on the counter. "Some folks don't like their corn bread sweet. You could have told them to get used to a new recipe."

"Except I like yours better, too."

Anna Beth ate her cookie, looking even more relaxed. "Well, if everything's all right here, I'll go back to the house. I'll plan on cooking on Tuesday, but there's no need for you to swap a day with me."

"I don't want to put you out, though it would be nice to have time to visit my horse. I'm boarding her up at Josh McKeon's rodeo school."

"You wouldn't be putting me out. There's plenty in my side of the freezer, including breakfast casseroles. I can even make the meatloaf ahead if I want." Anna Beth bobbed her head at Evan. "Good night, then."

"'Night."

Evan didn't say anything else for a long minute and seemed to be listening for the outer door to close behind Anna Beth. Then he chuckled, probably when he figured the retired marine was safely out of earshot.

"That was clever."

"Oh?" Billie gave him an innocent look. "I don't know what you mean."

"Anna Beth is proud of her cooking."

Billie sat at the counter with her cup of coffee. "So am I. But it doesn't hurt to let her know she's still in demand. I haven't won her over completely yet, but I'm working on it. The thing is, everyone wants to feel they're needed."

EVAN NODDED SLOWLY, realizing that being needed was something he'd missed over the years. He'd bailed on his family when he should have been strong for them, and he had made sure nobody truly needed him since.

His chest hurt at the memory of his boys grieving for their mother. *Alone*. He sure hadn't been any comfort to them, getting drunk all the time.

"What are you thinking about?" Billie asked.

"My wife. I messed up really bad after she died and I've never really forgiven myself for what happened. Talking about the past doesn't seem important to Jordan and Dakota, but Wyatt has a whole lot bottled up inside. He returned to Montana nearly two months ago and hardly says a word to me. Didn't before, either, the times he visited. And he told Jordan and Dakota that I shouldn't try to meet my granddaughter unless he says it's okay."

Billie's eyes were sympathetic. "Remember how long it took for you to come back? Wyatt could need a while to sort out what he feels. Maybe the timing also makes a difference. From what you've said, Jordan was happily married with a daughter and new baby son when you returned."

"But Dakota had been seriously injured on a SEAL mission and had to take a medical discharge. He still has trouble with his knee, yet he was thrilled to see me."

Billie poured cream into her coffee. "You also told me that he'd just fallen in love with Noelle. A real high point in his life, while Wyatt is a widower like you and has a little girl. He could be comparing how he's taking care of his daughter, to what you did."

Evan gripped his cup. Billie didn't pull her punches. She had some sharp edges, but he liked that she told the truth, even when it wasn't pleasant to hear. People tended to pussyfoot around him for fear he'd start drinking again. Dollars to donuts, she'd likely put her finger on the reason Wyatt was so standoffish. He was sure Jordan and Dakota knew, but he hadn't asked them. It wouldn't be fair—too much like asking them to take sides.

"Yeah, I think you're right," he said.

"Besides, your sons are all very different people," Billie added. "Surely if Jordan and Dakota can forgive you for the past, you can learn to forgive yourself."

"That still leaves Wyatt."

"Maybe it isn't about forgiveness. Maybe he just needs to be sure you aren't going anywhere before he's willing to trust you again."

"I'm staying here. And sober."

"You'd better," she warned.

Evan let out a laugh. Billie would probably douse him with a cold hose and kick him out in a storm if she ever found him drinking. Staying on her good side was another incentive to keep on the straight and narrow. And he felt better now that he'd told her about his AA meetings.

"It's funny," he said, his humor fading. "I don't even like the taste of whiskey or other alcohol."

"I never cared for it much myself. So, since I might have some time on Tuesday, would you like to go meet Lilly Jane?" she asked, briskly changing the subject.

It was a relief.

"I'd love to. Did you know that Tuesday is technically my day off?"

Billie blinked at him innocently. "I had no idea. How convenient that it's Eduardo's birthday, as well."

Evan chuckled and got up to pour more decaf for them both. "Luckily the weather reports suggest the next few days will be mild, so I should be able to get away for a couple of hours. I remember a few times we didn't have any snow after the first of March, but that isn't usual for this area. You really miss Lilly Jane, don't you?"

"She was my best friend for a lot of years. Finest barrel racer I ever trained and rode. She's still fit and able to work, but I didn't want to take a chance of her getting injured. Loath as I am to admit it, neither of us were getting any younger."

He sipped his coffee and wondered if it would be possible for Billie to keep Lilly Jane at the Soaring Hawk. The ranch hands had a barn for their horses and even if Billie was primarily a cook, she did her share of riding fences and doing other cattle work. She could ride Lilly Jane instead of one of the ranch's horses.

Problem was, it meant asking his son for a favor and that was something he'd been determined not to do. Still, if anyone else had been in charge, Evan wouldn't have hesitated. It would make Billy happy to have her horse closer. And it wasn't something he'd be asking for himself.

"HI, JOSH," BILLIE called to her old friend as they walked toward the rodeo school's horse paddock on Tuesday morning for the promised visit with Lilly Jane.

Josh McKeon was tall and strongly built. A few people had claimed he was too tall to effectively ride broncs and bulls, but he had been so successful that he'd become a rodeo champion in both the United States and Canada. Now he ran a rodeo school and was daddy to two pairs of twins, along with having a terrific wife who managed her family ranch and seemed oblivious to her own beauty.

"Morning, Billie. You're looking content."

She chuckled. "My feet are a little itchy for travel, but I also like sleeping in the same place each night." Billie gestured to Evan. "Don't know if you've met Evan Maxwell, Paige Maxwell's father-in-law."

"A time or two. Kelly and I bring the kids to the Soaring Hawk for playdays with Mishka and Daniel and vice versa. Welcome, Evan. I hear you're doing good work down there."

"Doin' my best."

The men gave each other firm handshakes.

"I brought Evan to meet Lilly Jane," Billie explained.

"She misses you, but she's become alpha mare of the herd," Josh said. "Absolutely calm and certain of herself."

Billie chuckled. "That's part of what made her a good competitor."

A loud neigh came from a shelter on one side of the paddock and Lilly Jane trotted over, demanding attention.

"Good girl," Billie murmured to the mare, rubbing her nose and neck, emotion nearly overwhelming her. For years Lilly Jane had been her best friend and companion and she missed her terribly.

"So this is the famous Lilly Jane," Evan said after a while.

She cleared her throat. "Yes. Lilly Jane, meet Evan Maxwell."

Evan put a hand out to let the mare get his scent. He spoke to her in a low tone and she cocked her head as if listening carefully. She then looked him over and bobbed her head, the way she signaled to say he was acceptable. Billie couldn't help being relieved. The mare had excellent intuition about people and it would have been disconcerting if she hadn't liked Evan.

Not that Billie expected their relationship to become more than friendship. Still, she was starting to care about Evan Maxwell more than any man she'd ever met. There were depths in him, a quiet thoughtfulness after everything he'd gone through, along with a sense of humor. A sense of humor went a long way for Billie.

She just didn't know if it was foolish to start thinking about a life with Evan. Or if committing herself was something she even wanted.

CHAPTER NINE

THE SUN WAS still well below the horizon and most of the crew were finishing their breakfast when Wyatt's father stepped into the ranch office on Wednesday.

Wyatt automatically tensed.

"May I talk to you?" Evan asked. "About Billie," he added quickly.

"What about Billie?"

"She's boarding her retired rodeo horse at McKeon's American Choice Ranch. I've seen Lilly Jane—she's strong and healthy. I know Billie doesn't work full-time as a ranch hand, but I wondered if she could keep the mare down here. There's room in the crew's barn and Lilly Jane looks to be an excellent horse. I'm sure she'd earn her keep, even just going out with Billie a few times a week."

"It's all right," Wyatt agreed. "But why didn't Billie ask herself? She isn't the type of person to need someone running interference for her."

Evan looked embarrassed.

"I'm not sure she knew it might be an option. But we've become friends. I thought I'd ask first to keep her from being disappointed if you didn't think it was a good idea."

"That was considerate," Wyatt said after regarding his father for a long moment, "but I wasn't likely to say no."

"I just wanted to be sure. Billie really loves that horse."

"It's fine. We have single horse trailers you can use. The two of you can go for Lilly Jane tomorrow morning if the weather permits. I consider it ranch business since she'll be using her horse on the job."

"Great. I'll let Billie know as soon as I get a chance."

Wyatt's tension eased as his father turned and left. Whenever Evan came around, there was a chance he'd bring up the past. Talking about it might be healthiest, but Wyatt wasn't eager to examine that long-ago period in his life, at least not with Evan.

Curiously, he wanted to ask Katrina what she thought about his father now that she'd gotten to know him better. She might respect his work as a fellow artist, yet she'd be honest. For someone who possessed such a positive outlook on life, she also had a solid grounding of common sense.

Of course, he already knew she questioned whether it was right to keep Christie and Evan apart, at the same time calling him a less-than-perfect grandfather.

Wyatt rubbed his temples and tried to clear his thoughts. He needed to focus. The crew should be done with breakfast and be getting ready for the day ahead. He got up and went outside to find they'd saddled his horse, along with Banana Split, the cutting horse Katrina would be using.

Across the way, he saw Katrina walk Christie to the main house to wait for Mrs. Bannerman to take her to preschool, then come down, a spring in her step.

"Hi, everyone."

A chorus of "Good morning," "Hi," "How are you?" and other pleasantries followed. The crew was fond of Katrina. They were tired after a long winter, but she seemed to lift their spirits. Just the other day while helping with the feeding she'd joked that the approaching storm was like a grumpy dragon, doomed to spit ice instead of fire. The bit of whimsy had made them laugh and they'd kidded about it the rest of the day.

Wyatt shook his head.

Maybe it was the artist in Katrina. She saw the world in a different way than other people. And she was probably the only one who could have talked about a grumpy dragon to the cowhands without being stared at as if she'd just dropped out of the sky.

"See you later, boss," Melody called as she mounted and rode out with three of the other ranch hands.

He nodded and refrained from repeating the instructions he'd already given them the evening before. They were headed west to herd the remaining pregnant cows on that side of the Soaring Hawk to the pastures around the main ranch. Those two teams had the biggest job. His brothers had already left going north, where they would move the cows wintering on the Circle M.

He and Katrina would handle the southern edge of the Soaring Hawk. She was a novice and he'd prefer having someone experienced along, but he was down an employee and had to leave at least one person at the main ranch. If there was an emergency, they would have to call on Billie and Saul.

"Is everything all right?" Katrina asked as

she fastened coils of a rope to the saddle horn and mounted Banana Split.

"Yeah, fine." Wyatt shook himself. "I hope Carmen's mother will be all right."

Carmen Melendez had rushed to the hospital in Bozeman in the early morning hours to see her mother, who was in intensive care with pneumonia. Carmen hadn't been able to say how long she'd be gone.

"Me, too. That new flu is nasty. Noelle told me it's making the rounds in Shelton County and they're concerned about it at the clinic."

"It's been helpful having a sister-in-law who's also a doctor. Ready to go?"

Katrina grinned and nodded. He didn't think he'd ever stop enjoying how excited she got about everything, even the long task of rounding up cows.

Luckily, another Chinook had developed and the temperature was moderate. The warmth was welcome and would make driving the cattle easier—not that he blamed pregnant cows for being reluctant to go anywhere in harsh weather. Their survival instinct told them to hunker down and endure. Yet an odd thought came to him. Wasn't that what he'd been doing since Amy died—hunkering down and enduring?

"Why did you decide to move the rest of the herd today?" Katrina asked.

Wyatt shrugged. "It's a balancing act. They have better winter forage still available on the outer sections of the ranch, but the rate of births are increasing. This way we'll need to feed them more, but they'll be closer to watch. And I don't need to tell you there's always the possibility of more storms coming in. I don't think winter is done with us yet."

"So a combination of intuition and knowledge."

"You could say that. We already have a fair number of cows near the ranch. Some moved earlier, and some wintering there. We'll do a running count on the ones we bring in today and if necessary, go out again tomorrow to round up stragglers."

"Sounds like quite a production. By the way, I've been practicing my roping. Saul claims I'm a fast learner, but I need experience with hitting a moving target," Katrina said, patting the coils of rope she'd secured to her saddle.

Wyatt frowned. "I don't want you roping cows, not yet. There are risks. And there isn't a real need today, regardless."

She rolled her eyes. "I don't plan on trying,

but Saul thought I should get used to having a rope on the saddle."

Wyatt wasn't sure if his grandfather was matchmaking by trying to turn Katrina into a cowgirl, or just liked having an eager novice to train. Curiously, it didn't bother him to think Saul might be getting ideas when it came to matchmaking. Nobody could force him to the altar if he didn't want to go, and it could be amusing to watch his grandfather's efforts.

He was glad to have Katrina on Banana Split. A good cutting horse was invaluable. With several of the ranch's dogs assisting, it shouldn't be too difficult getting the pregnant cows separated and back to the pastures around the main ranch. He might even be able to handle it alone—more than once as a teenager he had moved small herds by himself—but he'd promised that she could be involved.

Wyatt cast a sideways glance at Katrina. It was difficult to think of her as an employee. And after their kiss, he was particularly glad the ranch was paying her, instead of him. The more he thought about it, the more he wished that kiss had lasted longer.

Also that it had happened for a different reason.

"Um, I should apologize for the other night," he said.

"You mean for being upset about how I handled Christie's monster nightmare?"

"That and for everything else. I didn't think about the possibility of Tim overhearing the conversation."

"He doesn't always close his door and he has great hearing. I'm not trying to overprotect him, I just don't want him to misunderstand."

Wyatt hiked an eyebrow. "Why do I keep getting the feeling you think I overprotect Christie?"

Katrina pursed her lips. "You worry about her an awful lot."

"I'm supposed to, she's my daughter," he returned, exasperated. While he appreciated Katrina feeling free to express her opinion, he didn't see how being concerned about his child could ever be a bad thing.

"Yeah, but you seem to worry all the time. She's perceptive, she might be picking up on that. Surely there's a healthy balance between wanting to keep your child safe and being so cautious they're afraid of everything."

"Christie isn't afraid of everything."

"Really?" Katrina asked, a skeptical note in her voice.

He cleared his throat. "All right, she's nervous about a few things. But we've moved three times since she was born and with her mother gone..." He let his voice trail. He'd have to give it some thought. and consider what Katrina had said.

AS THEY RODE SOUTH, Katrina leaned over and stroked Banana Split's neck. She understood why Wyatt worried about Christie; she was all he had left of his beloved wife.

It was the kind of love Katrina had dreamed about as an adolescent and still wanted today. Absolute devotion and commitment. But apparently she wasn't the kind of woman who inspired that kind of emotion.

No.

She straightened in the saddle and scolded herself. She couldn't let what had happened with her ex-fiancé damage her self-confidence. It was right to consider whether she'd been too trusting and unobservant, but that was all. Nonetheless, it was difficult not to feel a niggling sense of doubt.

She stuck her chin up. "Remember what I said about losing something because of holding on too tight? You don't want Christie to rebel someday, do you?"

Wyatt slanted another look at her. "You mean the way my mother rebelled and married a man her father hated?"

"The feud between Saul and Evan was never a secret, though they've made peace now. I often see them talking around the ranch, like two old souls who've found common ground."

"And it only took them the better part of four decades." Wyatt's tone was dry.

"I realize it's different for someone looking in from the outside," Katrina said. "And I'm not trying to trivialize what you and the rest of your family went through."

"You aren't. The irony struck me, that's all."

Katrina sniffed the fresh air. Most of the snow had melted under the warm Chinook wind, leaving wet rangeland. There were few signs of grass starting to grow, but at the moment it felt like spring. How long that would last was another question.

"You've gotten to know my father by now, right?" Wyatt asked.

"He's interesting. Worked a lot of places and done various things. But we mostly talk about our art."

"Makes sense."

"By the way, I'm almost done painting that picture for Christie's room. It's going to be a sunrise with purple and Harlequin lupine on a hill. And a little girl on the crest of the hill with her arms thrown wide, embracing the rising sun."

"Sounds nice."

"I also have an idea for a mural on one of Christie's walls and wanted to see how you feel about it."

"With everything else you're doing, you want to paint a mural in my daughter's bedroom?"

"Sure. I can add puffy clouds to the blue background, along with trees, grass and wildflowers and mountains in the distance. Once Christie gets comfortable with the ranch animals, I could start adding them. Also rabbits and birds. Naturally I'd ask her before doing any of it."

Katrina wondered if she'd pushed too hard. After all, Wyatt might not want a mural. He'd already conceded quite a bit by changing the color he had originally planned to paint. Of course he'd also come unglued over how she'd handled Christie's monster nightmare, but had calmed down and listened to her reasoning, so that was good.

Oh, and she'd kissed him.

Except she didn't want to think too much about that kiss.

He'd sort of kissed her back, but likely more from shock than genuine response. It was her own fault. She should have explained earlier that Timothy didn't know why her engagement had ended. Kissing Wyatt to stop him from saying more had been the first option that came to mind.

Or maybe deep down she'd *wanted* to kiss Wyatt. He was strong and mature, trustworthy and kind. And he was a loving, devoted father. But she couldn't let her heart get involved. Coming second to a memory would be awful.

Katrina sighed. At least their interactions since that night had been pleasant enough.

"A mural is okay with me if it's all right with Christie," Wyatt said.

"Great. About Evan, I know what you said, but I'm sure he isn't trying to use me to get access to Christie. He's very careful. I can see how much he wants to ask about you both, but he doesn't. Maybe that's a point in his favor."

"I don't know. He scared me when I was a

kid, especially when the sheriff had to bring him home from the town bar. For a few days he'd start eating and didn't seem to be drinking, so I'd think everything was going to be okay. Then it would start again. Like being on an out-of-control roller coaster. And what about all those years he was gone without a word?"

No wonder Wyatt was having trouble dealing with his father's return. It reminded Katrina that she was lucky to have such a close family. They had their quirks, but she'd never felt the kind of fear Wyatt described—childhood qualms about imaginary animals under beds couldn't compare.

"The eating thing, is that important?" she asked.

"He didn't eat much when he was drinking. And he doesn't always eat now."

"You share quite a few meals out there with the ranch hands. It must be a little weird for him, working for his own son. Not that he's said anything about it," Katrina added hastily. Evan didn't seem to be underweight and she'd seen him munch on dried fruit and nuts at his workshop. Could someone do such beautiful wood carving if they were under the influence? He also serviced the heavy machinery on the ranch, though she didn't know how much he operated any of it.

"Evan does okay. Better than okay. Dakota says he had trouble facing us after everything that happened, but now that he's back, he just wants to reconnect and help out in any way possible. But I'm still leery about him being around Christie."

Katrina was flattered that Wyatt seemed to be seeking her opinion, though he might be figuring she'd give it to him, regardless. She *did* have a tendency to speak her mind.

"Something to consider is that Christie has some advantages you didn't have as a child—her daddy and a much bigger adult family," Katrina said, carefully choosing her words. Uncles, aunts and a great-grandfather and his wife. And Paige's mother, Margaret Bannerman, sees herself as a surrogate grandmother. She treats Christie the same as Mishka and Daniel."

Wyatt flashed a smile. "Christie also has a nanny."

"Right. See? She has a whole lot more support than you did."

"I'll think more about it."

His expression seemed to close, reminding Katrina again of that first day when she'd felt he was keeping the world at a distance. She'd thought it was new, but maybe she just hadn't seen that part of him all those years ago. It could also explain why he'd never dated any one girl for long. Having a relationship was difficult when there were barriers.

Still, he seemed to be loosening up, bit by bit, which was surely good for his daughter, as well as him.

"EXCITED?"

Billie rolled her eyes at Evan's question. They were driving up to the rodeo school again, but not to visit Lilly Jane this time. Instead they were taking her back to the Soaring Hawk.

"Obviously, I'm excited. Lilly Jane is happiest when she's with me and has something to do. This means I can see her every day and ride her when I have time or need to. Thanks for asking Wyatt. I didn't realize it might be possible or I would have asked myself."

"It wasn't anything."

Billie didn't take her gaze off the road, but she was sure if she looked, Evan's ears would be red, the way they turned when he was embarrassed. She'd almost kissed him when he'd given her the news and was sorry she hadn't.

The horse trailer Wyatt had loaned them was built with a quality suspension system, similar to the one she'd sold. Though the return drive down to the Soaring Hawk wasn't that far, she was glad Lilly Jane would be comfortable.

"How many miles did you travel with Lilly Jane?" Evan asked.

"Fifty to a hundred thousand a year for over a decade."

"That's a well-traveled horse. You told Josh your feet still get itchy for travel. Does that mean you're thinking of taking off again?"

Billie thought about it. "Not really, or I wouldn't consider bringing Lilly Jane to the Soaring Hawk. But I spent my whole life on the road. It's natural to be restless."

"Surely you took trips or visited your parents after they retired. You said they were in Great Falls."

"I'd stop for a day or two on my way from one rodeo to the next. But we mostly video chat on the phone. I think they miss me being a rodeo chaser because they could still feel like a part of the action that way. I understand. I don't miss road noise, but being on the go was fun. Life here is quiet."

EVAN DIDN'T LIKE hearing that Billie missed part of her old life, though people were often nostalgic, even if they didn't intend to return to how things once were.

His first thirty years had been great and things were getting better now, but he wouldn't care to relive the part in the middle unless he could undo his mistakes.

"Do you, uh…" He cleared his throat. "Do you ever think you'll go back to competing?"

Billie had turned onto the McKeon's American Choice Ranch road. Now she pulled to one side, stopped her truck and looked at him. "Any special reason you're asking?"

Evan squirmed under her gaze. He hadn't courted a woman since he was a wild teenager with fire in his engine and possessing unbridled confidence.

He hadn't thought about romance since becoming a widower, but he liked Billie and was still sorting out what that meant. It wasn't guilt about his wife; she would have wanted him to be happy.

Still, Evan didn't know how any of his sons would react to him being interested in a woman. It could be a lot to accept on top of the way he'd messed up their childhoods.

But Billie was special and surely his boys

could see that. She approached problems with solid good sense, which was interesting since she'd spent all those years chasing rodeos. In her case, it didn't seem to have been an expectation of becoming a champion, just enjoyment of the lifestyle and being around people with similar interests.

"I just wondered," Evan said. "You're making friends here and it might be hard to leave them behind, too."

"Did you have any particular friend in mind?"

He gave her an annoyed look. "All right, *me*."

"Oh."

Billie leaned forward and gave him an awkward smack on the mouth. She started to draw back, but he cupped the back of her neck and gave her another more thorough kiss.

When the kiss finally ended, he was quite certain both their faces were red.

"I'm not very good at this romance thing," she said, as if the admission was being dragged from her.

"Neither am I. You'd think it would be easier at our age, but it isn't."

"Yeah, but you were married."

"That was a long time ago. There hasn't

been anyone since. And romance during a marriage isn't like dating."

"How do you feel about holding hands?"

"I approve." Evan picked up Billie's hand and squeezed her fingers. She worked hard, but her calluses were softer than his own and he liked the sensation of her skin against his. "It's one of the first steps beyond friendship. How do you feel about *that*?"

"I'm okay with first steps. No promises otherwise."

"I understand."

Billie started the truck again and drove back onto the road. Evan was pleased, though it occurred to him that she hadn't really answered whether or not she would ever consider returning to rodeo competition.

He didn't want to push. After all, if he was in her shoes, he might question whether he should get involved with someone who had a drinking problem.

All he could do was try to show her the kind of man he was now, exactly the same as he was doing for his sons and grandchildren.

CHAPTER TEN

THE NEXT TWO weeks were frantically busy and Katrina took every opportunity possible to observe when Christie was in preschool.

According to Paige they were finally moving past the peak calving period, which should help. Although, something else would take its place. That seemed to be life on a ranch. But she wouldn't necessarily call Wyatt a workaholic. It was about the animals and the land and finding a place where he belonged. He belonged in Montana on the Soaring Hawk, the same as his brothers.

After teaching her online art course with Mishka's class, Katrina went upstairs to unpack more of Wyatt's moving boxes. He didn't seem to care if they stayed packed forever, but she'd been finding useful items, like extra towels and sheets and pans for the kitchen.

Before starting, she looked in on Christie. The three-year-old was lying on her stomach drawing a picture, knees bent with her feet waving in the air.

"Do you need anything, Christie?"

Christie regarded the stub of a crayon. "More blue, please."

"I'll look for another." Katrina found a new box in the cupboard and extracted the blue crayon. She wasn't surprised that Christie used so much of her favorite color—her pictures usually contained a lot of sky.

Christie's smile was as bright as sunshine. "Thank you, Aunt Kat."

"You're very welcome. I've been wondering if you'd like me to paint a picture on your wall. Maybe of grass and the hills and trees. A very *big* picture, where we could add things as we go along."

"Would it have little clouds in the sky?"

"Sure."

"Yes, please." Christie nodded vigorously. "I have dreams about sitting on a cloud. It's... *marvelous*." *Marvelous* was her most recent word from preschool.

"I used to have the same dream. Sometimes I thought I could fly, even when I was awake."

The three-year-old's eyes widened. "Me, too. At day care there was a slide inside the playroom, I climbed to the top and flew to the ceiling. Bunches of times. Then I couldn't."

"That's how it happened to me. One day my feet just stayed on the ground."

"Yeah." Christie heaved a sigh. "My kitties love to hear about my cloud dreams. They don't get to go outside, so I tell them how everything looks. Did you know trees are round from up high?"

"Yes, I do. Everything looks different from up above. I'll be working in the other room if there's anything else you need."

"Okay, Aunt Kat."

Katrina went down the hallway where one of the spare rooms still had a good number of boxes, partly because she'd deliberately left anything marked "personal" untouched. *Personal* covered a fair amount of territory—for all she knew, they contained items that had belonged to Wyatt's wife. It gave her a sinking sensation to think about, but he had every right to keep mementoes of the woman he'd loved so much, for Christie's sake as well as his own.

A cascade of mail fell as Katrina shifted one of the stacks. She collected everything from the floor and saw the envelopes were unopened. They each had forwarding labels and seemed to have been received shortly after Wyatt's move to Montana. She left them on his pillow except for a postcard from a veterinarian in Virginia. It was a reminder that Salem and Blinx had been due for their annual exams and vaccinations back in January.

Obviously they weren't going back to "Doc Beachey's Paw Palace" in Norfolk, so this was something she could take care of without invading his privacy too much. She looked up the phone number for the local veterinarian and dialed.

"Shelton Veterinary Clinic," answered an efficient voice.

"Hi. I want to make an appointment to do annual exams and vaccinations for two cats. They belong to Wyatt Maxwell. I'm his housekeeper, Katrina Tapson. That is, I need an appointment if the exams haven't already been done."

"Oh, hi, Kat. Remember me?" The voice changed from efficient to pleased. "It's Valerie Burke. Actually, Valerie Cantwell, now."

"You mean Harold finally woke up and realized he adored you?"

Valerie giggled. "Nope. I married his older brother, Elliott. I was working here at the clinic when Elliott returned for his veterinary residency. I can't believe I ever thought Harold was 'the one.' What are you doing in Shelton? I heard you were engaged."

"I returned his ring. It turns out 'the one' was hard for me to find in Seattle."

"That's too bad. Look, you can bring the cats for their exam, but we'll need Wyatt's permission. We already have their records from Virginia. He had copies sent before he moved back home, but he hasn't had time to bring them in."

"I take care of his daughter, so I have a general letter saying I'm authorized to act for him. Is that enough?"

"Perfect. How about two o'clock? There was a cancellation. We can put the charges on the Soaring Hawk account."

"See you then."

Katrina ended the call and went in to tell Christie they were taking her kitties to be checked by the cat doctor. "It's to help Salem and Blinx stay healthy," she explained.

"Can I stay with Aunt Paige?"

"They'll be much happier if you go with them because they know you best."

"Oh. O-kay."

Christie might not like meeting new people, but she adored her kitties and always made sure their food and water bowls were full. Katrina didn't mind her trying to take some responsibility, even if it meant cleaning up a few water puddles due to overfilling.

Thinking Wyatt should know, she sent a text saying she and Christie were bringing the cats to the vet for their annual exam. He responded almost immediately.

Thanks.

She waited a minute and saw the expected second text.

Wait. RU sure? It isn't your resp.

No prob, she texted back with a laugh emoji. He should have figured out by now that she was going to do what she thought was needed, whether or not it fit her so-called job description.

It would be great if he'd see her more as a partner, but that might be too close to the kind of relationship he wanted to avoid.

The next step wasn't so easy—getting Salem and Blinx into their carriers. She finally managed, though they glared through the wire openings in the doors. After all, they'd been pursuing their rightful feline duty of napping and playing and she'd had the *gall* to put them in prison. They grumpily settled down, their tails tucked tightly around their bodies. Luckily their language wasn't translatable, because she was reasonably sure it wasn't fit for Christie's ears.

"Sorry, pals," she said. "But this is for your own good."

Naturally they didn't care, they just spat at her. She'd have to give them extra treats when they got home or it might be days before she was forgiven.

Katrina was still uncomfortable about taking Wyatt's SUV, but it was what he'd asked her to do. And she couldn't deny the Volvo handled nicely.

They'd had several storms back to back, but for the last few days the temperature had been mild. If all went well, the grass would start growing and they wouldn't have more snow. Yet Katrina remembered Wyatt's conviction that they weren't done with winter. Maybe he'd meant the last two weeks, but snow in April wasn't uncommon.

At the Shelton Veterinary Clinic she greeted Valerie and nodded at a woman with a Great Dane puppy. Christie didn't seem too afraid of the dog, maybe because he was mostly clumsy legs and a goofy expression. He also seemed nervous and kept sticking his nose under his owner's chair. Katrina was happy to see his ears and tail had been left natural, instead of being cropped.

Suddenly the puppy was startled by something falling from a shelf. He let out a high yelp of alarm and raced to hide his face in a corner.

"It's okay." Christie ran over to reassure him. "I won't let anyone hurt you."

He slowly pulled his head out and let her pat his shoulder.

"Sorry," his owner apologized. "Scooter act like a clown sometimes."

"He'll probably grow out of it," Katrina said, though she thought the puppy was charming. She also thought it was sad the woman hadn't thought to reassure the dog herself. There seemed to be little connection between animal and owner.

The woman frowned at Scooter.

"I don't know what my brother was thinking when he gave me a Great Dane for my birthday. It has to be his idea of a joke. I can't even have Scooter in the boutique with me. He spends most of the time pushing up against me, or so scared of his shadow that he knocks things over when he runs away."

Katrina was trying not to dislike the other woman. Feeling bad about making a snap judgment, she went over and stuck out her hand.

"Hi, I'm Katrina Tapson. I just moved back to Shelton."

"Barbara Cullen. I'm a fairly recent transplant. I own the new boutique on Main Street called Dressing Right. I visited Shelton for the Christmas events two years ago and could see the town needed another clothing store." She eyed Katrina's casual jeans and puffy jacket. "Be sure to visit my shop. We're open five days a week, Tuesday through Saturday."

"Maybe when I have time," Katrina said politely, though she didn't think she'd find anything she liked at a place called Dressing Right.

Christie coaxed the puppy over to where they'd put the cat carriers and Katrina was concerned when she saw Scooter press his face to the wire door on Salem's kennel. But instead of swatting, the cat purred and gave him a lick. Blinx meowed and received a sniff from the dog as well.

"Look, Aunt Kat, he isn't 'fraid of my

kitties." Christie dropped to her knees and threw her arms around Scooter's neck. His tail whipped back and forth. "And they like him, too."

"They sure do, Christie. I bet they'd love having one of the puppies on the ranch as a friend."

Barbara got up with an excited expression. "What an excellent idea. Christie, do you want to have Scooter as your very own?"

"Oh, yes. *Can I?*" Christie cried.

Katrina's jaw dropped. "I don't think that's—"

"Please don't say no," Barbara pleaded. "I'm here because I'm going to ask the vet to re-home Scooter, but I'd much rather give him to such a nice little girl. He's very gentle and learns quickly, he just takes more time than I have, especially while trying to make the boutique successful. I feel bad for him. He needs someone who can give him more attention."

"It's okay, Aunt Kat," Christie said happily. "Daddy says I can have a dog."

Katrina gave Barbara a narrow look. She must know it was inappropriate to offer an animal to a child without asking permission first. On the other hand, Wyatt *had* mentioned wanting to get his daughter interested in adopting a puppy. He'd meant one of the puppies already on the Soaring Hawk, but surely he'd be happy to have Christie welcome any dog.

It was also true that Barbara had a faintly bewildered expression in her eyes, as if she'd landed in an altogether unfamiliar situation and didn't know how to rescue herself.

"Maybe we can take Scooter on a trial basis," Katrina said. "But the decision to keep him is up to Christie's father, so I'll need your address and phone number."

The woman handed her a business card. "I'm sure it'll be okay. Scooter is healthy, purebred and from a reputable breeder. Also fully housebroken. That basket on the chair has all of his things, including information on a prepaid dog training course." She turned and rushed out the door without even saying goodbye to the Great Dane.

Fortunately, Scooter didn't seem to care.

Katrina crouched and rubbed the puppy's floppy ears. He was lovely: a grayish black, with white-tipped forepaws, a blotch of white on his chest and a powerful tail. Maybe part of his appeal to Christie was the similar coloring to her cats. Also that he was scared of his own shadow.

"Maybe you can help Scooter be less afraid," she said.

Christie nodded with a grave expression. "I'll help him."

Katrina glanced at the reception counter and saw Valerie clapping a hand over her mouth.

"Don't laugh," she warned.

"You walked right into her trap."

"I wasn't expecting it. I mean, who expects someone to just give away a purebred Great Dane?" Yet Katrina wasn't entirely sorry. Barbara hadn't picked Scooter, he'd been a gift, one she obviously couldn't fit into her life. She'd planned to give up the puppy and Christie had fallen in love with him. This way he'd have a home where he was wanted.

"Well, she's right that Scooter is healthy. He's also fully up-to-date on his shots. We have all of his records and can give you care instructions."

The vet technician came out just then. She must have been listening because she appeared amused as well. "Please come into the exam room," she said. "All five of you."

Katrina sighed.

It might take a while to live this story down.

On the other hand, Scooter might be just what Christie needed, and that was worth a bit of teasing.

WYATT WAS DRAGGING by the time he got home after spending the previous night in the calving barn with nothing but short snatches of sleep.

The crew was over their colds, but this morning Rod Gaffney had come down with the much nastier virus making the rounds in Shelton—the same flu that had put Carmen Melendez's mother in the hospital. While Rod was temporarily moving to the old foreman's quarters to minimize exposing his coworkers, it was probably too late.

So far Evan didn't seem to be affected, but it was probably a matter of time before it caught up with him and the others. In the meantime, Wyatt had left his father in charge at the calving barn, with instructions to call if there was a problem.

He saw Katrina coming down the main staircase. "I'm guessing my daughter is already in bed."

"Er…yeah. Along with Blinx, Salem and Scooter and Fluffy Bob."

He nodded, then narrowed his eyes. "Wait a minute. Who or what is Scooter?"

She pursed her mouth. "Just a puppy we met at the vet's office. He's scheduled to start training classes and is housebroken, so no worries about that. The classes were prepaid and I'll take him myself. The owner was there to re-home Scooter and offered him to Christie, who was beyond happy about it. She reminded me that you'd told her she could have a dog."

Something in Katrina's expression and her rushed explanation made Wyatt suspicious.

He took the stairs two at a time and hurried into his daughter's bedroom.

And blinked.

It wasn't a small dog lying on the bed, like a Yorkie or Chihuahua, it was a Great Dane puppy, rivaling the size of his daughter.

A Great Dane.

On a ranch.

There couldn't be a more absurd combination.

Christie was sound asleep with an arm around the puppy, while the cats were curled up against her back. They all looked blissful. Fluffy Bob was on a corner of the bed, leaning against the headboard. Wyatt went downstairs again and found Katrina in the kitchen.

"That's a Great Dane."

"I know. The vet told me they're working dogs," she said. "So maybe Scooter can help on the ranch."

"There's no way that dog will be able to work cattle. I wouldn't dare let him near the herd. On top of that, he'll eat a hundred pounds of food a month and need jackets and booties in the winter if he's out for more than a few minutes. He'll be the laughingstock of the Soaring Hawk."

Katrina cocked her head and smiled. "Maybe, but did you see Christie's expression?"

Wyatt's annoyance fled at the memory of his daughter's peaceful, happy face.

"You should have seen her at the veterinary office," Katrina continued. "Scooter was startled by something and ran to hide—apparently he's shy and easily scared. Christie rushed to comfort him. She's very empathetic, so I've been thinking that helping Scooter overcome his fears might help her deal with her own. Besides, could you have said no? Especially when the owner offered the puppy to her out of the blue," she added. "Without even a hint to me of what she planned to do."

Wyatt began to smile, envisioning the situation.

"So you were outmaneuvered."

Katrina looked chagrined. "You could say that."

He couldn't resist, he leaned over and gave her a kiss. It was intended to be teasing, but she tasted so sweet he lingered, absorbing the scent and feel of her as if he'd never touched another woman.

Wyatt finally stepped back and cleared his throat. "Sorry. I shouldn't have done that. I don't want to make you uncomfortable."

"I'm not uncomfortable. Anyway, I sort of kissed you first. Remember? So we're even." She looked away, so he couldn't read the expression in her eyes. "But I think you should try to sleep. You're short on rest."

Wyatt hesitated for a long moment. More needed to be said, but maybe now wasn't the time.

"Okay. But I don't want Scooter in the bedroom with Christie until we know him better. Anyway, before long he'll be too big for her bed. He's almost too big now. He can stay in my room."

Wyatt climbed the stairs and went into Christie's room again. The night-light spilled a golden glow over his daughter and the animals cuddled with her. Blinx and Salem must be comfortable with Scooter's presence or they wouldn't be sleeping in such close proximity.

A Great Dane on the Soaring Hawk. It would be a sight to behold. He knew little about the breed except that they could be comical, affectionate and were known as gentle giants. Wyatt grinned at the absurd image of a full-grown Scooter trying to compete with the ranch's smaller, more agile cow dogs, who were bred for the job of moving cattle.

He stroked strands of hair from Christie's forehead and her eyes opened. "Hi, Daddy."

"Hi, sweetheart. I'm going to take your new friend into my room at night, at least until he's older."

His daughter stuck out her lip. "Scooter loves me."

"I know he does, but, uh..." Wyatt stopped, unsure of how to explain that puppies weren't always predictable, particularly nervous puppies. "He might scare your friendly monster. Remember, JoJo is so shy, he doesn't even let me see him."

"Oh. Okay." She petted the puppy until his eyes opened. "Go with Daddy, Scooter. Daddy loves dogs."

At Wyatt's urging, the puppy stepped down from the bed and followed him into the master bedroom. His eyes seemed to light up as Wyatt turned on the automated gas jets in the modernized fireplace. He promptly trotted over and curled up in front of the heat.

Wyatt shook his head as he dumped his clothes into the hamper and headed into the bathroom to take a shower. Thirty-six hours without any solid rest was too long. He was foggy, that had to be the reason he'd agreed to adopt a Great Dane and kissed Katrina.

Then again, maybe he had kissed Katrina because she was enticing and beautiful and he'd wanted to find out if it would affect him the way it had the first time.

The answer was, it had almost dropped him to his knees.

WYATT WAS BACK at the calving barn the next morning as the sun was rising, but all was calm.

In a way it felt as if he'd never been gone from Montana—his brothers and grandfather were here and the work was the same. Yet the others were married now. And beneath his crusty exterior, Saul had turned out to be a great guy, who not only had amazing insight when it came to raising cattle, but a special love for fine horses.

Wyatt shared that love. It was one of the reasons he'd wanted to ensure Katrina was a skilled rider who could safely handle a horse.

He just wished he had slept better after kissing her. Their first kiss had shaken him, but the second had rocked him to the core. If losing Amy had taught him anything, it was that life was uncertain and caring for someone meant the chance of being hurt. Yet he'd seen Saul's contentment with Anna Beth and his brothers' happiness with their wives and knew that being alone carried a cost as well.

A high cost.

"I'm glad Carmen's mother is out of the hospital," Stedman said, jarring Wyatt from his reverie. He'd taken over for Evan in the barn an hour earlier.

Wyatt shook himself. "Yes, though she still doesn't have any energy. Carmen is staying there to help out."

"We're taking up a collection to send flowers to Mrs. Melendez."

Wyatt nodded. The crew was supportive of

each other and Stedman seemed to have a soft spot for Carmen. Her mother also owned a large winter wear company in Bozeman and had an endearing habit of showing up with "seconds" of coats and other items to share with her daughter's coworkers. She brushed off any words of appreciation, saying they weren't worth shipping back to the supplier. Nobody was fooled, she was just a nice person.

"I want to contribute, if that's all right," Wyatt said. "I'll go back to the house and get some cash."

"Sure thing, boss. Everything is calm. Take your time. No need to be here if you have something else to do. We won't order the flowers until tomorrow."

Back at the homestead cabin the combined scent of maple and bacon filled the air. Wyatt found Katrina in the kitchen, once again dancing to the radio as she emptied the dishwasher. It no longer surprised him, but his day was brighter when he saw her spinning and twirling as she went about her various tasks.

He had asked how her former employer felt about that much exuberance and she'd made a face, saying it hadn't been the kind of place where people danced or even laughed that much. In her kind way, she'd added that they were simply conservative and found it difficult to understand employees who didn't fit into their mold.

Today an upbeat classic country tune was playing and Wyatt gave in to temptation—a fast waltz was one of the few dances he'd actually learned beyond square dancing and the polka. He bowed to Katrina and held out his arms. She looked surprised, then accepted and they danced around the large kitchen.

"I'm sorry if you hoped to see Christie, but she and Scooter are playing with Daniel at the main house," Katrina said when the music ended, sounding breathless.

He shook his head, hoping he didn't have a befuddled expression on his face. Impulsive kisses and dancing weren't like him. They needed to talk and clear the air. Preferably away from the ranch, where he could think more clearly.

"Actually, since the two of them are occupied, I wonder if you'd go into town with me?" he asked. "I'm not needed at the barn and I want to get some play clothes for Christie that aren't pink. Also, I was thinking we could talk," he added, so Katrina wouldn't suggest bringing his daughter.

She nodded. "Good idea. I'll get my coat."

Instead of driving straight to the Kid's Stuff store in Shelton, he stopped at the city park that served as the town square.

"I guess we're talking first and shopping second?" Katrina asked.

"I hope that's okay." He shifted and looked at her intently. "I've been thinking about last night. I shouldn't have kissed you and I'm sorry."

She pursed her lips in that cute habit she had of doing. And lately it made him think even more about kissing her.

"That's okay. You were thrilled to see Christie so happy and got carried away."

"It's just that—"

"Let's walk to the store from here," Katrina said abruptly, opening the door and getting out. "It's only a fewblocks and I want to stretch my legs."

Wyatt sighed and followed her. He didn't know what she was thinking, but it was obvious she wanted to avoid discussing anything personal.

"Wait, Katrina. I know you said it was okay, but I want to be sure I didn't upset you."

Katrina shook her head.

She wasn't upset, she was confused. Their

first kiss had been to keep her nephew from overhearing something he might misunderstand. But their second kiss had seemed more meaningful. The same with dancing around the kitchen. Her pulse had raced from the unexpected contact with Wyatt and their kiss had kept her awake long into the night while she replayed it in her mind.

On top of that her feelings for him kept growing, yet it seemed as if nothing had changed. He was strong and handsome and totally devoted to his daughter...and determined to stay single. A man like that was dangerous—a great package wrapped up in a guy whose heart belonged to a memory.

And now he was apologizing for their kiss. *Again.* It felt as if her heart was on a precipice, ready to fall. But Katrina didn't know if the fall would be wonderful or have a sudden, unpleasant ending. An ending, she suspected, that would be far more painful than the breakup with her ex-fiancé.

Traffic in town was busier than usual. The spate of good weather had brought people out to shop and take care of business. Passersby waved from their cars and trucks and called out greetings as they stood there, probably curious about seeing her and Wyatt together in

Shelton. It was a small town, curiosity came with the territory.

She started walking, knowing they might draw less attention that way.

"Why don't you want to talk about it?" Wyatt asked, easily keeping pace with her.

"What is there to say? I know you don't want to get involved with anyone. You've said it often enough. Do you need another assurance that I'm not getting ideas about us?"

"No. I'm quite certain you'll only accept a relationship with someone who loves you heart and soul. Someone you love that much in return."

Hmm. It was an interesting response. Neither a denial nor agreement. But it was also an affirmation of how important loving, and being loved, was to her.

"So we're agreed the kissing and dancing didn't mean anything."

"Well—" Wyatt stopped and she cast an inquiring glance at him. "I don't deny they were pleasant."

"Pleasant?" she repeated, annoyed.

"Very pleasant. For Pete's sake, Katrina, you're a beautiful woman. You make me laugh and want to be better than I am. I don't know. I'm all mixed up."

She opened the door of the clothing shop, trying to decide if she was insulted or discouraged. Yet a small edge of hope also rose. Wyatt wasn't trying to dismiss what had happened and seemed to be feeling more than he cared to admit.

"Make up your mind about what you want from me, Wyatt. In the meantime, let's get those clothes for Christie," she said, her tone deliberately brisk. "She could use a few rough and tumble outfits."

"Rough and tumble?" Wyatt asked, apparently getting the message that she was done talking about their kiss.

"Yeah. The kind kids wear on a ranch. She has a dog now, she needs denims and things that hold up better to mud and dirt and being active. Not that she'll necessarily decide she likes ranch life."

"What makes you say that?"

At the look on Wyatt's face, Katrina was pretty sure he'd never considered the possibility that his daughter wouldn't eventually become a ranch kid like her cousins. It was reassuring because it meant he didn't intend to keep her from riding horses and being otherwise involved.

"I'm just saying it's possible she won't like

the same things you do. Remember, I'm the maverick in my family who didn't go into teaching."

"But you're teaching an online art class and you're always showing Christie how to do stuff or illustrating a scene on the ranch for her."

Katrina found a rack of jeans for children and began looking for Christie's size. "There's a difference between teaching an hour-long class once a week and being a full-time professor or teacher."

"I suppose."

She hesitated a moment. "But in the spirit of encouraging Christie to embrace her new environment, how about letting me take her and Scooter to the barn to visit the pregnant mares? If she's willing."

"She's never been willing before."

"Except now she has Scooter to think about and teach to be less afraid. She seems very determined and I'd hate to see her lose momentum."

When he didn't say anything, she prompted, "How about it?"

"Sure, just let me know when you're going. I want to be there with you." He held up a hand when she started to say it wasn't necessary. "As added support and encouragement. I agree she needs to learn how to be comfortable around the Soaring Hawk's large animals. I don't want her growing up afraid for me. But I also need to be sure Scooter doesn't react in a way that frightens the mares."

"Does that mean you're ready to let her watch a calving?"

"It might be better for her to watch one of the mares give birth first. They rarely need help. But let's take things a step at a time. Let me know when you want to go and I'll meet you at the foaling barn."

"Sure. But I want to watch a foaling, too," Katrina said promptly.

"I figured."

"Can I help you?" asked a woman's voice.

Katrina returned the clerk's friendly smile. It wasn't someone she recognized, but in Shelton, there was a good chance they'd met before.

"Hi. This is Wyatt Maxwell." She gestured to him. "He needs play clothes for his daughter. She's three-and-a-half."

"Good timing. We just put out a new shipment. Keep in mind, you can always return items if they don't fit. Everything's right here."

"Thanks."

After the clerk left to help another customer, Katrina handed Wyatt three pairs of jeans to consider.

"I guess these would be softer and more comfortable because the denim is prewashed," he said, though his eyes were sad.

"Hey, what's bothering you?" Katrina asked gently.

"They look like adult jeans," he murmured. "Just smaller."

She gave him a sympathetic shoulder bump. "Christie can't stay a little girl forever."

"I know. But it seems like just yesterday I was changing her diapers."

Katrina looked through more choices on the rack and pulled out several. Butterflies were embroidered on the leg of one pair, the second depicted a kitten playing with a string, and the third was adorned with daisies.

"I get it. Maybe you'd like these better. They have elastic across the back, which would give her plenty of room to grow."

Some of the distress left his face. "Yeah, those are more like what I was thinking about."

They returned the other jeans to the rack and went to look at tops and sweats. Before long they had a nice selection in various colors.

Wyatt paid for his purchases and they went outside. He sighed.

"Thanks for understanding. It's hard seeing Christie grow up so fast."

"I'll feel the same way when I have kids."

He nodded.

Katrina tried to keep the mood light as they walked back to where they'd left the SUV. But she wanted to be more than an understanding friend, she was starting to want everything.

And kisses aside, *everything* with Wyatt still seemed like an impossible wish.

CHAPTER ELEVEN

"Come with us, Scooter. Don't be afraid."

Katrina was delighted by the way Christie was ignoring her own fear of the ranch in order to coax the Great Dane puppy farther away from the house.

He'd been okay rushing outside for a brief moment to do his business and hurrying back just as quickly. But as they walked toward the busier part of the ranch center, he whined and pulled on his leash as if saying *there are big things down there and people and stuff I don't understand.*

"What is *that*?" asked a voice. It was one of the ranch hands, pointing at Scooter and grinning broadly.

"He's mine," Christie announced, crossing her small arms over her chest. She was smart and had immediately realized that Scooter was being laughed at. "You stay away. He's scared. You'd be scared, too, if you were a baby."

"Excuse me, ma'am." Eduardo swept off his cowboy hat and bowed. "I was just surprised, we don't see many Great Danes on a ranch."

Christie harrumphed, sounding just like her great-grandfather. Saul could get a good deal of meaning into the sound and his great-granddaughter was a fast learner.

Wyatt walked over, his eyebrows raised. "Problem?"

"No, sir." Eduardo plopped his hat back on his head and nodded. "Just remarking on what an unusual puppy your daughter has adopted."

Wyatt got a resigned expression. He'd claimed Scooter would be a laughingstock and it appeared he was right.

"He's gorgeous," Katrina said quickly. "He just has to grow up more."

"Yeah," Christie agreed, patting Scooter who had nuzzled up to her for reassurance. She had her chin stuck out stubbornly.

A story for a picture book instantly began evolving in Katrina's mind about a Great Dane growing up on a ranch, trying to find a way to fit in with the agile cattle dogs. The illustrations would be so much fun to paint. She smiled wryly. Even though she was worried about the condition of her heart when it came to Wyatt, the change had been wonderful for her as an artist.

"I'll get moving." Eduardo was grinning as he walked away.

Katrina tried to look innocent as Wyatt narrowed his eyes at her. "Ready to go to the foaling barn?" she asked.

"You're enjoying this."

"'Joying what, Daddy?"

"Living on the ranch," Katrina interjected. "I really love being on the Soaring Hawk."

"Tim likes it. He says I should learn to ride. I dunno. Horses are *big*."

"But you're going to help Scooter stop being afraid of them, right?" Wyatt asked.

Christie bobbed her head and resolve grew again in her young face. They continued to the foaling barn, with Scooter having to be encouraged at several points to continue. Katrina supposed it was a question of perspective. She'd spent so many years in cities after living in a rural town that the Soaring Hawk felt wonderfully peaceful. But to Scooter and Christie, the place was filled with unfamiliar sounds, animals and activity.

"She's taking this very seriously," Wyatt murmured in an undertone as they went into the barn.

"That's good, right?" Katrina asked.

"Yeah, I've just never seen her so determined."

The pleasure in Wyatt's eyes gave Katrina tingles. He *was* lightening up, becoming less serious than before, and it was nice to think she was a small part of it happening.

"All the mares had been released into the paddock," he explained, "but I brought one back in for Christie and Scooter to meet. Mookie is quite calm."

The mare was in the first stall and she looked at them as they approached. Scooter stiffened and his ears shot out, making him resemble an alarmed cartoon character with his gangly legs.

"It's okay, Scooter, she's behind a gate," Christie assured her puppy. "She won't hurt us. Come on, let's go closer." She petted him and they stepped forward a few feet.

Wyatt went over and stroked the mare's nose.

Mookie was a beauty—a rich dark brown, with a crisp white blaze on her face.

"Good girl," he said softly. She nickered and both Scooter and Christie jumped.

"W-what does it mean when they do that, Daddy?"

"It's her way of saying hello," he explained. "Salem and Blinx meow and purr. Horses neigh and make other noises."

"Oh." Christie looked more interested now than nervous. "I hear them at home. And the cows moo-ooing."

"Animals make sounds for different reasons. Cows will moo when they're happy, but also to tell humans that something is needed, or to talk to each other. It's the same with horses."

Christie nodded. It was difficult to tell how much she actually understood about the ranch's animals. She would repeat things that Mishka or one of the adults had told her and look at the pictures Katrina painted and ask questions, but she remained uncomfortable about the risks they might represent, especially to her daddy. It wasn't surprising. They'd only moved to Montana in January and except for a few short visits to the Soaring Hawk, she had lived far away from the ranching world. Still, she seemed unusually mature for her age.

Katrina tied Scooter's long leash to a post and reached into her coat pocket for the sugar cubes she'd put in a bag.

"Christie, I'm going to give Mookie some

sugar," she said. "Horses should only be given a little as a treat, but today is special."

Christie watched with a mix of trepidation and interest as Katrina held out her open hand. Mookie's ears pricked forward and she nickered louder. She carefully took the cube from Katrina's palm and crunched the sugar between her teeth.

"She's kissing you," Christie giggled when the mare nuzzled Katrina's arm and neck.

"It's her way of showing affection and saying thank you," Wyatt explained.

Katrina stroked the horse, admiring her beautiful coat and healthy condition. "When do you expect her to deliver?" she asked.

"Late May or early June."

"So a while yet."

"The best timing is when there's plenty of green grass for a nursing mother to eat. We keep watch on the mares, but particularly when they're expected to foal. Luckily by then the calving period is basically over."

"You said horses usually don't have trouble giving birth."

"It's relatively rare, but we still keep an eye out. We also want them to be comfortable with a human presence."

Katrina tried not to be too aware of Wyatt

standing next to her. They were an unlikely pair—the artist and the rancher…even if he *had* danced with her. She couldn't help smiling at the memory of his carefree expression as they'd quickstepped around the large kitchen.

She turned around and focused on Christie.

Scooter was sniffing the stall gate, more curious now than scared. Mookie dropped her head, snuffling the new scent from the Great Dane, and their noses met unexpectedly in the gap between two of the boards.

Scooter made a surprised sound and plopped backward on his bottom. Christie giggled. Very carefully she put out a finger and touched Mookie's nose herself.

"Daddy, her nose is bigger than my hand."

"That's right. Did you know horses can only breathe through their noses, not through their mouths?" Wyatt asked.

Christie's eyes widened. "Uh-uh."

"That's right. And if you pay attention, they can show you how they feel with their faces and ears. She also has whiskers, a little like Salem and Blinx. They're very sensitive."

"Pick me up, Daddy. Pleeease. I wanna look."

Wyatt obligingly lifted her and she stared

as Mookie raised her head. The mare's peaceful eyes were just inches away from Christie as she peered at the whiskers on Mookie's face and muzzle.

"Her whiskers look funny."

"She probably thinks we look funny, too. Do you see how nice her coat is? In summer it will be shinier and smoother, but right now it's woollier to keep her warm."

"Oh." Christie stroked the side of Mookie's head. "She's soft. Nice horsy."

Wyatt shifted and caught Katrina's gaze; they both knew it was an important turning point for Christie.

"Yes, she is. And in a month or two, she's going to have a baby. Would you like to see it born?"

Christie nodded eagerly. "If it's before school is done, I'll get to tell everyone. Can I name the baby?"

"I'll find out. Mookie doesn't belong to us, she belongs to the ranch."

A SMALL WHINE came from Scooter and Wyatt put his daughter down so she could pet and reassure him.

He wasn't sorry to see her in the new jeans they'd purchased in town, but it gave him pause as he envisioned the years passing and Christie becoming a young woman.

He appreciated the way Katrina had immediately gotten his conflicted emotions while shopping. She had a blend of sensitivity and practicality that continued to amaze him. Yet she was also whimsical, imaginative and utterly beautiful.

"See, Scooter?" Christie hugged her puppy. "Horses are nice. We just have to be careful not to get under their feet cuz they're super *heavy*."

Katrina untied the dog's leash. "Come on, Christie, we'd better go back to the house so your daddy can go on with his work."

"Okay."

As they all emerged from the barn, a group of the ranch's dogs ran up, curiously sniffing the Great Dane puppy, who instantly cowered.

"Stop that." Christie shook her finger at the exuberant Aussie collies. "Stay away. Scooter doesn't know you yet. Sit down."

Wyatt's jaw dropped as the dogs obediently sat at her stern tone, eagerly whipping their tails back and forth along the ground. This was his daughter? Who had been terrified of newborn puppies and their mother?

He shared another look with Katrina. It was

amazing the way she was pulling him out of himself. Because of her, he was thinking more about the possibilities of the future, than looking backward. He just didn't know how ready he was to embrace those possibilities. Or if Katrina would be interested in sharing them with him.

In the crew's horse barn, Billie ran the curry comb over Lilly Jane, humming to herself.

The palomino gleamed in the sunshine flowing through the barn door. Palominos weren't rare, but Lilly Jane was a particularly beautiful shade of pale gold. She'd been magnificent in the arena, racing around barrels with breathtaking speed, light flashing off her coat. Yet she'd made it look easy, as if she was flying instead of running with all her might. Billie still remembered the excitement in the announcer's voice as they raced.

There goes Billie Bertram on her Lilly Jane. They're in fine form today, folks…

"Are you enjoying having Lilly Jane here?" Evan asked, pulling Billie from her memories.

"More than you can imagine. She's my best friend."

"What about me?" Evan asked.

Billie gave him a hug and grinned. "She's

my best horse friend. I'm not completely sure about you. I didn't make any promises about how *many* steps we were going to take beyond friendship."

It was one thing to have a pal with Evan's history, another to engage in more than light flirtation. Still, day by day she was coming to terms with what it meant to love someone.

Evan was proof that people could turn their lives around, even when they'd hit rock bottom and stayed there for years. He seemed reliable now and was a respected artist with his wood carvings. He'd be happier if his youngest son would talk and they could clear the air, but at least he understood that reconciling was something Wyatt had to choose. Aside from that, Evan seemed truly at peace and happy on the Soaring Hawk.

"I realize I haven't always been a solid citizen," he said seriously, perhaps reading the emotions on her face. "All I can do is try. Each and every day."

"Lilly Jane approves of you."

"I'm flattered. She's both smart and a real beauty."

"You should have seen us competing. She made it look easy, even if it was the result of hard work and hours of practice."

"Will she object if I help?" he asked, picking up the soft terry cloth Billie used to clean Lilly Jane's face.

"I don't know. She's always appreciated attention, but we haven't competed for several months and life has been quieter for her since then. You can give it a try."

EVAN SPOKE SOFTLY to Lilly Jane as he approached her head. She sniffed him, then neighed quietly. He stroked her face and ears, wanting her to accept his touch without a foreign object between them first.

Lilly Jane continued to check his scent, showing particular attention to the left side of his coat. "What is it, girl?"

"Might be that carrot I dropped into your pocket," Billie said as she brushed the mare's tail. "She loves carrots."

Evan chuckled and took out the carrot. The mare eagerly munched it down, then nudged his shoulder.

"Sorry, girl, I don't have any more."

He dampened the cloth in a bucket of clean water and carefully cleaned Lilly Jane's ears and face. Come summertime she'd probably appreciate getting wetter to cool herself off, but for now, he used just enough to do the job.

She would have a good life here on the Soaring Hawk, no matter what the season. The barn was heated in the winter, and in the summer the paddock had a pond in one corner shaded by black cottonwoods and quaking aspens. When they weren't working, the horses gathered on hot afternoons to drowse in the shade, tails swishing to chase away insects.

There were times he envied their easy contentment.

He cast a glance at Billie, thinking about the mix of challenge and contentment he felt whenever she was around. But like the situation with Wyatt, he mustn't push. Billie knew he cared about her and would have to make up her mind about how she felt.

Evan grinned as he recalled the smack on the lips she'd given him in the truck, followed by a longer kiss that had convinced him their chemistry was the real thing. They'd shared other kisses since then. Some sweet, some passionate. His own mind was made up and he thought she felt the same, even if she hadn't admitted it to herself or wasn't ready to commit to a man who had made so many mistakes over the years.

The cocksure teenager who'd courted Saul Hawkins's daughter was long gone, but Evan was okay with the person he'd finally become. And though he had regrets, he would simply have to live with them. Talking to Saul was helpful. The old guy had nearly as many regrets as Evan himself, but had found solace in trying to make his grandsons' lives as happy as possible.

Saul had gotten the boys home—that was the biggest thing. And because they'd come home, Jordan and Dakota were happily married. As for Wyatt? He seemed to be more cheerful under Katrina's lively influence, which was great.

Katrina was like a mountain spring, joyfully bubbling out in an unlikely place. How could his son resist?

"Hey, what are you thinking about?" Billie asked, breaking into his thoughts.

"Wyatt and Katrina. She's a wonderful young woman."

"Please tell me you aren't going to interfere."

"Absolutely not," Evan said promptly. "I know better than to stick my oar in where it isn't needed."

EARLY ON, Billie had recognized Evan would love to have Katrina Tapson as a daughter-in-law. Anything was possible, but she didn't want to see him disappointed.

It was a shock to realize how much she already cared for the rugged ranch hand. She just wasn't sure if they should be more than casual sweethearts. Maybe settling down in one place wasn't such a great idea. While she'd occasionally fancied herself in love, she had never expected temporary romances on the road to last, not with her footloose and fancy-free life.

Staying meant making decisions and everything felt different on the Soaring Hawk. This was a place where permanence held a special meaning. Maybe it was the solidity and consistency of the ranch—owned by the same family for generations, hanging on through good times and bad.

"Is something bothering you?" Evan asked.

"The differences between us," she said honestly. "Ranching represents roots and constancy. My life has been all about making it to the next rodeo venue and figuring out how to pay for the gas and other travel costs."

"Actually, I was a drifter for a long time," Evan admitted. "Without a purpose. I even stopped paying taxes on my own ranch, though it turns out I kept them up long enough that my boys were able to get it for themselves. But you *had* a purpose. Seeing friends at the next rodeo and practicing and competing in your different events. It required discipline and hard work."

"Some people say rodeo chasers are going after a pot of gold at the end of a rainbow we'll never reach."

"Josh McKeon proved it was possible."

Billie nodded. "But Josh's wife saw the other side. Her father was almost obsessed with performing at rodeos. Harry was moderately successful in the beginning, then he earned less and less and got injured more and more. He dreamed of being a champion. Instead he came close to bankrupting two ranches."

"Didn't you want to be a champion?"

"It would have been nice, but I can't say it was a particular dream." Billie ran a soft cloth over Lilly Jane's coat. "I usually earned a fair share of prize money, so I was okay for the most part, though I have to say getting a regular paycheck on the Soaring Hawk has been great. And I'm sleeping more. The beds in the bunkhouse are more comfortable than the one in my camper."

"Yeah. With room and board, the pay isn't

that bad. Enough to put some aside if your tastes are simple. I've thought about getting a small trailer to live in, rather than staying in the bunkhouse. Saul says he'd let me put one here on the ranch. It wouldn't be large, but private."

"Privacy can be nice."

"That's what I think."

Billie gathered up the grooming tools and stored them in the locker she'd been assigned. She had the feeling that Evan was trying to find out something from her, but she didn't have enough experience in this kind of relationship to be sure—if she even knew what kind of relationship it might be.

They'd progressed to hand-holding and kisses, but it could stay that way forever.

Then she looked over at Evan and saw him talking to Lilly Jane. He didn't resent her love for the mare, instead he'd helped bring Lilly Jane to the Soaring Hawk to live.

He was a good, decent, caring man.

With Evan she could have something deeper and more meaningful than a kiss-and-run romance on the road.

There would always be hurdles to overcome. But nobody could ever predict what would happen. You just did the best you could and went from there.

CHAPTER TWELVE

"ISN'T IT BEAUTIFUL?" Katrina exclaimed, gesturing to the landscape around them with one hand, the other hand holding Banana Split's reins.

"Whatever you say."

"Come on, Wyatt. Look at the mountains and the patterns of the quaking aspen and cottonwood branches against the sky. Everything is a different color this time of year, with different textures and scents. Every season is wonderful in Montana. Well, they are everywhere, but Montana is extra special."

Wyatt grinned. With Christie in preschool, he'd suggested they go riding for a couple of hours to check the winter fences and herd. There was little green in sight except for pines on a knoll and even though it was well into April now, the evergreens were still hunkered down in dark silence, waiting for spring.

To him it seemed dull and lifeless, but Katrina saw potential in everything. Just the evening before he'd seen a pencil sketch she'd done of his grandfather's hands, tying a knot in a rope. Though Saul's fingers were scarred and his knuckles gnarled with arthritis, she'd created a remarkable image that conveyed endurance and tradition. That sketch, and the painting she'd done for Christie's room, were all he needed to understand how gifted she was as an artist.

"Each to their own. The sunrise painting you did with the little girl is terrific. I noticed you added a very large puppy."

Katrina laughed. "Christie wanted Scooter in the picture, too. She knew it was supposed to be her on the hill."

Wyatt focused ahead, trying not to watch the changing expressions on Katrina's face. She compelled him, completely and utterly. His pangs of guilt at his growing feelings for her were lessening, but he didn't know how to resolve the emotion altogether.

Could guilt be what had kept Saul and his father alone for so long? Surely loving someone new didn't take away from the love you felt for someone you've lost. Or was it more a case of finally meeting the right person, like when Saul had met Anna Beth? And in his father's case, he thought Evan was getting serious about Billie Bertram, or at least his brothers felt it was possible. They were okay with the idea and so was Wyatt.

"It's good Carmen was able to come back to work," Katrina said, bringing Wyatt's thoughts back to the moment. "Especially since it means her mother is better."

"I told Carmen to take all the time she needed, but her father is there and I think her mom didn't like her hovering. Carmen also told me she wanted to resume a routine." He shook his head. "Some routine. So far Rod is the only one with the flu, but it's like waiting for a rocket to go off."

"All the ranchers around here are facing the same thing," Katrina said. "This can't be the first time a bad flu is circulating."

"No. Just the first time when I'm the one in charge. I'd hoped with April arriving it meant we'd dodged the bullet. Apparently not."

"Hey, don't borrow trouble. Rod could be the only one who gets sick. But whatever happens, I'll do what I can to help. And you know Tim will, too."

"That isn't what you signed on for, but if it's needed, I'll accept," he said before she could suggest he'd be doing *her* a favor. Katrina might be reveling in her first real taste of ranch life, but she was an artist, first and foremost.

Still, she had good instincts for horses and calving, which had convinced him it was possible to be both an accomplished artist and a dedicated rancher.

A wry sensation settled over him. After his adamant protestations to Katrina about never getting married again, he was looking for reasons she might want to stay. *Permanently.* He thought she liked him in return, but she liked everyone. And she had her own letdowns in romance to make her wary. He'd also done a good job of warning her away every chance he'd found.

Yet the memory of her comment in town had kept reverberating in his head.

Make up your mind about what you want from me, Wyatt.

It could mean nothing.

Or everything,

As they returned to the main ranch, Wyatt frowned at the small spikes of new growth he spotted in the sunniest part of the pasture. If he could be certain that spring had arrived, he'd be pleased. But if they got another blast of winter chill—as predicted by the weather services—the new shoots of grass would die and might take longer to come back later.

"Billie seems pleased to have her rodeo horse here," Katrina said as they passed the crew's horse paddock and saw Lilly Jane trotting around the perimeter. "It was nice of you to agree."

Wyatt wasn't surprised that Katrina knew about Billie's horse. Somehow she seemed aware of everything going on at the Soaring Hawk. Part of it was her curiosity about ranching, but part had to be the way she cared about people and made connections with them.

That, along with other things she'd said, was making him think about how he managed the crew. Yes, he'd wanted to earn their trust and respect. He also didn't want to be an authoritarian like his grandfather and had a different management style than his brothers. He needed to be in charge, but that didn't mean he couldn't trust people who'd never given him a reason to distrust them. And that included not looking over their shoulders constantly.

"I wasn't being nice to Billie, I was being practical," he said. "She does ranch work when she isn't cooking, so having her own horse here makes sense."

KATRINA DUCKED HER head to hide her amusement. Like her nephew, Wyatt didn't take compliments well. Maybe it was the "nice" thing for him. Her brother had told her guys disliked being called nice because "nice" men usually weren't seen as sexy.

She didn't understand why they thought the two qualities were mutually exclusive. Kindness and being nice were exceptionally appealing to her.

When she was in art school she'd once gone for coffee with a man, simply because he had stopped traffic to help her rescue a cat. He'd gotten scratched, she'd ended up adopting the cat, and they'd had a lovely hour drinking lattes and trading cat stories before he had to continue on his business trip. If he'd lived in Portland instead of Albuquerque, they might have had something.

"Why are you looking sad all of a sudden?" Wyatt asked.

"Just thinking about the cat I adopted in art school. He was around eight at the time, with a personality to match his size. He was huge, part Maine coon, with gorgeous, long tiger-striped fur. Slept on his back with his paws in the air, twitching and making various noises. He must have been having fabulous dreams about chasing mice and other fun stuff. Awake he liked to hang out on bookshelves, patting my head as I walked by or jumping onto my shoulder. When anyone came to visit, he insisted they make a fuss of him. No fear, totally bold."

"He sounds like a character. What happened to him?"

"Old age. There are worse ways to go than passing peacefully in your sleep at the human equivalent of a hundred years old, but it's never easy to say goodbye." She sighed. "That's another time I should have known Gordon was wrong for me. He acted as if it was no big deal when I lost Daredevil. But then, the two of them never liked each other very much, which should have been a clue, too."

Wyatt cocked his head. "Daredevil?"

"Another motorist and I rescued him from a freeway median. He wasn't injured, so he may have jumped from someone's car during a traffic jam. No one came forward to claim him and he didn't have a microchip, so he stayed with me. Daredevil was my best buddy for years, though when I moved to Seattle, I had to talk the landlord into allowing him at my apartment."

"I had trouble finding pet-friendly apartments after adopting Blinx and Salem—I could have used your powers of persuasion. Instead, I ended up paying gigantic pet deposits. But Salem and Blinx were worth it. They're great cats and they've given Christie continuity when we've moved."

"I don't know that I'm persuasive. I just talked to the landlord and he agreed after I explained everything."

"You have a way of talking to people that makes it hard to say no. Like with me and Scooter."

Katrina waved her hand. "You wouldn't have refused to keep Scooter after seeing him and Christie interact together."

"True. I've seen you taking them around the ranch. I appreciate what you've done for her. She's a different child lately."

For some reason Katrina's mood nosedived, probably because Wyatt had thanked her the way he'd thank any other employee for doing a good job—a reminder that she *was* an employee and unlikely to become more. For that matter, though he'd asked if he could call her Kat instead of Katrina, he hadn't done that, either. And after kissing her, he'd immediately apologized, saying he didn't want to make her uncomfortable. Then the next day he'd brought it up again.

Even if he felt more than friendship, it was a huge emotional leap to go from his flat statement that nobody could take Amy's place, to truly loving someone else.

Katrina tried to dismiss the hollow feeling in her midriff. She hadn't thought falling for Wyatt was a possibility. After all, she'd understood his position from the beginning and it hadn't been *that* long since the end of her engagement. Maybe it would be easier if he'd turned out to be difficult and unreasonable, but while he sometimes overreacted when it came to Christie, he usually listened afterward and they could come to an agreement.

Plainly, he felt things far more deeply than he liked to think. In fact, Katrina thought there was a volcano of emotion inside of him, just waiting for the right moment to come out.

"CAN YOU SPARE a minute?" Saul called to Wyatt after Katrina had returned to the homestead cabin.

Saul was navigating well these days, no longer needing a cane. The first time Wyatt had seen him after Jordan and Paige were married, he'd been shocked at how old and infirm his grandfather appeared. Saul's hip replacement had improved his mobility, but the best medicine had been Anna Beth and the rest of the family. He seemed to get younger every day and frequently declared he expected to see his great-grandchildren graduate from high school or even college.

"Sure, Grandpa, what's up?"

"There's a stallion for sale down south of Jim Bonner's old spread. I wondered if you'd like to go with me to check him out."

Wyatt was torn. It was a good opportunity to spend time with his grandfather, but how could he leave? Despite his resolution to stop being such a hands-on manager, it was hard to put that into action.

"I'd love to, but I've got a lot of work to do."

"You need a break and we wouldn't be gone more than two or three hours. I'd like your opinion and your brothers are fine with what we decide. They mentioned hoping to find another stallion to add to our breeding program. Anyhow, you're doing an excellent job. Liam Flannigan agrees with me—you've got everything in hand."

Liam Flannigan of Harmony Ranch was the third-party rancher who was supposed to decide how well Wyatt was doing under the agreement he'd signed with Saul. But Wyatt had the feeling that "approval" was more a formality than anything—Saul didn't have any reason to want his youngest grandson to fail, any more than he'd had a reason to want Jordan or Dakota to fail. His goal was to have family continue owning and running the Soaring Hawk long after he was gone.

Besides, Wyatt reminded himself that Jordan and Dakota had hired good people. Even their father had never shown himself to be unreliable. Evan did what he was asked and more.

Wyatt drew a deep breath. "All right."

"Excellent. Let's bring a trailer in case we decide to make the purchase. The stallion has good bloodlines and Macon is very reputable."

Saul looked so pleased, Wyatt was glad he'd agreed to go along. He hooked up a horse trailer to one of the ranch's trucks, then texted his brothers that he was going to see the horse Saul was interested in buying, sending a separate text to Katrina.

Something had happened while they were out riding fences that bothered her, he just didn't know what. He didn't think her sudden change in mood was solely due to thinking about her cat—she seemed to recall Daredevil with love and regret that he was gone, but understood that he'd led a long, full life. Maybe it was remembering her ex-fiancé's lack of sympathy about her feelings.

C U later, Katrina texted back.

It was illogical, but he wished she'd said more—something like "Have a good trip," or that she'd teased him about taking time away from the Soaring Hawk.

The ranch was across the Shelton County line. Once there, Saul shook hands with the owner and they spent several minutes in idle chitchat.

Wyatt began to get frustrated, then realized there was nothing idle about the discussion. They were evaluating each other and establishing a base of communication. It was an opportunity to learn the art of purchasing livestock from an expert and Wyatt knew he'd be a fool not to pay attention.

At length the rancher led them to the paddock where the stallion waited. Saul watched the animal move around for several minutes with a light, quick step, then went through the gate and approached him.

"Why are you selling?" Wyatt asked the

rancher when they were alone. It was the one question Saul hadn't asked.

Emotion twisted Macon's face. "Heart attack. I should make a full recovery, but the doctors want me to cut down my workload for a while since it's just me and my son running the place. But I won't sell to just anyone. Has to be to a horseman I can trust, like Saul Hawkins. Go on, check Moon River out," Macon said gruffly. "He won't disappoint you."

Wyatt crossed to where his grandfather was examining the stallion. "Did you know Macon is selling because of health issues?" he asked in a low tone.

"I heard. A darn shame, but it can't be helped. At least Macon isn't letting his spread get run-down the way I did before you boys returned."

Wyatt conducted his own exam of the stallion and was impressed. "Moon River is a great horse. He'd be an excellent addition to the Soaring Hawk and a good match for several of our mares." Yet Wyatt hesitated. "What if we offered to lease him for a season as a breeding stallion, with an option to buy? That way Macon could take him back if his health improves."

The pleased approval in Saul's face was all Wyatt needed to know. They sat down in Macon's dining room and negotiated a deal that was fair to both parties.

Soon a check was in Macon's pocket and they had Moon River in the trailer, driving back to the Soaring Hawk. As much as Wyatt would have liked to own the stallion, this seemed the preferable route.

"I hadn't thought of a lease," Saul said. "But that's better for Macon. Letting go of a horse you love is hard. Macon seemed happier when we left, knowing he hadn't given Moon River up for good."

"Do you know Macon well?"

"Mostly by reputation and through business deals. I missed out on friendship by being such a stubborn old codger. So don't turn into me."

"I wouldn't mind having at least half of your horse and cattle savvy."

A bark of laughter came from his grandfather. "You already have a good deal more than half. You know how to listen to your gut, even better than your brothers. That's important. But I'm not talkin' about being a rancher, I'm talkin' about what's going on in here."

Saul tapped his chest over his heart. "You still haven't made peace with your daddy."

"That's my business." Wyatt kept his tone mild, unwilling to cut him off the way he had with his brothers whenever they tried to push about their father.

It had nothing to do with the deal he'd made with Saul and earning part of the ranch, it just didn't seem right with someone of his advanced years. Besides, Wyatt had become quite fond of his grandfather.

"Maybe so, but you were always the kindest of you three boys. I'd hate to see you forget that with Evan. Besides, there's been too much trouble in this family. I blame myself, but there's no need to repeat my mistakes."

"You weren't the one buying liquor and getting drunk in front of your kids. You had nothing to do with that."

A sad expression filled Saul's face. "I still wish I'd handled things a better way."

"We can ask 'what if' forever," Wyatt said. "Look, I'll think about what you said. But no promises."

"All right, but you also have something else to think about. Katrina is quite a woman."

"So you approve?" Wyatt glanced at his grandfather and saw him shrug.

"My approval isn't important. But even if it was, I happen to think she's special. In fact, I've been wondering if you'd like the Hawkins engagement ring. I had it cleaned and the settings checked, just in case. It's been in the family for generations."

Wyatt wasn't sure how to respond. He was still sorting out his feelings for Katrina and having an engagement ring available wasn't going to make that any easier. "I appreciate it, but something like that should go to Jordan. He's the eldest. Besides, I don't know that I'm ever getting married again."

"I've already talked to Jordan and Dakota. They both want you to have the ring."

Saul seemed pleased and eager to be passing the family heirloom to a new generation and Wyatt couldn't say no.

"Then, great. Thank you."

Wyatt wondered if Saul would push harder about Katrina, but his grandfather seemed to be content with what he'd said so far.

Maybe he'd learned that saying too much was as big a problem as not saying anything at all.

BILLIE HUMMED AS she put spoonfuls of oatmeal chocolate-chip cookie dough on baking pans. They were everyone's favorite and she wanted to have plenty on hand in case she also got sick.

Drawn by the scent of baking, the cowhands working close by drifted in and out, getting coffee and handfuls of the warm cookies.

"Those smell good," Anna Beth said as she stepped into the kitchen for her own sample. Their relationship had gradually improved to the point that Billie now felt they were more of a team than adversaries. "How many batches are you making?"

"Six. The crew eats them so fast I'm not sure they taste anything on the way down."

Anna Beth chuckled and got a cup of coffee. "Looks like we'll need to be flexible on the days we cook," she said casually. "You'll be needed for other ranch work if more of the crew comes down with this flu bug."

"I understand. The livestock comes first." Billie pulled a batch of cookies from the oven and popped in another. "We're still in calving season and the mares will start foaling before too long."

"Right, and in the middle of all this, my husband has gone off with Wyatt, hoping to buy another horse," Anna Beth said in a tart tone. "You'd think there were enough horses on the Soaring Hawk already."

"For us horse lovers, there are never enough."

"So it would seem."

"Has living on a ranch been a huge adjustment?" Billie asked curiously. For her, she'd been around cows and horses at rodeos, so the sights and scents of the ranch were familiar. It would have been a different story for Anna Beth as a retired marine.

"Not too bad. In the Marine Corps I never knew what I'd be assigned to next. Here, everything is driven by the seasons and what the children and the rest of the family need. That's fine with me. I want to be useful, but aside from feeding the cowhands, I haven't gotten that handy on the ranch. I can clean a stable and run a hay mower, but that's as far as it goes right now."

Billie gulped some coffee. No wonder Anna Beth had objected to losing part of her role in cooking for the ranch hands. "Keeping stomachs fed is important."

"That's how I see it." Anna Beth leaned forward. "Which is why I'd be happier if we could do a more equal split on the cooking, with me taking at least one additional day."

Billie measured her expression. "I'm willing if Wyatt is willing. I love working with cattle and horses. But it pleased him to give you extra time with your husband and grandkids. And you've got two more great-grandbabies coming. Won't Noelle and Paige welcome any help you can give them?"

"Paige and Noelle have their mother across the way at the Blue Banner ranch."

"That isn't the same as a great-grandmother living right here. You're obviously very involved with the kids."

Anna Beth's face turned thoughtful. "We'll see what happens. I don't want Wyatt to think I'm unappreciative of what he's trying to do, but in his case, he has Katrina to take care of Christie. He doesn't need me to help with her."

"Katrina is a whole other story."

"Right. If he has any sense, he'll get off his duff and marry her before she finds someone else."

Billie sighed. Everyone wanted to see Katrina and Wyatt together, but no one knew what *they* wanted. "Any which way, I don't think Wyatt's goal was to turn you into a babysitter," she said, getting up to take the next batch of cookies from the oven. "He just wants you to have time for other things."

The door from the men's side of the bunkhouse opened and Evan came into the dining hall, freshly showered from the look of his neatly combed wet hair. He glanced at Anna Beth and back at Billie and seemed to relax since they clearly weren't at odds.

"Are the two of you plotting to take over the world?" he asked, going to the kitchen to grab a warm cookie from a baking tray and gulp a glass of milk from the fridge.

"What makes you think we haven't taken over already?" Billie asked, getting a thumbs-up from Anna Beth.

He laughed. "That's fine with me. I'm on my way to the horse barn. See you later."

"He's a fine-looking man," Anna Beth said when the door closed behind him.

"Hands off, you already have a husband."

The other woman chuckled. "Don't worry. Saul is more than enough for me."

AS EVAN WALKED to the horse paddock, cold air swirled around him. The sun was dropping and so was the temperature.

He would have enjoyed a chat with Billie alone, but they'd see each other later after everyone had gone to bed. Their late-night discussions had become important to him; he just wished they could be cuddled together in bed, pouring out their hearts, instead of talking over the crew dining hall counter and a cup of joe.

Time would tell if that would ever happen.

Evan brought the horses in two by two from the paddock since it was still too cold and windy to leave them outside for the evening. Coyotes had also been drifting down from the higher hills at night, harassing the herds and making the horses uneasy.

As he stabled the last two, a truck drove up near the barn door and he went out to see Saul and Wyatt.

"We leased a stallion for stud," Saul told him. "Moon River should be able to sire several foals."

Horse leases weren't as common in Shelton County as some places, but there were advantages to the arrangement. And the horse Wyatt led out of the trailer was a real beauty—coal black except for white stockings and a white blaze on the face.

"I need an empty stall between a couple of the geldings," Wyatt called. "He's a little jumpy."

"Just give me a minute."

Evan swiftly moved one of the stallions to

another stall, leaving a space between two of the mellowest geldings on the ranch. They made friends easily, which would be important for the new addition. It was hard for a horse to leave a familiar place and be put somewhere new. They were social animals and missed their friends.

Wyatt led Moon River into the stall, speaking gently to him. The stallion sidestepped and let out a short scream. It was his way of discovering if anyone he knew was there.

"Easy, boy. I know it's difficult."

Wyatt closed the stall and rested his arms on the gate, watching the restless horse.

"He's something," Evan said.

"Yeah."

They both stood there quietly until a long sigh came from Wyatt. "You're getting fond of Billie, aren't you?"

"ER, UH, YES. She's a fine woman."

Oddly, the discomfort in Evan's face made Wyatt feel closer to him. Because if there was one thing he was certain of, it was that his father had loved his mother.

"Do you feel guilty about caring for someone else?"

Evan's face was sad. "I feel guilty for not

taking care of you and your brothers after your mom was gone. I know she'd be disappointed in me, but she never would have wanted me to be alone. The truth is, she was the strong one. She would have kept the Circle M going and raised you boys if it had been me who was gone. No one could have stopped her, the way no one is stopping you from raising Christie and being a good father."

"But falling in love again when you've already lost so much?" Wyatt shrugged. "It's like asking for another broken heart."

"Anything worth having hurts to lose, but that doesn't mean it isn't worth every minute. Would you have refused to marry Amy if you'd known how it was going to end?"

Wyatt knew the answer. He would have chosen to be with his wife, even if they were only going to have a day together.

"You also can't assume the worst will happen," Evan continued. "I respect Anna Beth for the choice she made to marry Saul, though he was in poor health at the time and years older. And look what they have now. Noelle says Saul may be around another fifteen years or longer—as he's fond of reminding everyone."

"Amy was the love of my life."

"Yes, but you became a different person after she died. With a new life. That's what grief does. It rips our hearts apart and changes us forever. I'll always grieve for your mother and I don't love her any less, but I love Billie just as much. Surprised me, I can tell you that. Finding someone was the last thing on my mind when I came back to Shelton. Does it bother you?"

"Not especially, I just wondered how you got there."

There was another long silence as they both watched Moon River moving restlessly around his stall. His life had been upended and Wyatt felt a kinship with the unhappy horse. Moon River would make friends with other animals and people at the Soaring Hawk but he'd been taken away from his home and the human who had raised and trained him. Basically, he was grieving that loss.

"Your mother was everything to me, too," Evan said, almost as if talking to himself. "She never paid attention when we were in school, probably because I did such dumb stuff around the county. Then the day after graduation, we came face-to-face in town. It was like being hit by a bolt of lightning. Saul disapproved. I tried for a while to change his mind, but I was headstrong and got tired of trying to convince him that I could be a good husband, so we ran off and got married."

"And it took more than thirty-five years for him to forgive you and Mom."

"Actually, I suspect Saul forgave us pretty quick, but was too stubborn to admit it. That can happen when you take a position so fiercely—it's hard to back down, even if you turn out to be wrong."

"Pride."

Evan shrugged. "Pride. Stubbornness. Clinging to the past. I think as long as Saul thought he was angry, he still felt connected to his daughter, however illogical that might sound. Or maybe by staying angry, he didn't have to deal with losing her. Moving on can seem like a betrayal. But it isn't. Someone who loves you wants the best for your life. Why should that change when they're gone?"

Wyatt thought about the flashes of guilt he'd been feeling. He was changing the decisions he and Amy had made about raising Christie, realizing he couldn't do everything the way they'd talked about. He'd tried not to feel guilty for being attracted to Katrina, but he had. After all, Amy was gone, how could he even *look* at another woman?

Yet he'd known all along that Amy would have approved. When it became clear she probably wasn't going to pull through, she'd urged him to find someone else to love and be a mother to Christie. He just hadn't been willing to consider taking that chance again. And, as different as Amy and Katrina were, he knew they would have liked each other.

Evan tapped his hands on the stall gate and stepped back. "Do you want me to stay with Moon River this evening? I can do work around the barn and make sure he doesn't feel alone, while giving him a chance to start making friends with his neighbors."

"That would be great, but be sure to get dinner. We brought a load of Moon River's feed so we can transition him to what we use. It's in the horse trailer."

"I'll take care of it."

Wyatt nodded and walked out of the barn.

He'd had his first real conversation with his father and it hadn't turned out to be that difficult. As a matter of fact, Evan had given him a good deal to think about.

Particularly when it came to Katrina.

CHAPTER THIRTEEN

AFTER PUTTING CHRISTIE to bed, Katrina sat on the couch, sketching a picture of Wyatt wearing a cowboy hat and a heavy leather and shearling jacket.

It was pure indulgence.

Wyatt was a cross between a modern man and a traditional cowboy. Mixed with the modern man was a proper navy officer. The three were a compelling blend, one that was practically irresistible.

"You got it bad," she muttered.

Wyatt was his own man and a few kisses might mean nothing. She certainly didn't resent his deceased wife—without Amy there would be no Christie—but it was a shame that he was so committed to the past.

You knew that when you moved here, said her conscience.

Yeah, she'd known it.

But her heart had tumbled for him anyway. That was the trouble with hearts. They didn't use good sense and had a habit of getting their owners into trouble. She'd fallen for Wyatt, despite believing what he'd said about never getting married again. Her eyes had been wide open, unlike when she'd been dating Gordon.

Katrina dropped her head back on the couch cushion. She would just have to deal with her feelings the best she could. She'd continued working with Gordon, even after he'd lied to her and she had broken their engagement. Wyatt hadn't lied. He'd been up front and honest about his views, even apologizing after kissing her.

But hope was stubborn. And she kept hoping that the warmth in Wyatt's eyes and their growing closeness was more than friendship.

A light knock sounded on the front door and she got up to answer before the visitor could wake Christie or disturb Timothy while he was doing his homework. It was Paige Maxwell.

"Hey, Paige. Come in. What's up?"

"My brother-in-law has the flu," Paige announced as she dropped onto the couch.

Katrina's eyes widened. "Wyatt is sick? He isn't here. Don't tell me he had to be taken to the hospital."

"No, sorry, it's Dakota. The flu hit him like a freight train and Noelle has ordered him to stay in bed. He's grumbling, but from what she says, she isn't sure he could get farther than the bathroom, regardless. He got sick that fast."

"I thought Navy SEALs were indestructible. Including former Navy SEALs."

"Or so they'd like you to believe. I wanted you to know because someone else on the Soaring Hawk crew has come down with it. There's no telling who's next. We're going to have a rough few days ahead."

"I'll do whatever I can to help."

"Thanks. Part of Dakota's problem is that he's worried because Noelle is pregnant. He doesn't want my sister coming near him, which she's ignoring, of course."

Katrina didn't need to call attention to the obvious—Paige was pregnant as well.

"Jordan fusses, too, but luckily, Bannerman women rarely get sick," Paige added as if in response to Katrina's thought.

"I don't, either."

"That's good to hear. Anyway, I just wanted to update you on the status. You may not see much of Wyatt for a while unless *he* gets sick.

And even then he'll probably try to work through it, no matter what."

"Wyatt thinks he has to keep tabs on everything going on. Totally stubborn."

Paige made a face. "Obstinacy is a Maxwell brother trait, likely inherited through their Hawkins genes." She got up, her agility still unaffected by pregnancy. "I know you were going to do the afternoon tea next week, but all things considered, maybe you should put it off until the end of April. Hopefully by then everything will have settled down."

"That sounds best. I'll send a text to Noelle and your mom, changing the date."

Paige picked up the large sketch pad from the couch and looked at the pencil drawing of Wyatt. "This is amazing."

"There are a wealth of amazing things to draw around here." Katrina went over and flipped the heavy pages. "Here's one of Jordan with Mishka and Daniel."

Paige's eyes softened. "How beautiful. None of the pictures I've taken capture what you've drawn."

"Just a sec." Katrina went to her studio and got a large plastic sleeve, then came back and gently detached the sketch from the pad and slipped it into the sleeve. "I'll matte it for you later, but you can take it home in the meantime."

"Thank you, it's perfect."

Katrina leaned against the door after it closed and sighed, wishing she'd covered the drawing of Wyatt before answering Paige's knock. She knew everyone saw her as a potential wife for him and they didn't need more fuel for their speculation. It would just make things harder.

She determinedly threw off her moodiness and took her sketchbook and supplies back to her studio. But before she could begin working, a small whine came from behind her and she turned to see Scooter. He came to her when he needed to be let into the yard, so she took him to the side door. Scooter stuck his head out and peered around cautiously before going outside; he was still wary of the unfamiliar ranch.

A couple of minutes later he came racing back and Katrina realized a coyote was calling, the long, haunting howl lingering on the breeze. She crouched and scratched behind his silky ears. Scooter wriggled with delight. "That coyote is a long way away, my friend."

He licked the tip of her nose and she laughed.

"Let's make a deal. You continue helping Christie be less afraid, and I won't tell Wyatt you've destroyed three of his socks."

"Too late," said a voice near her. "I already know."

Katrina stood and saw Wyatt had come in. He was grinning.

"I guess we need more chew toys for him. Ones disguised as your socks."

WYATT HAD BEEN utterly enchanted at the sight of Katrina trying to make a deal with a Great Dane puppy, who probably was going to destroy a whole lot more than socks before he was grown.

Feeling reckless, Wyatt walked over and kissed her. Her lips were soft and she tasted like coconut—her lip balm, he supposed. When he drew back, she was staring at him, her eyes wide.

"Uh, what was that for?"

"I—" He stared back at her like a deer caught in headlights. "You're just really incredible. ."

It wasn't like him, but he'd been thinking about what his father had said—about becoming a different person when you've lost someone you loved. He *felt* different with Katrina.

She made him laugh and see the humor and beauty around him. Only Katrina could have looked at his grandfather's hands and seen the timeless strength in them. She radiated life and determination and was wholly connected to Montana, despite her years in the city.

What he felt with her was surely worth the risk of what could happen in the future.

"You're acting strange," Katrina said. "Maybe I should take your temperature and make sure you aren't coming down with the flu. I hear it hit Dakota really hard."

"It did but I'm fine," he said, still staring at the woman he was beginning to fall in love with.

Or had fallen in love with, which was the truth if he was completely honest.

"Okay, but whatever you need me to do, I'm happy to help. Tim will, too, within limits. I mean, he'd skip school and work on the ranch twenty hours a day if I let him, but I can't. He's twelve, not twenty," she said. She seemed to be rambling a little, avoiding the enormity of what had just happened—inside him, at least. Not that she knew what he was feeling, unless she felt it herself.

The possibility encouraged him.

"I know. We're okay for now. The calving

season has been fairly easy on us this year, though there's no telling what will happen."

"I understand." She nodded. "*Oh,*" she said suddenly, digging into her pocket for something. "Take a look at what I found on the floor today in the kitchen. Apparently it simply fell out of the fireplace."

She handed him a large greenish-blue translucent stone. His eyes widened. "That's a Montana sapphire. A *big* one."

"I know. Go look at the stones on the right side of the fireplace."

Wyatt followed Katrina and realized there were a number of sapphires embedded within the rocks used to build the fireplace and chimney. Montana sapphires came in all colors and these were the variable blue-green shade of Katrina's eyes. Faceted, they would sparkle like them, too—clear and bright, with untold depths.

Untold depths?

That almost sounded poetic and he definitely wasn't the poetic type.

He cleared his throat. "These are really something. Montana sapphires are usually found in river deposits. I've never seen them embedded in rocks."

"I looked it up. They *can* be found in a

stone matrix, but it's rare. This is like having a nest egg of family heirlooms hidden in the chimney. I don't think they're found in rocks around here, unless there's a vein no one knows about. Who knows how many miles your ancestor hauled these stones to build a comfortable home for his wife?"

"My great-something-grandmother refused to leave when her son built the new place. Maybe she knew about the sapphires and didn't want to leave them unguarded."

"Nah, I'm betting she wouldn't leave because this was the home her husband had built for her. She felt closer to him here."

Something flickered in Katrina's eyes, almost a wistfulness, and then the emotion was gone.

She was difficult for Wyatt to read when her reactions were zinging all over the place. The challenge didn't bother him, the way it had with some women he'd known. Instead, he was intrigued.

As a boy, he'd learned early to guard his feelings. The biggest problems in his marriage had stemmed from his inability to share his deepest emotions. His worst mistake had been believing he had to be strong and encouraging for his wife when she got sick, only to discover she'd needed to know she wasn't alone with her fear.

He didn't want to make that mistake again.

Life was complicated—he had to accept that. Maybe it was even part of what made everything else worthwhile. The thought of losing someone he loved again still made his stomach churn, yet it was being replaced by the realization of what he'd lose if he didn't take a chance.

And really, did he have a choice? His heart had made the leap without his permission.

"I would never sell a family heirloom unless it was a last-ditch effort required to save the ranch," he said. "And even if we're short-handed for a while because of the flu, we're in no danger of losing the Soaring Hawk."

"That's good."

Wyatt stepped away from the fireplace, thinking he'd never properly looked at the massive structure, which now housed a modern woodstove instead of being a functioning fireplace. He'd seen a few pictures of his great-great-grandmother Ehawee, including one here in the kitchen. She'd been a beautiful woman, always with a gentle smile, but stubborn about not leaving her home. Maybe her stubbornness was why she'd lived to such an advanced old age.

"Are you working tonight, or sleeping?" Katrina asked.

"Sleeping. Melody can call my cell phone if I'm needed."

Katrina put a hand over her heart in mock shock and staggered backward. "You mean you're trusting her to keep an eye on everything by herself? The world may spin off its axis."

"Very amusing."

"I think so. You can't have control every minute, Wyatt. It just isn't—" She stopped abruptly.

"Go ahead. Spit it out."

She shook her head. "Never mind."

"You want me to sleep, don't you? Otherwise I'll stare at the ceiling, wondering."

Katrina eyed him. "Nothing I say or don't say is going to keep you awake. You look ready to drop on your feet."

"Then go ahead and tell me."

"Fine. Maybe you've been trying to regain a sense of control over your life by keeping a tight watch on every aspect of the Soaring Hawk. It would be natural after everything that's happened."

"It's possible," Wyatt admitted. "But I've already decided to alter my management style. Or to try. And at least one thing is certain."

Katrina cocked her head in inquiry.

"No one will ever control you," he said with a grin.

"I know. Thank you."

He grinned wider, but hesitated, wondering if he should tell her what he was feeling. Considering her obvious deflection after the kiss, he decided it wasn't the best time. "Okay, I guess I'll be heading for bed now."

"Sweet dreams," Katrina called after him as he climbed the back staircase, Scooter following.

Wyatt stopped at his daughter's doorway and noticed Fluffy Bob was on the bedside table, not even on the bed. Maybe she didn't need to have the large teddy bear as close now that she wasn't quite as fearful.

His brow creased in a frown. Could he actually be the reason she'd become so nervous and uncertain of herself?

It was what Katrina had suggested and he was finally willing to concede the possibility. Christie had been so small when her mother died, he'd almost been afraid to touch her. He'd sat up with her at night, counting her breaths, worrying constantly, unable to bear the thought of losing her as well.

Going back on duty and leaving her at a day-care center had practically killed him, but the navy only granted so much leave and he'd used every minute available.

He'd gotten baby monitors and baby cams and found day care that provided twenty-four-seven video observation. When she started walking, a bump or tumble had sent him running with her to the emergency room until they'd finally lectured him on not going overboard. They probably would have agreed with Katrina that he'd been an unintentional part of making Christie afraid.

Control *had* become important to him. But as Katrina had said, nobody ever really had control of their lives.

Wyatt pulled the large, rough sapphire from his pocket and turned it over in his hand. He would send it to a gem cutter and see what they suggested. Considering his grandfather had given him the family engagement ring, he didn't think Saul would object to him having the sapphire cut and set into something special for Katrina.

He went in and kissed Christie's cheek before heading for a shower and bed himself. Yet his last thought before falling asleep wasn't of his daughter, it was of Katrina and her beautiful eyes. He had remembered what they'd reminded him of when she first arrived—the glowing, changing color of the sea off a Caribbean beach.

Wyatt remembered a trip to St. Thomas and how he'd loved the warm crystalline water, unlike anything he'd experienced before. He hadn't wanted to leave.

And now he wanted to fall into the warmth of Katrina's eyes and stay there forever.

BILLIE PREFERRED COOKING fresh meals for the cowhands, but when she woke up on Friday morning, she was glad she'd filled her side of the freezer with food prepared ahead. Now that a particularly nasty flu had found the Soaring Hawk, she would be needed more than ever to help with the regular ranch tasks.

From what she'd heard, one minute Wyatt and Dakota had been talking in the horse barn, and the next Wyatt was practically carrying his brother home. Rod Gaffney was on antibiotics for bronchitis. Stedman had gotten sick the previous morning and Eduardo and Carmen had been pale and unusually quiet at dinner. They hadn't finished their meal and would probably be on the sick list today. She already knew Melody was ill.

It was unfortunate so much of the crew wasn't feeling well, but Billie was glad to be useful. Wyatt had told her and Anna Beth it was okay to work things out between them, so they were coordinating, making sure food was prompt at mealtimes, while hot soup was available to everyone at all hours. They were also providing comfort foods to tempt poor appetites.

"Wyatt wants to build a new bunkhouse so the cowhands have individual rooms," Anna Beth said as they talked over a cup of coffee, just before dawn.

Billie nodded. "Too bad it wasn't available this year. What does your husband think about that?"

"He wasn't thrilled when Wyatt first brought up the idea, called it molly-coddling, but now he's seeing the wisdom of having less communal living."

"Noelle must have been working on him."

Anna Beth chuckled. "Helps to have a doctor in the family. Noelle is the one who convinced Saul to do the proper exercises after his hip replacement. You know, I went from having no family and a few good friends, to being part of a large family here on the Soaring Hawk with many friends. Not bad for an ex-marine in her seventies. You could do worse."

Billie made a face. "Except Evan hasn't proposed."

"I proposed to Saul. We're modern women, we don't have to wait."

"I'll give it some consideration."

Billie got up to check the breakfast burritos staying warm in the oven. They were a meal-in-one, but she didn't know how many hands would be eating them. Melody had had toughed it out until Evan came to take over for her, but had been utterly miserable by the time she'd crawled into her bunk.

"I'll get going now," Anna Beth said. "Let me know if I'm needed to take over."

"I already know you'll be needed for lunch and dinner. Wyatt came through earlier and said a blizzard is brewing. They need to put out feed. Not too many of us are upright at the moment, so I expect to be on the haying or caking crew. I've made sandwiches to take with us, but a fresh pot of soup for the patients would be good."

"Gotcha."

When Billie was alone she thought about

what Anna Beth had said about proposing. It was an option, but Billie thought it was best to let Evan move at his own pace. She wasn't too concerned about him getting stressed and starting to drink again, but he still needed to navigate the situation with his youngest son. It was a relationship that needed to be repaired, if possible, and she didn't want to interfere.

KATRINA HAD WOKEN up periodically through the night, mostly thinking about Wyatt and his latest kiss.

With a sigh, she got dressed before 5:00 a.m. Wyatt was already out and her nephew was on his way to the horse barn when she checked the weather conditions. A blizzard was on its way—at least fifteen to twenty inches of snow were anticipated. *In April.* Not that it surprised her—as a kid, one storm had dumped three feet on the area over a four-day period.

She might not be an expert on ranching, but she already knew that much snow meant putting out feed for the cattle.

Katrina dialed Paige, knowing she'd be awake along with most everyone else.

"What's up, Katrina?"

"Is it all right if I bring Christie over? I

want to see if there's anything I can do to help with the storm coming in."

"That's fine. I'd appreciate it since I can't go myself. Daniel is too active to leave with Saul and I'm sure Anna Beth will be busy in the dining hall."

"Tim is already working at the main horse barn. I told him it was okay, he just needs to be on time when your mother arrives to take him and Mishka to school."

"He's a good kid. But in case you haven't heard, there's going to be an early closure. They want the children home well before the storm hits. My mom has it in hand. She'll pick them up at noon. Earlier if the weather front comes in sooner than anticipated."

"Great. I'll have Christie there in a few minutes, along with an overnight bag, just in case. Oh, I'm afraid this also means taking care of Scooter again."

Paige laughed. "I figured. No problem. Dixie will be out working and her puppies have all gone to their new homes, so Scooter should be fine. Especially if he's with Christie. It's adorable the way she encourages him."

"Wait until you see her scolding the other dogs when they get too curious. She's *fierce*."

"That will be a treat to watch."

"Just keep any socks away from him. He has a thing about socks."

Before long Scooter and Christie were at the main house. Christie was still sleepy from being woken early on a day she didn't attend preschool, and Katrina was headed for the equipment barn. The healthy adults available to work were limited—just Wyatt and Jordan and their father, along with Billie.

"Paige is watching Christie. What can I do?" she asked Wyatt.

He flicked her a glance and kept working as he fired out instructions. "Keep an eye on the calving barn. Bring any calves inside that might be struggling. The cows still pregnant have been moved to the pasture behind the barn. This will be a real blizzard, so secure anything that isn't tied down. If you have to go out after the storm hits, use the safety ropes we put up between the buildings."

"Isn't Melody going with you?"

Wyatt shook his head as he continued to fill the caking truck with the protein supplement. "She got sick a few hours ago. When this flu hits, it knocks you flat."

Katrina gulped. She wasn't afraid of tackling the calving barn by herself, but she *was* worried about Wyatt being away from the main ranch with so little support. What if one of them got sick or injured out there? Or all of them? It wasn't impossible. Would they even have the strength to get home?

"I'll do my best," she said, backing away. He didn't need to deal with her concern along with the rest. Besides, the storm shouldn't be here until late afternoon; they had time to prepare. She also knew Paige had a unit in her home office that tracked all the satellite phones on the ranch. With her husband out there, she'd be watching with extra care.

At the calving barn Katrina took a minute to evaluate how much space was available. It was at least two-thirds empty. The cows inside were probably close to delivering, but they looked comfortable. A few of the pens needed cleaning, so she got the wheelbarrow and dealt with them, replacing soiled straw with fresh.

Outside, she collected pails and anything lightweight that might fly around in the wind. She wasn't sure what needed to be tied down, but she fastened the tarps tighter over the nearby stacks of hay and straw bales and made sure all the gates were secured.

Then she began checking the newest calves in the field. There were a few that looked as if they were suffering more from the cold than the others, though the ones with protective mothers seemed less of a concern—they knew it was their job to take care of their babies.

"I'm here, Aunt Kat. After an hour in class, they decided to send us home."

Katrina looked up to see her nephew coming toward her, pulling a kind of cart on wheels. It was a relief—though just twelve, he had more experience than she did with cattle after watching and helping his grandfather on the Big Jumbo.

"I'll bring the weaker calves in," he told her. "I think one of the heifers in the barn is close to calving, but I don't know if she needs help."

Katrina cast a look toward the mountains. Though the storm hadn't hit, they were becoming less distinct. "Okay, go ahead. Just be careful. Some of the mama cows don't like us interfering," she said before hurrying back inside to check the heifer Timothy had mentioned.

It was going to be a long day. And even longer knowing Wyatt was out in the storm.

BY LATE AFTERNOON, the wind began blowing harder and Katrina and Timothy had pulled their third calf.

They'd brought more pregnant cows into the barn as a precaution, though several had delivered their babies in the pasture without assistance. Maybe it was silly, but Katrina had made room inside for all of the new mothers and babies. Surely it would just be for a few days and they seemed so vulnerable out there in the wind.

The activity kept her from thinking too much about Wyatt.

Everything was in a quiet lull, so she left to check the horses, using the brightly colored safety ropes installed to help navigate between the buildings. The wind was blowing hard enough that the ropes helped keep her on her feet. She found Saul and Anna Beth in the main barn.

"Don't worry, we're watching after the horses," Saul assured her. He looked quite happy as he went from stall to stall to evaluate the food and water supply in each. "We've already checked the pregnant mares, along with the crew's horses. We should have called to let you know."

"Then I'll get back to the calving barn. How are the flu patients?" Katrina asked Anna Beth in a low tone.

"The medical clinic closed early, so Noelle's looked in on everyone. They should be fine if they stay in bed and do as they're told. Everybody is keeping an eye on each other and will call if needed." Anna Beth patted the pocket where she kept her cell phone. "We're much better off than ranches without a resident doctor. Be sure to stop by the dining hall kitchen and fill a thermos with hot soup. And also get coffee."

Feeling reassured, Katrina stopped for the soup and coffee and returned to the calving barn. She insisted that Timothy eat and managed to swallow a few bites herself. The coffee tasted the best to her.

"Can I have some, too, Aunt Kat?" he asked.

She nodded. Timothy was taking the responsibility of an adult; he deserved to be treated like one. But the coffee didn't stop him from yawning and she finally suggested he lie down with a blanket on a pile of clean hay.

"It isn't late and you need me, Aunt Kat."

"I'll wake you up if something happens. We can spell each other."

"Okay."

The biggest problem with Timothy being asleep was now she was alone with her thoughts. She was trying to trust her instincts about men again and thought Wyatt cared for her in return. But what if it was partly proximity? After all, she was living in his house and taking care of his daughter.

That wasn't enough for her. She wanted *more* than a convenient romance—she wanted Wyatt's *whole* heart.

Katrina walked through the barn again, checking the cows, then cracked the door open an inch and peered out. She couldn't see much because it was dark now and snow was blowing horizontally, carried by the wind.

And the man she loved was somewhere in the middle of all that.

CHAPTER FOURTEEN

As Wyatt shoveled out the protein supplement in the worsening storm, he tried not to think about the calves and cows that could be struggling back at the main ranch. While the busiest part of the calving season was over, there were still a number of pregnant cows.

Katrina was there and she'd do her best, but she was a novice.

Still, she was amazing. Offering to help without hesitation and not being offended by the rapid-fire instructions he'd given her. Knowing she understood there wasn't a minute to spend on niceties was reassuring.

"That should do it," Wyatt called as they finished their latest run. He wanted to get everyone back to the ranch center before the storm turned into the predicted blizzard. Besides, he'd heard Jordan coughing a few times and suspected he was getting sick.

Lights were on in the barns and houses when they got close, and by unspoken accord, they stopped at the calving barn. Wyatt went in, fearing the worst.

"Oh my gosh, I was worried about you." Katrina dashed over and flung her arms around his neck, hugging him for all she was worth, then just as quickly backed off, looking embarrassed. "Sorry."

"No more apologies. I finally know what I want. And I hope you want the same thing," he whispered. He opened his arms and she stepped right in. He then gave her a long kiss, not caring that his brother and father were watching with amused approval.

At length, Katrina drew away again, her eyes wide and brimming with emotion. He sent her a smile meant just for her.

"Um, we've had quite a few calves arrive," she said. "All seem to be fine, though one heifer is looking stressed. I was just going to put her in the calving chute."

"Right."

It was a reminder that they still had the storm and ranch chores to get through. For a moment he wished the Soaring Hawk would disappear.

He turned to his brother. "Jordan, you're sick. Go home," he ordered.

Jordan put a hand on a sawhorse, obviously

to steady himself after another bout of heavy coughing. "But—"

"No excuses. Paige will never forgive me if you come down with pneumonia. Dad, Billie, could you make sure he gets there?"

Evan nodded and pulled his eldest son's arm over his shoulders, while Billie took Jordan's other side.

A loud bellow from a nearby pen captured Wyatt's attention and he strode over. Katrina was right, the heifer needed help. She had a narrow pelvis and a large baby. They moved her into the calving chute and together helped deliver a huge calf. His tongue was swollen and blue by the time he was out and they turned him to rest on his sternum, head and neck stretched forward to facilitate breathing. After his condition improved, they carried him to an empty pen.

"I need to get to the horse barns," Wyatt said, sinking on the floor and breathing hard.

"Your grandfather and Anna Beth are keeping an eye on the horses. Tim has been helping here. He's asleep right now because I made him take a nap, but he's starting to stir." It was a subtle reminder they didn't have any privacy.

Wyatt leaned his head against a post, unable to believe how beautiful Katrina looked, even with her hair mussed and a smear of dirt on her forehead. Seeing her concern for him after being out in the storm was a reminder that he wasn't the only one worried about losing someone important to them. Love took courage, no matter what you'd experienced in the past.

She got up and stretched. "I'll give the baby its first vaccine and put his mama in with him."

"I'll do it."

"*No.* You're going to rest and have a cup of coffee first. There's still plenty left in the thermos."

Wyatt was bemused as Katrina poured him a cup, then gave the calf a vaccine and casually released his mama and used a pole to direct her through the gate. She immediately began licking her baby with the contented moo he loved hearing.

Katrina's smile showed she loved it as well.

He became aware it was warmer than he would have expected and got up to look across the large expanse. There were quite a few cows and calves filling the pens—that many bodies crowded together added a good amount of heat to the air.

"Did you bring the entire herd inside?" Wyatt asked.

"That would hardly be possible. But it's cold out there and a lot of calves were being born. I realize it's going to be a mess to clean up after them, but I thought they should be out of the wind. They've all got food and water."

"That's okay. You did what most of us want to do."

"So, did you have a chance to talk with your dad?"

Wyatt smiled wryly. "It wasn't a chatting situation. I spoke to him a few days ago, though. Not a lot, but some. I think we're going to be okay. He's getting fond of Billie."

"We all saw it coming. He's probably wondering where to go from here, though, being as they live in a bunkhouse."

"Actually, I have an idea about that."

"Care to share?"

"I need to talk with my brothers about it first." He leaned closer. "I haven't had a chance to say so, but thank you for looking after things here."

"My pleasure."

Wyatt gave her another kiss. "No, it's mine," he whispered against her lips.

IT WAS LATE when Billie got back to the bunkhouse for a shower. She was as quiet as possible, trying not to disturb Melody and Carmen, who were curled in their bunks, looking miserable.

As she scrubbed off in the hot water, she mused that plumbing was one of the things she enjoyed the most about staying in one place. Her camper had a marine toilet and shower she'd installed a few years ago, but it wasn't the same as having a full-sized hot water tank and generous stream of water pouring over her.

When she was dressed, Billie went into the bunkhouse dining hall. As usual, she was tired, but not sleepy.

Everything was tidy—Anna Beth wouldn't leave it in any other way. But the level in the regular coffeemaker was low and there was no decaf made, so Billie dealt with both and did prep for breakfast in the morning. Soon, the scent of fresh-brewed java filled the air, one of the most enticing scents in the world.

"Thought I'd find you in here."

She turned and smiled at Evan. "You'd think feeding cattle all day in the cold and wind would make us sleepy."

He shrugged. "Sleep is overrated."

Maybe, but she suspected when two people in love were cozied up together in bed, sleep came easier. Or at least it made being unable to sleep less tedious.

"Were you able to attend your AA meeting?"

Evan shrugged. "It was over, but I found another one."

Billie sat next to him at the counter. "I heard Wyatt call you 'Dad' several times today."

"I think everything is going to be all right with him. He's a fine man. Kind and decent. I don't blame him for not trusting me around Christie. My drinking must have terrified him as a child. He was the youngest and most vulnerable."

She squeezed his hand. "I know, but he's on a good path now. Wyatt is the one who married young and was a devoted husband for years. Maybe he'll have a second chance with Katrina."

"Speaking of second chances..." Evan straightened. "Is there any possibility you could see me as a husband?"

"A husband, or *my* husband?"

"Yours, of course."

"You mean you're proposing?"

"OF COURSE I'M PROPOSING," Evan said, annoyed until he spotted the twinkle in Billie's eyes. "All right, as proposals go, that wasn't the best."

"At least it proves you don't do it that often."

He grinned and lifted her hand. "Billie, I love you with all of my heart. Will you do me the honor of marrying me, even if I don't get down on one of my battered old knees to ask?"

"You aren't old."

"Older than when I did this the first time. That was a disaster, too."

Billie leaned over and kissed him. "I wouldn't call this a disaster. If we can't laugh, what kind of life will we have together?"

"Is that a yes?"

"Definitely a yes." She kissed him again.

"Good, because this doesn't fit me." Evan held out his hand and she saw a ring lying on his palm. "A friend in my artists' guild made it to order."

Enchanted, Billie let him slide the gold ring on the third finger of her left hand. It was simple and wide, with laser-cut horses running around the band.

"It's beautiful, Evan."

"I know it isn't a traditional engagement ring."

"No, it's better."

KATRINA HATED LEAVING Christie at the main house over the next few days, but she was realistic. Mishka would help keep her cousin and brother entertained and Paige's husband was sick in bed, so she'd want to stay with him, regardless.

The ranch was shorthanded, but Katrina wouldn't let Timothy work too many hours at a stretch or go outside alone, even using the safety ropes.

"I know what I'm doing, Aunt Kat," he protested. "And I'm bigger than you, so you'd be knocked off your feet by the wind easier than me."

She'd stared in surprise, realizing it was true. Timothy had surpassed her in height when she wasn't looking.

"I suppose," she had admitted, "but you still can't go out by yourself in a blizzard."

Her no-nonsense tone had ended his protest.

There was little time to talk with Wyatt, but nothing could stop her from thinking about him.

He'd said he finally knew what he wanted from her and that he hoped it's what she wanted, too. But until they had a chance to really talk in private, she couldn't be completely sure of what it meant.

The storm finally blew itself out on the fourth night and the sun was bright the next morning, sparkling on the new snow. Wyatt and Evan didn't waste any time. They hitched the ranch's two draft horses to an ancient sleigh and started hauling hay and protein supplement out to the cattle.

Wyatt seemed pleased when they only found one chilled calf. The cattle had stayed by the windbreaks, huddled together to stay warm. The temperature also hadn't dropped as drastically as predicted, so none seemed too worse for wear aside from being hungry. Katrina worked on warming and feeding the chilled calf and it was ready to go back to its mother when Wyatt and his father returned for a new load of feed.

"You're amazing," he murmured, giving her a quick kiss. "Have I mentioned that I'm head over heels about you?"

"Actually, I think this is the first time you've mentioned it."

"I'll have to rectify that." He leaned close

to kiss her again, when he was interrupted by Timothy.

"Eww," her nephew muttered in disgust as he cleaned an empty pen. "Can you please not do that in front of me?"

Though disappointed to see the moment put on pause, Katrina shared a grin with Wyatt before he lifted the calf and took it out to the sleigh.

Things were looking bright.

"DAD, GOT A MINUTE?"

Evan turned and smiled at Wyatt. Life was settling down. The snow had melted and new grass was growing furiously. Before too many more weeks passed, they'd probably be moving the herd to summer grazing land, higher in the hills, followed by haying and other summer tasks.

Best of all, he was engaged to Billie. Knowing word would spread quickly, he'd made sure his sons heard it first.

"Of course, son."

"Now that things are starting to get quieter and everyone is healthy again, I wondered if you and Billie would like to come to Saturday dinner up at the main house? So, um, you can meet your youngest granddaughter. Youngest so far, at least."

Evan's throat got tight. He'd hoped that he could get to know Christie, though it was more than he deserved.

"We'd love to come."

"By the way, I know you've mentioned buying a small trailer to live in, but I've been discussing options with Jordan and Dakota. The foreman's quarters are available and we can fix them to be snug and comfortable. There's a kitchenette and enough room for a double bed and some easy chairs. Not spacious, but roomier than a trailer. Naturally we'd update the bathroom and kitchen."

Using the foreman's quarters hadn't occurred to Evan—it would have seemed presumptuous. His sons didn't owe him anything. He would never forget that he could have made things easier when their mother died, instead of so much harder. It wasn't a case of punishing himself; he just didn't want to become complacent.

"That sounds like a fine plan," he choked out.

"Then we'll get working on it. Let us know if either of you have color preferences, or anything like that. Oh, and Paige tells me dinner will be at four. She and Noelle want to have a regular family meal each weekend—very casual. The Bannermans will be coming, too."

Evan resisted asking what Katrina wanted. If Wyatt was interested in anyone's opinion, he'd ask for it.

AFTER THE MEAL on Saturday, Katrina stood back, watching Christie and her grandfather interact. Wyatt was hovering nearby, but she thought it was because he wanted to be sure Christie was comfortable being around so many new people, rather than being concerned about what his father would say.

Christie *had* been shy initially, but she already knew Margaret Bannerman and had seen Evan and Billie around the ranch. Now she seemed intrigued that she had a grandpa and would soon have a new grandma. And that she shared that grandpa with her cousins.

"Christie is a delight," Scott Bannerman said to Katrina. "Margaret adores her."

Katrina looked up at the tall, lean rancher. He'd been a quiet presence during her childhood, along with his wife and sons. Her family had always attended Noelle's early-December birthday party, complete with a hayride and other entertainment. But the Bannerman birthday parties for their other four children had also been memorable—they were a family that liked to entertain.

"Margaret seems to see Christie as an honorary grandchild."

Scott chuckled. "The more grandkids, the better, as far as we're concerned. We feel fortunate to have both our daughters so close on the Soaring Hawk. Say, do you remember our son, Shane? He's single. You should talk and get to know each other again."

Single?

Katrina restrained a laugh. Matchmaking was a sport in Shelton County. Few could resist.

Scott called Shane over and soon his brother Elijah joined them. It was a boost to her ego having two handsome men talk her up, each trying to outdo the other.

"Enough of that," Wyatt said finally, stepping to Katrina's side.

"Enough of what?" Shane Bannerman asked with a wicked grin.

"Don't be a dunce," Elijah said, pushing Shane away.

Katrina glanced at Wyatt and saw he was smiling. "You're in a good mood."

"We're past the flu season and everyone is back on the job. We didn't lose many calves. And I finally have at least five minutes to breathe before we start moving the herds again and mowing for hay." He gestured toward Elijah and Shane. "I hope the Bannerman brothers weren't bothering you too much."

"Nope. I'm the only unattached woman present and they like to flirt."

"That isn't the only reason they were flirting with you."

"If you say so."

Wyatt's eyes crinkled with humor. "You're a tough sell. But trust me, a guy can tell when another guy is attracted to a woman. It's a guy thing."

"A guy thing? Wow, that sounds very scientific."

"Totally. Would you like to go for a ride? The moon is full tonight and I thought the view might appeal to your artistic instincts. Christie is sleeping over here with Mishka."

Katrina felt a rush of anticipation. "That sounds like fun."

"Good. You deserve some fun. Dakota and Noelle have already gone home, so things are starting to break up here."

"I'll change into my boots. Scooter needs to be checked, anyway."

"Daddy," Christie called and Wyatt gave Katrina an apologetic smile before going over to his daughter.

Katrina sighed, watching him for a minute. He was wonderful and she was totally in love with him. On top of which, a moonlit ride sounded more like a date and a chance to talk, not time spent together working.

And he *had* said he was head over heels for her. Surely that meant what she' thought it meant.

She said goodbye to the Bannermans and hurried to the homestead cabin. Scooter was waiting at the door to go out and do his business. He was mellower now and less uptight about being outside. He'd even made friends with a couple of the ranch's Aussie collies, though he towered above them. And, aside from his penchant for chewing Wyatt's socks, he was gentle and cooperative. Basically, he was a big couch potato.

"Done?" she asked the Great Dane when he strolled inside the mud porch with a decided lack of haste.

She grinned and closed the door behind him. Scooter went to his dog bed in the living room and lay down with a pleased sigh. She crouched and ruffled his ears. He blinked at her lazily and rolled over onto his back, his legs splaying crazily.

Yup, a big ol' couch potato.

Happy and comfortable.

Katrina put on her boots and draped a light jacket over her arm, stepping outside in time to see Wyatt walking toward the horse barn. His stride and the set of his shoulders were distinctive in the silver moonlight.

She tried to quell the butterflies in her stomach as she headed to the barn herself.

There had been a look in his eyes when he asked her to ride with him that suggested this was the "later" he'd promised in the barn during the blizzard.

CHAPTER FIFTEEN

WYATT FINISHED SADDLING Banana Split for Katrina.

He didn't know if it was the right moment to propose, but it was getting more and more difficult to wait. And he *had* told her how he felt, more or less.

"Hey, Banana Split, did you miss me?"

He turned and saw Katrina feeding the mare an apple.

"I'm sorry you haven't been able to ride lately," he said.

She shrugged. "That's okay. We've all been busy. Besides, I've never gone riding at night, so this is a treat."

"Horses have great night vision. We'll find time to do it more often."

As they rode north, the moon was so bright it cast shadows across the ground. The air was almost warm and the scent of growth surrounded them, as if everything was trying to catch up after the end of the long winter.

At the crest of a hill marking the property line between the Soaring Hawk and the Circle M, Wyatt reined in his horse. "I don't know if you can see it, even with the full moon, but the house where I was born is down this valley to the east."

KATRINA LOOKED CURIOUSLY and saw buildings in the distance, with a single pinpoint of light.

"Is the electricity turned on?" she asked, trying to verify if she was seeing what Wyatt seemed to want her to see.

"Yes. The buildings have all been kept up or repaired. The barn is useful since we're using the Circle M land for grazing and hay production. We leave a light on in the house. It seems..." Wyatt's voice trailed and he shrugged. "I don't know."

"As if you're reminding the universe that your mother was there," Katrina said softly. "Deserted homes always seem sad, echoing with memories. Did you mean you were actually born in the house?"

"Yeah. They didn't even make it to the truck. Mom had one contraction and there I was. She used to call me her eager beaver. It's one of the few things I remember about her."

Katrina thought about all the places Wyatt must have been in the navy, yet here he was, living just a few miles from where life had begun. It wasn't too different for her—though she'd been born at the hospital in Bozeman, her roots were firmly planted in Shelton.

"That's a nice memory to keep."

"Yeah."

Wyatt dismounted and stood gazing down the moonlit valley. Katrina did the same, wondering if he was moody or just contemplative. Next to her, Banana Split dropped her head and along with Wyatt's horse, began eagerly nibbling on the grass. After a long winter of hay and grain, it must be a treat for them to eat the spring bounty.

"Do you like the homestead cabin?" Wyatt asked unexpectedly.

"Very much. Your brother and Noelle did a wonderful job of renovating and making the house comfortable, but it still has a lovely historic feel."

"Right, including a fireplace with sapphires embedded in it. That's unique. But you don't like my furniture."

"I shouldn't have said anything about that," Katrina said contritely. "On my first day here, no less."

"I'm glad you did. I agree, the style doesn't fit on the ranch. Anyhow, I was wondering if you'd help me pick something else out. Particularly for the living room and master bedroom."

"Um, our tastes are very different, Wyatt. I don't know how much help I could be."

He cleared his throat. "Sorry, I'm doing this badly. I just didn't know how to start after all the times I've said something to push you away. The thing is, I want the house to feel like *our* home, not a leftover from my navy days."

Katrina gulped.

Our home.

"I love you," Wyatt added simply. "Head over heels, just like I told you the other day. And I really, really hope you feel the same. Will you marry me?"

Though Katrina knew he had feelings for her, doubts remained.

"Wyatt, you said you couldn't imagine loving anyone but Amy. I know you're fond of me, but I can't marry someone because I'm convenient. I want the kind of love your brothers have with their wives. Absolute devotion and commitment."

"I've said a lot of dumb things." Wyatt rubbed the back of his neck. "Mostly out of self-protection. Taking a chance that I would get hurt again was more than I wanted to face. So I decided it wasn't possible to give my heart to someone else. Then you arrived, full of laughter and opinions."

"Some people wouldn't see the opinions as a good thing."

"Not me. I love you, just the way you are. You made me think. You shook me out of the rut I'd fallen into and brought color and light into my life. I've never known anyone with so much joy and enthusiasm. I couldn't keep your face and smile out of my head. Or my heart."

The warmth in Wyatt's voice sent tendrils of pleasure through Katrina. He wasn't asking her to change or become someone she wasn't. "So, what are your feelings about having a larger family?" she asked.

"Entirely pro. And I know Christie would love to have more brothers or sisters."

"That's encouraging."

ENCOURAGING?

Wyatt wished Katrina would fling herself into his arms and say she loved him, too, but he didn't blame her for being cautious.

Him and his big mouth, declaring to anyone who'd listen that he was remaining single, now and forever, that there was no way he could ever fall in love again. Who could have guessed that a childhood friend would become more important to him than the air he breathed?

"I wanted to believe it was simply friendship between us," he continued, "but even when I was denying it, a part of me knew it was more. I felt guilty at first and it was like waking up after a long sleep. But for the first time in years, I've been truly alive. So I had to decide if I was going to let fear get in the way of a potentially wonderful future."

Katrina began to smile. "When did you make up your mind?"

"My heart made the decision before my head. But my head made the leap the night I saw Scooter lick your nose."

"Scooter?" She grinned, looking delighted. "Nice try That isn't very romantic."

"How does a moonlit ride stack up romantically?"

Katrina reached out and brushed the line of his chin. "Everything stacks up with you, Wyatt. I wasn't completely comfortable with the boy you once were, but I'm utterly in love with the man you've become. So yes, I'll marry you."

"Thank goodness," Wyatt breathed. Then he caught her close in a fierce kiss.

KATRINA WAS DIZZY by the time Wyatt lifted his head, mostly from delight and surging anticipation.

"Grandpa Saul gave me the family ring." Wyatt reached into his shirt pocket. "I know it's old-fashioned, so feel free to tell me if you'd prefer something different. There are diamonds and a couple of sapphires in it, but I don't think the sapphires are from Montana."

He slid the ring over her finger and she turned her hand back and forth in the silver light, seeing flashes of muted fire from the stones, along with a beautifully ornate gold setting.

"It's lovely," she said. "How could I want something else?"

"I also had this made for you. I hoped it would be your 'something new and something blue' at our wedding. The color matches your eyes."

Something new, and something blue…

Katrina's breath caught as the moonlight seemed to be captured and intensified by the brilliant greenish-blue stone on Wyatt's palm—a large trillion-cut gem in an unobtrusive setting.

"Is that the sapphire from the fireplace?" she gasped.

"Yeah. I sent it to a gem cutter and jewelry designer. He got this back to me yesterday. Go ahead, put it on. There are earrings, too, but they're back at the house."

The gold chain was long enough to go over her head and Katrina looked down at the pendant, resting over her heart. It was beautiful. Knowing the stone had come from the homestead cabin and was intertwined with the history of the Hawkins made it even more special.

Katrina put her arms around Wyatt's neck. "I hope you aren't interested in a long engagement," she whispered against his mouth.

"Not a chance." He whirled her around, his laughter ringing out. "I'd marry you tonight if I could."

They kissed again and Katrina's heart felt as if it was overflowing. But that was the great thing about love: there was always room for more.

WYATT STOOD ON the crest of the hill above the homestead cabin, waiting with Jordan, Dakota and Evan for his bride to appear.

The air was warm and a light breeze rippled the wildflower-studded grass like ocean waves. It wasn't going to be a traditional wedding, but his bride hadn't wanted a fancy church ceremony.

He smiled as he remembered his mother-in-law-to-be's protests. Edith Tapson was a formidable woman, but no match for her daughter. Katrina had declared that their wedding would be simple and just the way she and Wyatt wanted it. So even though they'd needed to pick a date far enough ahead so her sister and brother-in-law could attend, she'd refused to order flowers, choose a wedding cake or interview caterers from Bozeman or Helena, preferring to spend her time in other ways.

One of those ways had been choosing new furniture with her fiancé. They'd settled on Mission-style furnishings that were much more suited to the homestead cabin. The old stuff had gone to a benefit shop in Bozeman.

Instead of a formal reception, they were having a barbecue after the ceremony. The

Bannermans and McKeons had volunteered to handle that part—the two families were experts when it came to grilling. Katrina had ordered food from the local deli, but Anna Beth, Billie and Wyatt's sisters-in-law had insisted on making salads and other side dishes. Other guests had called to say they were bringing a contribution as well.

Katrina's one concession to her mother had been letting her choose and bring a wedding cake, so that would be dessert, along with ice cream.

Like pieces of a puzzle falling into place, their childhood friend, now Reverend Nick McGill, had heard they were getting married and offered to drive down from Helena to do the ceremony. He waited on the hill next to Wyatt.

"Nervous?" Nick asked quietly.

"Not a chance. Katrina has already changed my life for the better. I'm just sitting back and enjoying the ride."

His brothers and father chuckled.

Evan and Billie had gotten married a few weeks earlier in Great Falls at her parents' home. They'd all gone, including Saul, who was pleased that his former son-in-law was happy. Like Katrina, Wyatt was impressed that the two men had become so close.

Saul had told Wyatt the night before that a third of the Soaring Hawk was already in trust for him. He'd arranged the paperwork as soon as Wyatt signed the agreement to return for a year.

"I just wanted my grandsons to come home," his grandfather had explained. "To give me a chance to make amends. You were always going to inherit the ranch—I never had any other intention. But when something happens to me, which is inevitable at my age, I just ask you to keep including Anna Beth as part of the family."

"Anna Beth couldn't get rid of us if she tried," Wyatt had assured him. "But I hope you're here for a very long time. We need to make up for the years we've lost."

They'd hugged and Saul had unashamedly wiped tears from his eyes.

Wyatt glanced at Nick and saw a solemn expression on his face. He'd truly cared for Katrina when they were teenagers, but he was happy for them.

Eduardo began playing a romantic folk tune on his guitar and everyone turned. Paige and Noelle walked forward. They were followed by Katrina's sister, Mary. Mishka and Christie came next with baskets of wildflowers. A ripple of chuckles went through the group of guests at the sight of Scooter solemnly walking between them with a teal bow around his neck. By now he was nearly as tall as Christie herself and more than twice her weight.

Christie had been over the moon about Katrina becoming her mother. She'd immediately asked permission to call her mommy and had proudly announced to her preschool class that she was going to have the "bestest new mom in the whole world."

Wyatt's breath caught as Katrina stepped out next to her father, so beautiful he could hardly believe he was so lucky.

He'd half expected her to show up in jeans and a batik top. Instead, she wore a simple, white satin wedding gown that flared in a full sweep over her hips and ended midcalf. Her bouquet was made of sunflowers she'd collected earlier in the morning. The sapphire pendant and earrings she wore glinted green-blue fire in the sunlight, but they were nothing compared to her dazzling smile.

Then he grinned in delight, realizing she was barefoot.

KATRINA LOVED THE feel of the grass against her feet as she walked up the small hill on her father's arm.

From Wyatt's smile, she knew he'd spotted her bare feet. There wasn't a hint of censure in his face; instead, he seemed to enjoy her determined self-expression.

She'd almost painted a spray of sunflowers on her dress, but had preferred the simplicity of the gown as it was—an off-the-rack dress that even her mom had liked.

She and Wyatt were going to have a week-long honeymoon in Yellowstone National Park, then go for a longer honeymoon in the fall. Paige had managed to secure a suite for them in the park with a view of Yellowstone Lake. Katrina would have been happy in a tent, but couldn't deny that a room in the hotel would be nice.

At the top of the hill, her father put her hand in Wyatt's before going to stand with her mother.

Katrina handed her bouquet to her sister, then rose on her bare toes to kiss Wyatt, unable to wait until their *I do's* had been said.

"I guess you're ready," Nick chuckled.

Christie was so excited she was hopping

from one foot to the other. Katrina held out her hand and Christie ran to her.

"Now we're ready," Katrina said.

Then, with their daughter standing between them, the ceremony began.

* * * * *

For more charming romances from Julianna Morris and Harlequin Heartwarming, visit www.Harlequin.com today!

Get 4 FREE REWARDS!

We'll send you 2 FREE Books plus 2 FREE Mystery Gifts.

Both the **Love Inspired®** and **Love Inspired® Suspense** series feature compelling novels filled with inspirational romance, faith, forgiveness and hope.

YES! Please send me 2 FREE novels from the Love Inspired or Love Inspired Suspense series and my 2 FREE gifts (gifts are worth about $10 retail). After receiving them, if I don't wish to receive any more books, I can return the shipping statement marked "cancel." If I don't cancel, I will receive 6 brand-new Love Inspired Larger-Print books or Love Inspired Suspense Larger-Print books every month and be billed just $6.49 each in the U.S. or $6.74 each in Canada. That is a savings of at least 16% off the cover price. It's quite a bargain! Shipping and handling is just 50¢ per book in the U.S. and $1.25 per book in Canada.* I understand that accepting the 2 free books and gifts places me under no obligation to buy anything. I can always return a shipment and cancel at any time by calling the number below. The free books and gifts are mine to keep no matter what I decide.

Choose one: ☐ **Love Inspired Larger-Print** (122/322 IDN GRHK) ☐ **Love Inspired Suspense Larger-Print** (107/307 IDN GRHK)

Name (please print)

Address Apt. #

City State/Province Zip/Postal Code

Email: Please check this box ☐ if you would like to receive newsletters and promotional emails from Harlequin Enterprises ULC and its affiliates. You can unsubscribe anytime.

Mail to the **Harlequin Reader Service:**
IN U.S.A.: P.O. Box 1341, Buffalo, NY 14240-8531
IN CANADA: P.O. Box 603, Fort Erie, Ontario L2A 5X3

Want to try 2 free books from another series? Call 1-800-873-8635 or visit www.ReaderService.com.

*Terms and prices subject to change without notice. Prices do not include sales taxes, which will be charged (if applicable) based on your state or country of residence. Canadian residents will be charged applicable taxes. Offer not valid in Quebec. This offer is limited to one order per household. Books received may not be as shown. Not valid for current subscribers to the Love Inspired or Love Inspired Suspense series. All orders subject to approval. Credit or debit balances in a customer's account(s) may be offset by any other outstanding balance owed by or to the customer. Please allow 4 to 6 weeks for delivery. Offer available while quantities last.

Your Privacy—Your information is being collected by Harlequin Enterprises ULC, operating as Harlequin Reader Service. For a complete summary of the information we collect, how we use this information and to whom it is disclosed, please visit our privacy notice located at corporate.harlequin.com/privacy-notice. From time to time we may also exchange your personal information with reputable third parties. If you wish to opt out of this sharing of your personal information, please visit readerservice.com/consumerschoice or call 1-800-873-8635. **Notice to California Residents**—Under California law, you have specific rights to control and access your data. For more information on these rights and how to exercise them, visit corporate.harlequin.com/california-privacy.

LIRLIS22R3

Get 4 FREE REWARDS!

We'll send you 2 FREE Books plus 2 FREE Mystery Gifts.

Both the **Harlequin® Special Edition** and **Harlequin® Heartwarming™** series feature compelling novels filled with stories of love and strength where the bonds of friendship, family and community unite.

YES! Please send me 2 FREE novels from the Harlequin Special Edition or Harlequin Heartwarming series and my 2 FREE gifts (gifts are worth about $10 retail). After receiving them, if I don't wish to receive any more books, I can return the shipping statement marked "cancel." If I don't cancel, I will receive 6 brand-new Harlequin Special Edition books every month and be billed just $5.49 each in the U.S. or $6.24 each in Canada, a savings of at least 12% off the cover price, or 4 brand-new Harlequin Heartwarming Larger-Print books every month and be billed just $6.24 each in the U.S. or $6.74 each in Canada, a savings of at least 19% off the cover price. It's quite a bargain! Shipping and handling is just 50¢ per book in the U.S. and $1.25 per book in Canada.* I understand that accepting the 2 free books and gifts places me under no obligation to buy anything. I can always return a shipment and cancel at any time by calling the number below. The free books and gifts are mine to keep no matter what I decide.

Choose one: ☐ **Harlequin Special Edition** (235/335 HDN GRJV) ☐ **Harlequin Heartwarming Larger-Print** (161/361 HDN GRJV)

Name (please print)

Address | Apt. #

City | State/Province | Zip/Postal Code

Email: Please check this box ☐ if you would like to receive newsletters and promotional emails from Harlequin Enterprises ULC and its affiliates. You can unsubscribe anytime.

Mail to the **Harlequin Reader Service:**
IN U.S.A.: P.O. Box 1341, Buffalo, NY 14240-8531
IN CANADA: P.O. Box 603, Fort Erie, Ontario L2A 5X3

Want to try 2 free books from another series? Call 1-800-873-8635 or visit www.ReaderService.com.

*Terms and prices subject to change without notice. Prices do not include sales taxes, which will be charged (if applicable) based on your state or country of residence. Canadian residents will be charged applicable taxes. Offer not valid in Quebec. This offer is limited to one order per household. Books received may not be as shown. Not valid for current subscribers to the Harlequin Special Edition or Harlequin Heartwarming series. All orders subject to approval. Credit or debit balances in a customer's account(s) may be offset by any other outstanding balance owed by or to the customer. Please allow 4 to 6 weeks for delivery. Offer available while quantities last.

Your Privacy—Your information is being collected by Harlequin Enterprises ULC, operating as Harlequin Reader Service. For a complete summary of the information we collect, how we use this information and to whom it is disclosed, please visit our privacy notice located at corporate.harlequin.com/privacy-notice. From time to time we may also exchange your personal information with reputable third parties. If you wish to opt out of this sharing of your personal information, please visit readerservice.com/consumerschoice or call 1-800-873-8635. **Notice to California Residents**—Under California law, you have specific rights to control and access your data. For more information on these rights and how to exercise them, visit corporate.harlequin.com/california-privacy.

HSEHW22R3

THE NORA ROBERTS COLLECTION

Get to the heart of happily-ever-after in these Nora Roberts classics! Immerse yourself in the beauty of love by picking up this incredible collection written by, legendary author, Nora Roberts!

YES! Please send me the **Nora Roberts Collection**. Each book in this collection is 40% off the retail price! There are a total of 4 shipments in this collection. The shipments are yours for the low, members-only discount price of $23.96 U.S./$31.16 CDN. each, plus $1.99 U.S./$4.99 CDN. for shipping and handling. If I do not cancel, I will continue to receive four books a month for three more months. I'll pay just $23.96 U.S./$31.16 CDN., plus $1.99 U.S./$4.99 CDN. for shipping and handling per shipment.* I can always return a shipment and cancel at any time.

☐ 274 2595 ☐ 474 2595

Name (please print)

Address Apt. #

City State/Province Zip/Postal Code

Mail to the **Harlequin Reader Service:**
IN U.S.A.: P.O. Box 1341, Buffalo, NY 14240-8531
IN CANADA: P.O. Box 603, Fort Erie, Ontario L2A 5X3

*Terms and prices subject to change without notice. Prices do not include sales taxes which will be charged (if applicable) based on your state or country of residence. Canadian residents will be charged applicable taxes. Offer not valid in Quebec. All orders subject to approval. Credit or debit balances in a customer's account(s) may be offset by any other outstanding balance owed by or to the customer. Please allow 3 to 4 weeks for delivery. Offer available while quantities last. © 2022 Harlequin Enterprises ULC. ® and ™ are trademarks owned by Harlequin Enterprises ULC.

Your Privacy—Your information is being collected by Harlequin Enterprises ULC, operating as Harlequin Reader Service. To see how we collect and use this information visit https://corporate.harlequin.com/privacy-notice. From time to time we may also exchange your personal information with reputable third parties. If you wish to opt out of this sharing of your personal information, please visit www.readerservice.com/consumerschoice or call 1-800-873-8635. Notice to California Residents—Under California law, you have specific rights to control and access your data. For more information visit https://corporate.harlequin.com/california-privacy.

NORA2022

Get 4 FREE REWARDS!

We'll send you 2 FREE Books plus 2 FREE Mystery Gifts.

Both the **Romance** and **Suspense** collections feature compelling novels written by many of today's bestselling authors.

YES! Please send me 2 FREE novels from the Essential Romance or Essential Suspense Collection and my 2 FREE gifts (gifts are worth about $10 retail). After receiving them, if I don't wish to receive any more books, I can return the shipping statement marked "cancel." If I don't cancel, I will receive 4 brand-new novels every month and be billed just $7.49 each in the U.S. or $7.74 each in Canada. That's a savings of at least 17% off the cover price. It's quite a bargain! Shipping and handling is just 50¢ per book in the U.S. and $1.25 per book in Canada.* I understand that accepting the 2 free books and gifts places me under no obligation to buy anything. I can always return a shipment and cancel at any time by calling the number below. The free books and gifts are mine to keep no matter what I decide.

Choose one: ☐ **Essential Romance** (194/394 MDN GRHV) ☐ **Essential Suspense** (191/391 MDN GRHV)

Name (please print)

Address — Apt. #

City — State/Province — Zip/Postal Code

Email: Please check this box ☐ if you would like to receive newsletters and promotional emails from Harlequin Enterprises ULC and its affiliates. You can unsubscribe anytime.

Mail to the **Harlequin Reader Service:**
IN U.S.A.: P.O. Box 1341, Buffalo, NY 14240-8531
IN CANADA: P.O. Box 603, Fort Erie, Ontario L2A 5X3

Want to try 2 free books from another series? Call 1-800-873-8635 or visit www.ReaderService.com.

*Terms and prices subject to change without notice. Prices do not include sales taxes, which will be charged (if applicable) based on your state or country of residence. Canadian residents will be charged applicable taxes. Offer not valid in Quebec. This offer is limited to one order per household. Books received may not be as shown. Not valid for current subscribers to the Essential Romance or Essential Suspense Collection. All orders subject to approval. Credit or debit balances in a customer's account(s) may be offset by any other outstanding balance owed by or to the customer. Please allow 4 to 6 weeks for delivery. Offer available while quantities last.

Your Privacy—Your information is being collected by Harlequin Enterprises ULC, operating as Harlequin Reader Service. For a complete summary of the information we collect, how we use this information and to whom it is disclosed, please visit our privacy notice located at corporate.harlequin.com/privacy-notice. From time to time we may also exchange your personal information with reputable third parties. If you wish to opt out of this sharing of your personal information, please visit readerservice.com/consumerschoice or call 1-800-873-8635. **Notice to California Residents**—Under California law, you have specific rights to control and access your data. For more information on these rights and how to exercise them, visit corporate.harlequin.com/california-privacy.

STRS22R3

COMING NEXT MONTH FROM

HARLEQUIN

HEARTWARMING

#463 HER AMISH COUNTRY VALENTINE

The Butternut Amish B&B • by Patricia Johns

Advertising exec Jill Wickey knows all about appearance versus reality. So why does she keep wishing that spending time with carpenter Thom Miller—her fake date for a wedding in Amish country—could be the start of something real?

#464 A COWBOY WORTH WAITING FOR

The Cowboy Academy • by Melinda Curtis

Ronnie Pickett is creating a matchmaking service for rodeo folks—but to be successful, she needs a high-profile competitor as a client. Former champ Wade Keller is perfect...but could he be perfect for her?

#465 A COUNTRY PROPOSAL

Cupid's Crossing • by Kim Findlay

Jordan's farm is the only security he's ever had. So when big-city chef—and first love—Delaney returns home with suggestions for revamping it, Jordan isn't happy. But Delaney has a few good ideas...about the two of them!

#466 A BABY ON HIS DOORSTEP

Kansas Cowboys • by Leigh Riker

Veterinarian Max Crane didn't expect to find a baby on his porch—or for former librarian Rachel Whittaker to accept the job caring for his daughter. Now, most unexpectedly of all, they are starting to feel like a family...

YOU CAN FIND MORE INFORMATION ON UPCOMING HARLEQUIN TITLES, FREE EXCERPTS AND MORE AT HARLEQUIN.COM.

HWCNM0223

HARLEQUIN PLUS

Try the best multimedia subscription service for romance readers like you!

Read, Watch and Play.

Experience the easiest way to get the romance content you crave.

Start your **FREE TRIAL** at www.harlequinplus.com/freetrial.

HARPLUS0123